I0452092

THE LIGHT AT THE END OF THE WORLD

Copyright © 2012 by J.A. Cummings

All rights reserved. Except as permitted under the U.S. Copyright Act of 1976, no part of this publication may be reproduced, distributed, or transmitted in any form or by any means, or stored in a database or retrieval system, without the prior written permission of the publisher.

Irish Horse Productions
664 Forest
South Lyon, MI 48178

First eBook Edition: January 2012

Cover illustration © iStockphoto, Inc. Cover design by Chantel Y. Cummings

ISBN-13: 978-0984474752

CHAPTER ONE

B^{elow}

It was in the ninth month of his twenty-first year when Alexander's mother came to him in his bedroom, waking him with a light touch between his shoulder blades. He opened his eyes in the red-tinged darkness and rose up onto his elbows, pulling his face out of the silken pillows he had been sleeping on, listening as she bent low to whisper into his ear.

"Be very silent and say nothing. Follow me where I lead you."

There was gravity in her voice that he was unaccustomed to hearing, and it woke him fully with a shock of anxiety. She was only this serious when they were being hunted. Her lair should have been secure, and knowing that there was something strong enough to breach her defenses made him very nervous. He rose and dressed quickly.

In his head, her voice directed, *Pack the three things most precious to you and bring them. You will not be coming back.*

Without giving the matter too much thought, he grabbed his three treasures: a photograph of his father, a protection talisman on a neck chain, and his dagger. His mother smiled when she saw his collection, pleased by his choices. He packed them into a haversack and slung it over his shoulder. She nodded to him and beckoned him to follow her.

She led him out of the lair and down a narrow corridor that ran deep into the rock walls. The stone around him breathed and shuddered, warm with the anguish of the compressed human souls that made the landscape around them. As he passed a particularly dark, damp stone, it sighed, tickling the small hairs around his ear. He ignored it.

In the distance, he could hear screaming from Anuria's lair, and he recognized the voice as David, her half-breed son. He was Alexander's age, and, despite their instinctive competition, they had been as close to friends as anyone could be here in the Abyss. Hearing David dying made him sad, but it also told him what was happening and why his mother was so intent upon hiding him: the incubi were hunting.

His friend's screams rang off of the moist stone around them, echoed by the rocks themselves, a chorus of agony. Alexander hurried to follow his mother more closely. She led him around a corner and up to a flat, featureless area of bedrock that had not yet been covered over with the damned. His mother touched the stone, and a travel sigil appeared, pulsing and glowing a soft blue in the darkness. He glanced over his shoulder, afraid that the light would be echoed by the moisture on the walls behind them, giving them away but there was no reflection.

Hurry, she urged. *Step through.*

He took a deep breath and stepped through the sigil, which slurped around him like the mouth of an eager lover, taking him up. He felt his mother coming through behind him, and the tunnel squeezed them gently. This mode of travel was fleshy and warm, distracting with reminiscences of bodily pleasures. It was inappropriately exciting in light of the danger his mother was avoiding, but he was the child of a succubus. He had no shame.

Ahead, the other travel sigil shone, and he left the delightful passage for another dark corridor lined in pure bedrock. His mother emerged immediately after he did, and the sigil vanished, its power spent. He pulled his bag closer and looked around.

There was no screaming to be heard here, and the damned did not blanket every surface where they stood. The floor, walls and ceiling were all pure stone, without the soft moans or the weeping of human tears that marked the walls around their home. It was disquietingly empty and bare.

"We are very near the surface," his mother informed him, evidently feeling safe enough to speak aloud. "I am sending you to your father."

His brow puckered. "But – ."

"It's time, Alexander. You've grown too old and too powerful, and I can't hide you from the King any longer."

"He's the one who's hunting."

"He's killing all of my sisters' part-blood sons. He fears the prophecy."

Alexander shook his head. "That's ridiculous. No part-blood could ever challenge the Incubus King for his seat! None of us has the power."

"The prophecy says otherwise." She kissed him, her lips soft against his own. "I will do what I can to keep him from seeking you, but you have to leave the Abyss. My sisters are sending their sons out, as well. We can no longer protect you."

"Will you follow?"

She smiled. "I'll try."

He took a deep breath. He had heard so many stories about the surface, so many wild tales. He had listened to what his mother had said about humanity and the Earth, both the good and the bad, and, while he had always been entranced by the rumors and innuendo about the place, he was afraid to go there. He saw the anxiety in his mother's eyes, though, and he knew that there was no arguing and no place for his trepidations. He knew that when his mother ordered him, he had to obey.

Lifting his chin with all of the strength and maturity he could muster, he said, "Tell me what to do."

"I have some loyal friends among the Utukku who will help you navigate the passage between the Abyss and the Earth plane. We will try to get you as near to your father as we can. Go to him. He will know what to do."

He nodded and embraced her for what he hoped would not be the last time. Behind him, he heard a shuffling sound, followed by the characteristic snorting of the Utukku. He parted from her, and the worker demon took him gently by the elbow.

"Be safe, my love," his mother bid him. "I will see you when I can."

They shared one more smile, and then she retreated into the darkness, leaving him with his guide. Alexander turned to look into the beady black eyes that stared at him from the porcine face of the Utukku. "I'm ready."

"Come," the drone said, its voice deep and gravelly. "Come fast."

They scrabbled upward through a narrow passage in the bedrock that had been carved by hand. He could still see the finger marks scratched into the stone, feel the impressions of millions of human souls who had labored here. The quarter of his blood that was itself human ached in resonance with the imprinted sorrow and suffering that he could sense in those narrow finger channels, but he had no time for misplaced compassion now.

The Utukku led the way in silence, and the passage narrowed and twisted until Alexander no longer knew which way was up. He knew that "up" and "surface" were only semantic figments, but it still made him feel closer to the Earth plane to climb.

Unfortunately, the path they were following was beginning to dip.

His mother trusted this drone, but he was suspicious. He had lived in the Abyss all of his life, and he had learned that duplicity was as common as heartbeats here. He slipped his hand into his sack and clutched his dagger, ready to defend himself if the Utukku was leading him into an attack. The tunnel evened out in a place where bluish light shone weakly, reflecting off of the coal-chips of the drone's eyes. Another Utukku grunted to them, and his guide responded in kind. In the dim light, he saw two more drones gesturing him forward.

"Go," his first guide said. "Go with them. I go away."

Alexander watched the guide melt into the rock around them, disappearing into the wall like a ghost. The remaining Utukku gestured to him impatiently, and he stepped toward them.

"Come," one of them said, unwittingly echoing his brother's earlier words. "Come fast."

This time, he was led into a blunt-ended cavern where the ceiling was so low he had to crouch. His wings were brushing uncomfortably against the walls, so he retracted them, folding them into the hidden pouches in his back where they could hide. The Utukku nodded, and one of them commented, "Good. Look like man. Now we go."

One of the drones took a tool from his shoulder pouch and began scratching into the stone, sparks flying from the working edge. Alexander had never seen the sigil that he was carving, but he could feel a change in the space around him, as if air were rushing into the chamber and whirling about his feet. He pulled his treasures closer and watched as the second Utukku held out a chubby, two-fingered hand.

"Come now. I take you." A flash of red light glanced off of the carving tool, and they all winced. The atmosphere in their little cave grew anxious, tense with waiting, and Alexander could feel a thread stretching, ready to snap. Something told him that this was going to be unpleasant.

The Utukku grabbed his hand and pulled him closer, nearly smothering him in the creature's musty, stale-sweat smell. Alexander stifled his reflexive gag and turned his face away from his companion.

The other drone finished his carving and uttered a word that sounded painful to speak and was certainly painful to hear. Alexander's ears throbbed beneath the weight of it, the pressure in his head growing until he was ready to scream. Just as he was becoming certain that his skull would burst, he and the two Utukku were swallowed by a brilliant white flash and wave upon wave of mind-numbing sound. It was agonizing, and the three of them screamed in pain. As suddenly as the explosion had come, it was gone, and Alexander collapsed in the sudden lack of sound and pressure.

He awoke lying on his stomach in puddle of cold water, his cheek pressed against rough concrete. His head was splitting, and before he could stifle it, he moaned. Strong hands gripped his shoulders and flipped him over onto his back, and he raised his hands defensively, still disoriented. A disheveled human crouched over him, his long, matted hair hanging in his bearded face, dripping water down onto Alexander. Behind the man's dull gaze, he could see another pair of eyes, dark and beady, and for a moment he saw the human and his Utukku guide at the same time. He closed his own eyes hard for a heartbeat then looked again, this time perceiving correctly that his guide had possessed some poor unsuspecting bastard on the surface.

The surface! Then he had made it, and he had somehow survived the trip. That had to be good news. He sat up shakily, and the Utukku moved back to give him room.

"Hard to bring a body up," his guide said with something like sympathy. "Ulug came as spirit. Easier."

"That's one trick I can't manage," he said softly. He looked around them. They were in a narrow, stinking alleyway between two grey brick buildings. A dumpster overflowing with reeking trash stood to his right. To his left, behind where Ulug was crouching in his borrowed body, there was a single wooden door, bolted shut on the outside with a steel bar. A heavy padlock secured the crossbar, and Alexander wondered what the owners of that lock were trying to keep in. A steady drizzle was falling from the cloud-covered nighttime sky, insistently soaking him to the bone. His haversack was beside him, and he clutched it to him. "Where are we?" "New York," Ulug said. "Your mother sends us at night. Easier light. Sunlight will come, will burn. Come. Come fast."

He rose with assistance from his guide – his bodyguard, he supposed – and brushed himself off. He profoundly hoped that the puddle he'd been laying in was only rainwater. "I need clothing, and a way to make myself presentable before I meet my father."

"No time. Sunlight will come."

He had never seen sunlight. He had seen images of it, and his mother had explained it to him, telling him about her difficulties with adjusting to the brightness the first time she had left the Abyss. She had told Alexander that the light would be bright, but not painful. His guide's attitude seemed to suggest otherwise. He decided that discretion was definitely the wisest course, so he nodded to Ulug. "I'll follow."

His response seemed to satisfy the Utukku, who rose smoothly and began to amble toward the locked door. He looked at Alexander, then grasped the steel bar and wrested it clear of the wall. Chunks of masonry and mortar crumbled from the places where the bar had been attached, the sound loud in his ears. At the other end of the alleyway, a taxi cab drove by, its windshield wipers slapping as it rolled through the rain. Its headlights flashed toward them as it turned, piercing Alexander like a knife. He gasped and threw a hand up to protect his aching vision.

"Just little lights," Ulug said, amused. "Wait until sunlight. *That*'s bright."

The Utukku turned the door knob, snapping the locking mechanism, and pulled the door open. It swung out into the alley, and the demon stepped aside, gesturing for Alexander to go in. He did.

He stepped through the doorway into darkness almost as absolute as that in the Abyss. He could still see, though, his Hell-born vision revealing elegant furnishings, a bowl full of fruit, and a door to another room holding a king-sized four-poster bed draped with silk curtains and piled high with colorful pillows. The scent of perfume wafted around him, embracing him like a lover, and he recognized the scent of a succubus immediately. He had barely registered the familiarity when two arms wrapped around him from behind. The succubus pressed herself against his back, one hand on his chest, the other on his waist, and she purred to him, "Welcome to the surface, Alexander. Your mother told me to make you welcome." Her right hand ran lower, skimming his skin. "We need to get you some human clothing and acclimate you to this world. I know just what to do."

He smiled, his incubus blood singing in his veins. "I'm sure you do. Is this your lair?"

"No," she whispered, kissing his ear. "It's yours. We set it up for you when we knew you were coming."

"We?"

A naked human woman stepped into view, her dark hair curling around her heart-shaped face. She took his hand and held it against her body. He could feel her heart beating against his palm, could feel the life force rushing through her. "You need to eat," she whispered.

He had never heard a human woman speak before; the alien tones, so different than the voices of the demons he had known all of his life, sent a thrill through him. Behind him, the succubus chuckled, adding another shade to his growing desire. The three of them swayed their way to the wide bed. Alexander may have been only three-quarters demon, but he was a demon of lust.

Finally, he was on familiar ground.

Above, Below and Between

The blank walls reflected the brilliant late morning sunlight against the white tile floor, which amplified the brightness to tear-inducing levels. If the patient had any discomfort from the light, it was impossible to tell. She sat quietly, her hospital gown tied tightly closed and covered with a light summer blanket. Her pale hands, delicate as birds, held one another in her lap, clinging to each other like long-lost lovers. The doctor adjusted the vertical blinds to cut down on the glare and returned to his straight-backed wooden chair at the bedside. The patient watched him quizzically, as if she couldn't quite understand what he was doing.

He sat down with a sigh and reopened the manila file holding her records. He turned to a blank page and picked up his mechanical pencil, clicking it once to bring out more lead. He had a feeling this was going to take some time.

"So, Miss – what did you say your name was, again?"

"I have no name, Doctor."

"You mean you don't remember it?"

"I mean I have none."

He glanced at the label on the file. 'Jane Doe.' *All righty, then.* "They're calling you Jane Doe on your records. Do you mind if I call you Jane?"

She smiled gently. "You may call me whatever you would like, Doctor."

"Okay, Jane." He scribbled a quick note. "How did you come to be here at Saint Martha's?"

"I was found and brought here by a kind man."

He knew from the intake history in the chart that she had been found wandering naked in the street in the early morning hours four nights ago. The kind man she referred to had been a police officer, specifically Patrol Officer Carl Shea, who had picked her up, wrapped her in a blanket and brought her to the hospital. Amazingly, she had shown no sign of injury or abuse, and seemed to be in the prime of physical health. She was even clean, so she must have come from somewhere nearby. Shea and his fellows were still trying to track down where she'd come from.

He considered his patient, and she considered him, her large eyes innocent and guileless. She barely moved, only turning her head to watch him. Her body stayed in the same contained, prim pose that it had maintained all morning. Her stillness was unnatural, and he was beginning to think that she suffered from a form of catatonic schizophrenia.

"Where were you before the kind man found you?"

"I was in Heaven, Doctor."

"You mean someplace that was like Heaven because of how happy you were?"

"No, sir. I mean that I was in Heaven, with God and His elect."

So this is where the schizophrenia shows itself. "Are you a ghost? A spirit?"

"No, Doctor. I am an angel."

"An angel?"

"Yes, Doctor."

He looked at her for a moment, wondering how he could pierce her illusion. She looked back at him, blinking slowly, her face still passive and serene. Finally, he asked, "So where are your wings?"

She hesitated. "I... I lost them."

"You lost them?"

"Yes."

"How could you lose your wings?"

"They must have broken off when I fell."

"So you're a *fallen* angel?"

"Oh, no. Not in the way you're thinking."

"But you said you fell."

She nodded. He noted the movement. "Yes, Doctor. I must have lost my balance."

He smiled. "So it was an accidental fall?"

"Yes, Doctor. But I wasn't hurt at all." She canted her head, her dark hair crimping where it caught between her shoulder and her ear. "May I go now? I have work that must be done."

"We need to make sure that you aren't ill," he said gently, using his best soothing voice. "We can't let you go just yet. What work do you have to do?"

She fixed him with a gaze so filled with conviction that he was certain she believed every word she was saying. "The portals to Hell are active, and the Light Bringer is trying to breed the Antichrist."

He made more notes. "Where are these portals to Hell?"

"There are many portals." She turned slowly and looked at the window. The drawn vertical blind blocked the view, but she stared out at the light anyway. "The nearest is in the ocean, just off the coast of this continent. I believe the place is called 'Maine'."

"Maine is a portal to Hell?"

"No, Doctor. It is near the closest portal. That is where I need to go."

He shifted on the wooden seat. "And what will you do when you get to Maine?"

The patient looked at him as if he were simple. "Why, I have to close the portal, of course."

"How?"

Her serenity slipped a fraction, revealing a moment of pure anxiety behind the mask. "How?" she echoed.

"Yes. How? How will you close the portal to Hell? If you've lost your wings, don't you think you might have lost your other powers, too?"

He was treading on dangerous ground, stripping away some of the elements of her illusion. He saw her struggling with the thought that she might be less than omnipotent, saw the way her eyebrows twitched and knitted in her milky brow. Finally, she whispered, "I suppose that I will have to pray for an answer to that question, Doctor."

He leaned forward. "What will you do if it turns out that you're here on Earth as a human being, and that you aren't an angel at all?"

"But I am an angel," she objected mildly.

"Perhaps you are," he allowed, "but you're an angel without supernatural abilities, living in the body of a very mortal young lady."

She bit her lip and chewed it for a moment, clearly disturbed by the thought. Her slender body began to rock slightly back and forth, as if she were comforting herself. He had seen autistic children do the same thing. Her silence stretched on for a long moment, and he watched her closely. The emotion slowly drained from her face, which eventually froze into an impassive and expressionless mask. Her hands released their hold upon one another to rest flatly, palm down, on her thighs.

"I will pray about it, Doctor, and when you return, I will have an answer for you."

She had come close to the unraveling of her delusion, he decided, and she needed some time to catch her breath. Well, here at

Saint Martha's, they had nothing but time. It wasn't as if either of them had anywhere else to go. He closed the chart and rose, careful not to snag his expensive linen slacks on the splintery edge of the chair. This interview had clearly come to an end.

"I wish you luck, Ms. Jane Doe." He nodded to her. "Good day."

She replied like an automaton. "Good day, Doctor."

He went to the door and knocked lightly, signaling the orderly waiting on the other side to open the lock. The click came with obliging swiftness. Smiling once more over his shoulder at Jane, he stepped out into the hallway and promptly slipped on something wet. He fell heavily, landing on his back and staring up in horror at the figure that loomed over him, the orderly's head dangling from one clawed hand, the door keys in the other. The creature leaned over him, its red skin shining in the light from the windows, its leathery wings beating slowly. It snorted at him, its upturned nose twitching above the twisted, fang-studded maw. He scrambled away, sliding on his back through the rapidly cooling pool of the orderly's blood, keening as he went. The creature dropped its gory burden and reached out to the doctor, grasping him by the throat.

It spoke. "Quiet, ape."

They were the last words the doctor ever heard.

Inside the room, the patient heard the snapping of the doctor's neck, and she rose to her bare feet, facing the door. She was powerless, without her wings, without a weapon. She knew that she would be next to die.

The demon strode into the room, stepping sideways to get through the doorway without damaging its wings. When it saw her, it laughed, the sound low and obscene.

"Little angel," it mocked, "who will help you now?"

She knew that help was not coming. Praying for a swift death, she closed her eyes as it approached.

Between

14

Jessica Norgren stretched, her legs spread wide and her torso lowering to the dojo mat. She rested her hands on her ankles and her forehead on the ground, concentrating on breathing. It had been a horrible day. First she had slept through her alarm, which meant that she had to run to the nearest station and try to catch the train. Naturally, she had arrived just as the train was pulling away, so she had to wait for the next one. Her neighborhood wasn't what a person might call well-serviced by the municipality, so it took fifteen minutes for the next train to arrive. She still might have been able to beat her boss to the office, until the conductor announced a "pedestrian incident" and the train ground to a halt. Leave it to her to pick the track where someone wanted to commit suicide that morning.

She got to the office just as her boss was grumbling about having to make his own coffee, and his mood was as black and foul as the bottom of a sewer worker's boot. She spent the day hiding from him in the law library, ostensibly researching case law for their latest round of ambulance chasing.

That wasn't when the day turned bad, though. The day turned bad when she got the call from her doctor.

"Congratulations," the nurse had chirped. "Your test results are back. You're going to be a mommy."

Pregnant?

She remembered muttering something vague and trying not to drop the phone, even though her fingers had turned into jelly, insensible and just as shaky.

How can I be pregnant? I haven't had sex in months.

Thirteen months, to be exact. It had been thirteen months since she'd relocated to this rancid city after finally – finally! – graduating from university with her pre-law degree. She'd taken a position as a law clerk with a private practice attorney, and she was taking night classes at law school. Even if she'd had the inclination or the energy to get laid, she just didn't have the time.

Sperm doesn't live for thirteen months, and anyway, he used a condom. She pressed her forehead into the mat just a little harder. *It has to be something else. I absolutely cannot be pregnant.*

She felt more than heard Tsung Li settle onto the mat across from her, doing his own stretches in preparation for their karate katas.

He was her favorite sparring partner. As a third-degree black belt, she had trouble finding an opponent at her level, and it took a lot to make her stand up and take notice. Li was a bona fide kung fu monk all the way from China by way of Tibet, and he more than made her take notice; he usually made her want to take a sick day. He was a challenge in the best bruise-causing sense, and she loved him for it.

"You sad?" he asked, his quiet baritone voice soothing.

Jessica straightened and took a deep breath. "I guess I'm just stressed. It was a bad day."

He smiled at her as he limbered up his impossibly flexible body. "You have more bad days than good days, I think."

"That's life in the big city."

"That's *your* life in the big city. My experience is much more... serene." He leaned into one of his pre-sparring contortions and said mildly, "I could teach you to meditate."

"No stupid monk tricks, Li," she said. "Besides, I already know how to meditate."

Li clicked his tongue. "You are feeling very aggressive. Very harsh energy from you today." He smiled again, broadly, like a cross between a barracuda and the Cheshire Cat. "I think I'm going to have to kick your ass for that."

"Ha! You can try."

Her friend bounced up onto his feet and beckoned her to follow. "Do, or do not. There is no try."

"Great. Just what I needed: kung fu Yoda."

"We can practice kung fu later. We're here for karate today," he helpfully reminded her. "You ready?"

She rose and shook her hands and shoulders. "I'm as ready as I'm going to be."

"Good." He dropped into his opening stance. "Let's dance."

Jessica shook her head and followed suit, but she could not resist one more comment before their workout began. "Li," she said, "you watch way too many movies."

CHAPTER TWO

elow and Between

B

    Alexander yawned and rubbed his aching eyes in the flickering light from the television. Lily, the succubus who had helped set up his lair and who was still acting as his hostess, had suggested that the best way for him to acclimate himself to the surface was to watch the humans in action. He had watched everything the electrons could provide: movies, television episodes, talk shows, news, and local commercial advertisements. When the exercise had first begun two weeks ago, it had been thrilling and new; now he was tired of watching and he wanted to get involved first-hand.

    Lily sat beside him, her hip comfortably against his, and she lightly caressed the back of his neck with her fingertips. "I know it gets dull, just watching," she told him, "but if you're going to go out there, you need to know how to behave, and more than that, you have to be ready for the light."

"I'm ready for it," he said, even though he was less than convinced. "Shouldn't I go out and find my father now? My mother said I needed to find him."

"Rachel is very wise," she allowed, "but perhaps not as wise as she might think. I'm not certain that your father is the right person for you to be meeting on your first trip to the surface."

He looked at her then. "First trip? Does that mean there's a chance I might be going back to the Abyss?"

She smiled and kissed him. "If all goes well, darling, you can go back as the King."

Alexander frowned. "I don't think I want that."

Lily laughed at him. "That's just because you don't have the power in your hands yet. Once you have it, you won't want to give it up. It's in your blood."

The door opened, and Ulug came lumbering through, walking like a disjointed marionette in the third human host he had possessed since they'd emerged on earth. His hands were full of grocery sacks, and a satchel hung from his shoulder.

Lily rose to meet him, diving enthusiastically into the bags. "Did you get it all?"

"Everything," the Utukku said, nodding his borrowed head. "I used money."

"Good boy," she praised. "You're learning."

"Easier to just take."

"Yes, dear, but then you attract unwanted attention." Ulug grunted and went about putting the groceries away while she dug through his purchases. She finally came up with what she was looking for with a happy exclamation. "Ah! Here we are. Alexander, come here, darling. I want to show you something."

He turned off the television and came to her side, curious. She was holding a magazine and flipping rapidly through the pages. He bent so that he could read the title.

"*Sports Month*," he read aloud.

She found the page she'd been searching for and held it out to him. "Look at this. What do you see?"

Alexander looked closely. There was a color photo of two men wearing brightly-colored costumes that seemed to be heavily padded. Their heads were encased in helmets, and in their hands they brandished long, curved sticks. They appeared to be balancing on knife blades that were somehow attached to the bottoms of their feet. One of the men, the one in the background wearing the lighter-colored shirt, was deeply ugly, his face a roadmap of scars. His open mouth revealed several missing teeth, and he was apparently shouting when the photograph was taken. The man in the foreground, though, was a different story. He was extremely handsome, even in his current ridiculous get-up, and there was something compelling about him. His presence echoed off of the page and into Alexander, and he recognized him immediately.

He blinked, surprised. "My father," he said, his voice quiet. He stared at the picture for a moment longer, then blurted, "What is he *doing*?"

"He's playing hockey," she answered. "It's a game that mortals play. He's paid very, very well for it, too."

She took the magazine back and turned the page. There was another picture of his father, this time in a neatly tailored suit, looking like a model in a fashion spread. Alexander was struck by the resemblance between himself and the man on the page.

"He's handsome, isn't he? Rick Buchanan," Lily said, pillowing her cheek against his shoulder. "Rachel chose well when she selected him to be your father."

"If you say so."

"Don't be disrespectful. A succubus always chooses her children's sires very carefully. It's not a decision to be taken lightly."

Ulug shuffled back to them, taking the satchel from his shoulder and thrusting it out at Lily. She took it in one hand and led Alexander back to the couch with the other. He followed her, but his attention was on the picture, and he nearly knocked his shins against the coffee table before he sat beside her. Ulug wandered out of the main area of the lair and into the bedroom, but neither lust demon was particularly interested in what their guardian was doing. He was ignorable, like the family dog, just there to do errands and bark at intruders. For his part, the Utukku was fine with the arrangement, too. He was antisocial by nature.

She pulled a laptop computer out of the bag and set it up in front of him. "I have your father's e-mail address. I want you to open a line of communication with him, ask to meet him." She took the liberty of booting up the laptop, and while it whirred through its start-up sequence, she added, "He's famous, and he probably gets dozens of e-mails, but it's a start. Hopefully he'll respond."

Alexander nodded absently, going back to the beginning of the article and beginning to read. His mother had told him some things about his father, but he'd never even known the man's name. He was amazed by how nervous he felt to be confronted with this Rick Buchanan's reality. The language in the article was sometimes lingo-heavy and hard to understand, but pertinent bits and pieces of information stood out, at least a little. He'd been born in Canada, raised by his maternal grandparents. His mother had died when he was very young. Apparently he had been kidnapped by his father when he was a child, but had been recovered after a few months. Alexander wondered if the kidnapper had really been his incubus sire, or if some human had taken him. He wondered if his father even knew the truth.

He read the whole article, then re-read it while Lily waited patiently. He finally put the magazine down and looked at her. "He says he doesn't have any children. Didn't mother tell him?"

"Of course not. You'll be the best kind of surprise for him." She pushed the laptop toward him. The internet e-mail site was up on the screen, with an account already created for him. She had opened a new message window and typed Buchanan's e-mail address (DevilRay69@gmail.com) in the "to" line. The cursor blinked at him, waiting. She put a hand on his knee. "Start typing. Tell him who you are. Tell him that you want to meet him."

He put his fingertips on the keys, but found himself hesitating. "I don't know what to say."

"Say anything. Just arrange a meeting."

"I...." He typed a word, deleted it, typed another, deleted that, and then managed to type an entire phrase. He deleted that, as well. "Help!"

Lily laughed and pulled the laptop back to herself. She read aloud as she typed, "Mr. Buchanan, please contact me. I need to meet with you to discuss a mutual acquaintance, my mother, Rachel. You can reach me at this e-mail address. Sincerely, your son, Alexander B." She sent the e-mail with a satisfied smirk. "There. All done."

"Alexander B.?" he asked. "What's the 'b' for?"

"Buchanan. On the surface, children take their fathers' last names as their own."

"How odd."

"It is. The humans tend to view family in a very patrilineal way, at least in this part of the world." The bedroom door opened, and Ulug emerged, carrying the lifeless corpse of their last meal. The man's life force had been drained completely, and his dead hands flopped against the Utukku as he dragged him toward the door.

"And where do you think you're going with that?" Lily asked.

"Throwing it away, like the others." He continued his slow passage through the living room, the dead man's head lolling grotesquely over his shoulder.

"Where?"

"Train tracks," Ulug said, shrugging. "Same as the others."

"Very well," she sighed, gesturing dismissively. "Just make sure nobody sees you."

He gave her a scathing look. "I'm not stupid."

She decorously waited until he had gone out of the lair and closed the door behind him before commenting. "I doubt that."

Alexander turned to her. "On the television, they prosecute humans for killing other humans. They call it "murder." Is what we do murder? Are we committing crimes?"

Lily threw her head back and laughed. "Oh, darling, you're such an innocent! No. Absolutely not. We're *predators*, dear. Their little rules don't apply to us. We're above them. Their only purpose is to serve and feed us. Don't worry your pretty head about such silly philosophical details."

"If we're doing nothing wrong, then why are you always warning Ulug to be careful?"

"We're superior, but we're outnumbered. Their herd will be happy to come tear us apart if they know we're here. That's why it's so important to have a secure lair. You can never let the apes know where you are, because they'll object to being used for food, and then it will go very badly for you. Even superior beings can be overcome by overwhelming numbers."

Alexander looked at the photo of his father, still face-up on the coffee table. "So I descend from mere meat?"

"He's part incubus," she said gently. "That makes him somewhere between them and us. He's not as powerful as a true demon, but he's more than a herd animal, unlike the people we bring here for dinner." She took his face in her hands. "And you are *much* more than just meat, my dear. You have a great future written in the stars."

He let her kiss him, but it did nothing to quiet his mind.

Between

Detective Lloyd Herman frowned fiercely into his case file. Maybe if he could glower hard enough at the photo of the murdered psychiatrist, he could scare the man's ghost into telling him who'd killed him. When no such testimony was forthcoming, he tried the same maneuver on the photo of the orderly from the mental hospital. No luck, and no surprise. He picked up his mug and finished off his ninth cup of coffee for the day, grimacing at the way it had gone cold and even more bitter than it had been when it was hot. He put the mug aside with a grumble.

He had one more photo to glare at, and this one actually disturbed him. It was the patient, a young girl who'd had delicate features and tiny bones. Each and every one of those bones had been broken by her killer, and her blood smeared across the camera's landscape, making the entire picture a mess of lumpy scarlet. Just looking at the photograph made him remember the smell of the blood and bowel contents that had permeated the room. His stomach twisted, and he put the photo beneath the others. He normally didn't react this way to crime scene photos, but the way this girl had died, and something about the girl herself, made this particular murder obscene as well as gruesome.

The girl had no past that anyone could determine, but if there was one thing he knew, it was that people didn't just appear out of thin air. Somebody someplace was missing a daughter, or a sister, or a girlfriend. There had to be someone who was looking for her. The thought of that person searching in vain with a heart full of lead made him hurt inside. He knew how that family felt. There had been a time when he'd stood by the phone, too, waiting to hear news from a search party. The news he'd been given had been grim, and he remembered his wife pulling away. She had never come back.

He shook his head and rubbed his eyes. The case was getting to him. Maybe he'd been working too hard. Maybe it was just that it was getting close to the anniversary, close to Christmas, and that always made him sensitive and melancholy. Maybe he was just burnt out.

One thing was certain; he was getting nowhere squinting at the case file. He had to do something. He abandoned his rancid coffee and turned to his computer, intent on searching one more time through the missing persons reports. She had to have come from somewhere.

Between

Jessica finished shelving the last of the books that she'd had scattered around the law library, listening as her boss read someone the riot act over the phone. She felt bad for whoever was on the other end of the line, but at the same time, she was glad she wasn't on the receiving end of the screaming this time. Working for Edgar Winters, Esq., was a source of constant delight. She was certain that sucking chest wounds would have been more enjoyable.

Unconsciously, she rested her hand on her lower abdomen as she looked around the room for more books, hoping for a reason to stay sequestered and out of Edgar's way. She had gone to a new doctor and had received the same unwanted news. She was pregnant, and she had no idea how that could possibly be true. Logic had failed her, and now she was hoping that denial and a stepped up workout schedule with Tsung Li might solve the problem.

Her cell phone buzzed on the table, vibrating in quiet mode and skimming across the polished wood. She picked it up and looked at the number. The display said only "Caller Unknown." Hesitantly, she answered.

"Hello?"

"Jessica Norgren?"

It was a man's voice, mellow and smooth and redolent of sexuality and promises of fleshy pleasures. Just the way he'd said her name was somehow sinful. She cleared her throat. "Yes. Who is this?"

He laughed softly, and the hairs on the back of her neck rose. There was nothing mirthful in that laugh. If anything, there was pure menace in the sound. "This is the father of your child."

She snapped the phone shut, shocked into acting on instinct. The phone rang again in her hand, again registering as "Caller Unknown." She answered again. "Hello?"

"That was very unfriendly, Jessica. You might hurt my feelings."

"Who are you?"

He laughed again. "I already told you."

"Who are you?"

"If you really want to know, why don't we meet up for dinner? How about seven o'clock at Mario's in the Village. Do you know where that is?"

It was her favorite Italian restaurant. Her palms began to sweat. "I know it."

"Good." He sounded smug. She hated him. "I'll see you then."

"I never said I'd meet you."

Again, he released that filthy laugh. "Oh, but you will."

This time, he hung up on her, leaving her shaking and staring at the silent cell phone. She sat in the nearest desk chair and put her head in her hand, blinking back frightened tears.

What's going on?

Above

Ariel folded his wings and bowed to the Archangel Michael, who barely nodded in response. The superior angel was busy cleaning his sword, which still flamed and smoked with the blood of a recently-slain demon. The less powerful angels knew better than to even approach Michael's weapon, which was beyond the power of any of them to wield. He kept a respectful distance until his commander was ready for him.

When Michael finally spoke, his tone was grave. "It has begun. Your mission starts now."

He bowed again. "By God's will," he responded obediently. "I am yours to command."

The Archangel touched him, and he shuddered as he was suddenly encased in a fleshy frame. The change was stark, and the abrupt limitation of his powers and perceptions gave him a moment of despair.

"Courage," Michael encouraged him. "Find the woman. Stay by her side and protect her."

Ariel ducked his head and prepared to receive the touch that would send him to Earth, and to endure the inevitable pain that leaving the Garden always caused.

The End of Days had begun.

Between

Jessica hesitated on the sidewalk outside the abortion clinic, and steeled herself to the inevitable unpleasantness ahead. She went inside, ducking around the wild-eyed protesters brandishing gory images of dismembered fetuses. She tried not to look at the pictures as she went around them, and she studiously avoided eye contact. The last thing she needed was a confrontation with some fundamentalist crackpot.

Unfortunately, one of those fundamentalist crackpots decided that a confrontation was in the cards, and she stopped her progress with a vise grip on Jessica's elbow. "Do you realize what you're about to do is murder?"

Jessica pulled away, looking into the woman's craggy face. "Leave me alone." Their eyes met, and the woman recoiled as if she'd been slapped.

"You… you're the one," the woman said, gaping. "It's you! You've been Chosen!"

"Get away from me! Jesus!"

"Yes, yes!" she raved. "Call on Him! Call on Him to save your soul!"

She pushed the protester away and hurried into the clinic. The nurse receptionist met her on the inside, helping her to shut the door and bolt it from the inside. "We'll just wait until the freak show leaves," she told Jessica, smiling. "Sorry about that. The closer it gets to Christmas, the weirder they get."

Jessica took off her coat and hung it on a free peg near the door. "I need to see the doctor."

"Sure thing. I have some paperwork for you to fill out, and then I'll need your insurance card."

"I don't have insurance."

"How are you going to pay?"

She opened her purse. "Cash." It would take everything she'd had in savings for next month's tuition, but she was certain it was worth it. If she didn't pay for this now, she'd have no school next term, anyway.

The nurse handed her a clipboard and a pamphlet. "Here. Read this, and then fill this out, both sides. When you're done, bring it back up to me. Okay?"

"Okay."

The paperwork was amazingly innocuous, like the forms she'd filled out in a hundred different doctors' offices a hundred times before. The pamphlet was some sort of propaganda about women's health treatment, and she barely looked at it. Her head was ringing, and something inside of her was coiling and angry. She felt like her heart was being battered from the inside out.

She brought the clipboard with the completed forms back to the desk, and the nurse took her into a lab triage room, where she took her vital signs and a blood sample. She gave them a urine sample for a confirmatory pregnancy test, and then returned to the waiting room.

Another woman, a Latina with kind eyes and a bracelet made of chunky turquoise beads, came out of the inner rooms and held out her hand. "Jessica? I'm Ana. I'll be your counselor. Please follow me."

Jessica shook her hand and numbly followed her into a consultation room that had been decorated to be deceptively homey. She sat on the floral-upholstered couch and clenched her hands on her knees while Ana consulted her skinny file. It was all so normal, but still so unreal. She couldn't believe that she was actually here, about to abort a child that she could not have conceived in the first place.

What did that old woman mean, I'm Chosen?

Her stomach lurched and flopped, and she pressed a hand to her forehead. Ana looked up at her, concerned.

"Are you all right?"

"I...."

She was shaking again, and the room was too hot, the walls too close. She began sweating. She wanted to run. Another wave of nausea washed over her, and she could feel a throbbing in her head. A sound like whispering was in her ears, making the headache worse. She rose.

"I have to go," she said. "I'm sorry."

Ana did not go after her. The nurse watched from behind the desk as Jessica literally ran out of the counseling room, grabbed her coat, and bolted for the door. She barely remembered to throw the lock before bashing her face against the door's frosted glass window, but she unlocked it just in time. She burst out of the clinic and back onto the sidewalk, where she fell to her knees, vomiting. The sound in her ears was louder, dozens of voices whispering mixed with the buzzing of a thousand locusts. She shook her head to clear it, to no effect. The crazy-eyed protester lady bent to help her, and Jessica swatted her hands away.

"Run," the woman hissed. "He knows you're here."

Somehow, she made it back to her feet. She was dazed. Her body began to move without her telling it to, walking steadily and resolutely for the train station without her conscious control, and all the while her mind whirled in a foggy haze. It was only when the subway doors opened and she stepped out at the station nearest her apartment that she regained something like control.

All she wanted was to go to bed. *I'm just stressed. I just had some sort of panic attack, that's all.* She just needed to sleep.

In her head, the voices quietly agreed.

CHAPTER THREE

*B*elow and Between

Shick shick keeee shick shick shick

Rick Buchanan's skate blades cut across the hard morning ice as he warmed up before practice. The sound was music to his ears, proof that everything was right in his world. As long as he was in a rink and flying across the ice, he was sure he was alive.

He was the only member of the New York Devil Rays to show up this early. He loved having the rink to himself, to have the entire, pristine sheet of white his and his alone. He lived for the feeling of skating, the way his legs pumped as he picked up speed through the crossovers in the corner, the thrill of creating his own wind as he raced from blue line to goal line. All he ever wanted to be and everything he'd ever been existed here in the cold.

He turned around and skated backwards, his stick trailing along with him, blade down and leaving a track of its own. He smiled to himself and turned around quickly, facing the visitor's crease and continuing his north-south flight. His smile died when he saw it.

Sitting on top of the net, skinny legs dangling from the crossbar, was a tiny black form. It was humanoid without being remotely human, its face both reptilian and simian. Scrawny wings beat slowly around it, keeping time with the way it kicked its clawed feet. He drove into to a snowplow stop, spraying the imp with ice shavings and demanding, "What do you want?"

It brushed the snow away with an indignant squeak. "Your father wants to see you," it said.

"Well, I don't want to see him."

"He says it's important."

"Too bad. Now get out of here before somebody sees you."

The imp's wings flapped, and it rose into the air, its red eyes glaring at him. "You're still rude."

"And you're still not welcome."

It disappeared with a spark and a puff of sulfur. Rick slapped his stick on the ice in annoyance. Leave it to Yeter'el to ruin a perfectly good morning skate.

He went back to the bench and took a swig of Gatorade out of his squeeze bottle, more out of habit than out of any kind of thirst. He hated when his father sent his little minions to check up on him. He'd told Yeter'el years ago that he wanted nothing to do with him, and he had every intention of continuing to distance himself from his demonic sire. He wished he could divorce himself from the Abyss all together, but it just kept coming back into his life.

He had been fine, just fine, until he'd gotten that e-mail from some maniac claiming to be his son by Rachel. He doubted it could be possible, but part of him had to admit that the e-mailer could very well be telling the truth. He knew that time passed differently in the Abyss, and a child conceived last summer might indeed be an adult now. What that child was doing on the surface now, and why he wanted to make contact, though – those were the questions of the hour.

"Think of the devil and she shall appear. Or something like that."

The familiar voice came close by his ear, and he heard her before he felt her pressed against his back. He turned and found himself facing her in a loose embrace.

"Rachel," he greeted. "Long time no see."

She kissed him, deep and insistent, and he could feel her taking just a lick of his life force. He gently pushed her away, but she released him without complaint, smiling up at him and purring, "It's been too long." She plucked at his jersey, smiling at the cartoon stingray on the logo. "My Devil Ray. Has Alexander contacted you?"

He pulled away. "I should be upset with you about that. Why didn't you tell me you were going to conceive?"

Rachel pouted prettily. "I wanted to surprise you. You told me that you love surprises."

"I meant sneak-attack blow jobs. I didn't mean babies."

"Well, so? I gave you both." A tense silence passed between them, and she approached him again, her hands on the hip pads of his hockey pants. "Angry with me?"

He sighed. They both knew that he was, just as they both knew that he wouldn't stay that way for long. "I should be."

"I'm sorry." She kissed him again, and this time it was only a chaste peck. "Forgive me?"

"Let me think about it."

She ran a hand through his hair. "You never wear your helmet."

"I do during games." He heard noises coming from the locker room, and he pulled away farther, skating slowly toward the red line. "You'd better get going. They're going to be coming out soon. Maybe I'll see you later…?"

"What about Alexander?"

Rick took a deep breath. "Bring him."

Her smile was wide, beatific, and devastating. It was all he could do not to rush to her and take her in his arms. "Wonderful! I'll see you this afternoon, when you go home for your pre-game nap."

She vanished, and he shook his head. He would live to regret this.

Jessica jolted awake with the shrilling of her alarm clock and decided that there was no way she was facing her boss today. She grabbed her cell phone from the bedside table and called his voice mail in the office, leaving a suitably croaky-sounding message to take a sick day. Her phone helpfully reminded her that she had five unheard voice mail messages, all of them from "Caller Unknown." He had started calling her when she'd stood him up at the restaurant and showed no sign of stopping. She made sure that the phone was still set on vibrate and put it aside.

She lay in silence, her eyes closed, for a long moment. The buzzing and whirring in her ears was finally gone, but now there was a dull tap-scratching sound instead, insistent and repetitive. She lay and dozed and listened to the noise for nearly an hour before she realized that it was real and coming from her kitchen. Jessica got out of bed and reluctantly went to investigate.

On her kitchen window sill, huddling in a wet and forlorn ball, was a white cat, its green eyes staring through the glass. It reached out a soggy paw and tapped on the window, begging to be let inside. She hurried over and opened the window, pulling the animal in to safety. It clung to her, shivering.

"How did you get up there?" She looked out at the sill. There was barely a ledge, and no way the cat could have climbed all the way up a three-story building. "Where did you come from?"

Its only answer was a scratchy meow. She held it close in one hand while she grabbed a dish towel with the other.

"You're soaked, poor baby! How long have you been outside?" She rubbed the cat dry, and it purred and rubbed its head against her ankle in appreciation. It wasn't skinny, and seemed to be in good health, at least for now. "Hopefully you haven't just managed to catch pneumonia." She put her hands on her hips. "Let's see if I have anything around here that you can eat. How about tuna? I think I have some tuna. I've never known a cat to turn up his nose to that."

The cat meowed again and sat down, licking its paws. Jessica got down a dessert plate and opened a can of tuna, dumping the whole thing out for her little visitor. As soon as she put the plate on the floor, the cat dove in, eating as if it had never seen food before. She stroked its back a few times, then stepped back to lean against the kitchen cupboard, her ankles crossed.

"So…it looks like now I have a mystery baby *and* a mystery cat." She ran a hand through her messy hair. "My life just keeps getting weirder and weirder."

Abruptly, the cat arched its back and let out an angry yowl, its eyes toward the living room. It hissed fiercely and moved to stand between Jessica and the couch. She took a step back from the animal, convinced that it had lost its little mind, then looked up to see what was causing it such upset. To her shock, she saw an elegantly dressed and startlingly beautiful man sitting on the worn upholstery, his hands folded mildly in his lap. He smiled at her and crossed his legs casually, his black trench coat crinkling softly as he moved.

"Who are you?" she asked, her voice little more than a frightened squeak. The cat growled furiously.

The man smiled. "I think you know who I am."

The voice was familiar, and it made her shiver. "Caller Unknown."

"You can call me that, I suppose, but I'd prefer it if you used my name. We are very intimate by now, after all." He glanced at the cat and laughed. "Oh, that's amusing."

The cat took a step toward her unwanted visitor, and Jessica grabbed it up into her arms to keep it from attacking, more to protect the cat than the man. "What's your name?"

"I have many names," he said, "but you can call me 'Baby Daddy.'"

"Fuck you."

"You already have." He gestured toward her with one perfect hand. "How do you suppose you ended up in your…peculiar condition?"

The animal in her arms hissed again, but it did not claw her. It seemed to be standing in her embrace, guarding her. She felt safer holding it.

"Get out."

He laughed. "Really, Jessica. So unwelcoming. I should be upset with you. You know that, don't you? First you won't take my calls, then you stand me up at that delightful Italian restaurant – excellent chicken piccata, by the way, good choice of meeting place – so that you could try to abort our son." He clicked his tongue, tsking her. "You've been very naughty." He canted his head, once again looking at her and the cat with a mocking smile. "We have much to discuss, you and I."

She held the cat closer and stepped back farther into the kitchen, trying to put some distance between herself and this frightening stranger. She shifted her grip on the cat to just one arm, reaching toward the knife block with the other. "I don't have anything to say to you. I don't know who you are, or how you got in here, but you can just get the hell OUT!"

She had barely finished speaking when the cat launched itself away from her, leaping onto the man's chest and slashing him with its claws. Brilliant red light lanced out through each wound, and the man howled in pain. He threw the cat aside, its tiny body bouncing off of the living room wall, and he jumped to his feet, bleeding badly from dozens of angry, glowing gashes. The scratches were much more serious than she'd thought a cat could inflict. He took one step toward Jessica, his face a mask of rage, and the cat attacked again, protecting her. The man knocked the animal aside once again, then vanished into thin air, leaving only her snarling guardian and a scent like burned toast.

Jessica ran to the cat and scooped it up, checking it for injuries. It shivered in her arms, shaking in its righteous fury, but rubbed its head against her chin. It was streaked with blood, but none of it seemed to belong to the cat itself. To her unprofessional eyes, her cat was unharmed, and she hugged it tightly, sobbing into its soiled fur.

Below and Between

Rick took the long way home from the rink, avoiding the impending meeting with Rachel and her son. He wasn't ready to be a father. He wasn't ready for any of this, not a child, not a reconnection with his demonic summer fling, and certainly not the re-emergence of his father. He could sense that something deeply unpleasant was happening.

He took the train back to Manhattan and got off one station early, walking the rest of the way to his apartment. A man on the street recognized him and shouted his name, and he acknowledged him with a smile and a wave. Sports fans were everywhere in this town, it seemed, and since he was currently the Devil Rays' scoring leader, his face was familiar to them. He was grateful that the man did nothing more than holler at him. Normally he liked meeting his fans, but today was not the day for such things.

He stopped at the corner deli for a cup of coffee and some chicken soup before continuing on to his building. The concierge greeted him with a tip of the hat and a cheery, "Afternoon, Mr. Buchanan."

Rick smiled and tucked a twenty into the man's hand. "Afternoon, Billy."

"Thank you, Mr. Buchanan," Billy said, opening the door for him. "Good luck in the game tonight."

"Thanks."

"Go Rays!"

Rick smiled at him again, albeit weakly, as he passed into the marble-floored front elevator lobby.

The ride up to the penthouse level was disappointingly fast. He had really hoped for a mechanical breakdown or some other failure that would help him prolong this foot-dragging. Instead, the elevator was prompt as always, smoothly depositing him in his semi-private vestibule on the 95th floor.

Rachel was already there, sitting on the red-velvet upholstered couch beside a young man with Rachel's violet eyes. Rick's heart sank when he saw a certain resemblance between Rachel's companion and the face he saw in his own mirror every morning. The young man bounced to his feet, eager and smiling.

"You must be Rick Buchanan," he said, his voice almost melodic. "I'm Alexander... your son."

Rick looked at the hand that Alexander extended toward him, andgripped it reluctantly. "Yeah, uh... good to meet you."

He unlocked his door as Rachel came forward and kissed him on the cheek. She smiled at him and brushed by, strolling into the apartment ahead of the two men. Alexander followed her, looking around him with open curiosity. Rick was the last to cross the threshold. He put his keys on the console table in the front hall and hung up his coat.

His Canadian upbringing kicked in, and he politely asked, "Can I get you anything to drink?"

"Water would be great," Alexander requested.

Rachel met Rick's gaze. "Why don't you let me get your drinks while the two of you get to know each other? I remember my way around."

"No, no, that's okay. I'll be right back." He nodded to the couch. "Have a seat. Make yourselves comfortable."

He vanished into the kitchen, leaving Rachel and Alexander to occupy themselves in his living room. He filled two glasses with ice, then added water to one and scotch to another before he returned to his guests. Rachel was waiting for him with a glass of wine in her hand.

"I see you found the bar."

"I did." She sat down, crossing her long legs, demurely keeping her pencil skirt from riding up. "So... what do you think?"

He handed the water to Alexander, then drained his scotch in one go. The burn helped him focus and gave him strength. "Of what?"

"Of our boy. Don't you think he looks like you?"

Rick looked at Alexander, who smiled. "Yeah, I guess so. A nicer-looking version, though."

Rachel shrugged. "He's three-quarters incubus. That accounts for any additional attractiveness." She sipped her wine. "Still mad at me for making him?"

"Not mad, per se," he allowed. He felt awkward, talking about Alexander in the third person when he was sitting right there in the room with them. "I know that a succubus can decide when and where she gets pregnant, but I always thought you'd let the sperm donor know."

"I told you I wanted to surprise you," she pouted.

"You know that the Incubus King has forbidden this."

"I also know that the Succubus Queen has said nothing of the sort. His rules might apply to you, but not to me."

Alexander pointed out quietly, "His rules also apply to me. That's why I'm here." He looked back at his father. "The King had his men killing all partial-bloods in the Abyss. He's afraid of the prophecy."

Rick scratched his head and wished he'd poured a double. "Demons are big on prophecies. Which one are we talking about?"

"The one that says a partial-blood will destroy the King." She shrugged. "That one's not important. It's the other prophecy that brings me to you."

"Which other one?" Rick sat on the edge of his lazy boy. "Please, my head is already hurting. Could you start being less opaque?"

She put her wine glass aside and leaned forward. "The one about the End of Times."

He blinked. "End of Times? As in, the Apocalypse?"

"Exactly."

Rick stood and held up his hands wardingly. "Leave me out of that. I don't need any of that noise. If you're here to bring me into that, I am definitely not interested."

"I'm not convinced you have a choice."

"Why not?"

"Because you're a descendant of the bloodline who will sire the Anti-Christ, and the time for siring has come."

His mouth dropped open, and he looked from Rachel to Alexander and back again. He pointed to the young man. "Is he…"

"Alexander, the Anti-Christ? Oh, no. But he could be his father. And so could you." She rose. "And Yeter'el thinks he can be, too."

"Shh! Don't speak his name out loud! Do you want to call him? He's going to hear you." Almost reflexively, Rick rushed across the room to make sure that the salt line at the base of the picture window was intact.

Rachel waved her hand dismissively. "He can't hear me all the way from the Abyss, not in here with all of your wards and protections."

"He's not in the Abyss," Rick said, irritated. "He's on the surface."

Alexander let out a cry of surprise and turned to Rachel. "Mother!"

"On the surface?" Her beautiful face set into a harsh expression of concern and anger. "What makes you say that?"

He went to the door to check the talisman on the coat hook. "I say that because he sent his appointment secretary to see me this morning at the rink. He wants to arrange a meeting."

Rachel crossed her arms. "This won't do. This just won't do. He's not supposed to be the sire! He can't be. There has to be human blood for the Anti-Christ to be born."

Her son asked, "But if he's on the surface, doesn't that mean he could just breed with a human woman?"

Silence fell over the group, and Rick shook his head in irritation. "He probably already has."

"Terrific," Alexander said, slumping in his seat on the couch. "We're fucked."

"Don't be so gloomy," Rachel chided.

"How else is he supposed to be?" Rick asked. "How are we supposed to stop my father? If you say he's already caught on to this whole End Times vibe, then who's to say he hasn't already gotten busy with some babe and made a kid?"

The succubus strode toward the door. "I know someone who will know, but he'll be very hard to find. I'll be in touch." She opened the door and went through, vanishing as she stepped through into the hallway.

Alexander jumped to his feet, startled to have his security blanket ripped away so abruptly. He looked at Rick, who looked back. They regarded each other silently for several long, painful moments until finally Rick did the only thing he could think of to do.

"You want a beer?"

"I'd love one."

CHAPTER FOUR

B*elow and Between*

Alexander sat on the couch and looked at his father, still amazed that he had finally met the man face-to-face. He was nothing like he had imagined he would be; he was rough-talking and had a brusque and energetic manner that did not match the elegance Alexander had always thought his father would have. Rick Buchanan had more of an incubus tang to his scent than the average half-blood would have, which he supposed was due to the power of the incubus who had sired him. They came from very exalted demonic stock.

Rick squirmed beneath his son's appraising gaze, and he picked at the label on his beer bottle. "I never expected to have a kid," he said, "much less one that's all grown up."

His words stung, but Alexander gave him the benefit of the doubt and chose to believe that he had intended no insult. "Are you sorry that you've met me?"

"No," he said quickly. "Not at all. I'm just... still getting my head wrapped around it." He looked down at his hands as if he'd just realized that he was fidgeting. He put his beer aside, untouched except for the mangled label. "Where do you suppose your mom went?"

Alexander shook his head. "I have no idea."

"I'll bet you wish she'd taken you with her."

"I'll bet that makes two of us."

He didn't deny it, and that stung, too. Alexander put his beer aside without tasting it. Rick flashed a smile, his teeth white and even and all present, despite what people on the radio and television said about hockey players. His father ran a hand over his dark brown hair and said, "So... tell me about yourself. Since you're grown, I assume you were born and raised in the Abyss?"

"Yes."

"Must have been hard."

Alexander shrugged. "It was all I knew. It was...Abyss-like. Screaming souls, rocks that wept, demons up to mischief. The usual sort of Abyss things. Mother tried to keep me in her lair and away from the worst of it. She pretty much secluded me from everyone but her sisters and their children." The expression on Rick's face was an unreadable combination of relief and something strange that Alexander could not identify. "It wasn't a bad upbringing, all things considered."

His father hesitated, rubbing his palms against his pants. He was sweating; Alexander could smell the first whiff of it from where he sat. "Did she... tell you about me?"

"Absolutely. She told me that you are an athlete, and that you live on the surface in New York City, in a place called Manhattan. She said you were gentle and good-natured."

"Gentle? Really?" He shook his head. "Wow."

"She found you to be a very satisfying lover."

Rick's face turned an alarming shade of pink. "She told you that?"

"Of course." Alexander wasn't certain why his father would be embarrassed to receive such a complimentary review. He should have been gratified. "She even gave me your picture, so I would know you when I saw you."

His father rose and walked to the picture window, looking out over the city. The harsh afternoon light outlined his body like a halo. Alexander had to look away from the painful brightness. "So she always intended for you to know me."

"Yes." He sighed. "I know this is a very big surprise to you, and probably an unwelcome one. Perhaps this was a mistake."

"What 'this'? Me finding out about you?" Rick turned to face him. "Why did she bring you here?"

"To meet you, and to keep me safe from the Incubus King."

"Why? What does this have to do with the End Times? What's she planning? She's a demon – she's got to have some sort of plan."

Alexander blinked as if Rick had just slapped him in the face. In a way, he had. "She's protecting me because she loves me. She's my mother. Even demons love their children." He stood and headed toward the door. "Perhaps it would help you to remember that you're also part demon. If you're capable of feeling, then consider that she is, too." He put his hand on the knob, sensing the uncomfortable vibration from the talisman on the back of the door. "And so am I."

His words fell heavily into the silence between them. Speechless, his father just watched him leave.

Above and Between

Jessica dialed Li's phone number, hoping that he wouldn't think she was crazy and hoping even more that he might have some experience in his monkish past that could help explain what was happening. The cat sat purring in her lap, its feet curled beneath itself, finally dry after its ordeal on the window sill and seemingly unhurt despite its battle with the... whatever it was that had been here. She shuddered and stroked the soft fur, listening to Li's cell phone ring.

Finally, he picked up. "Hello?"

"Li? I, uh… I need your help."

"Jess?" He sounded concerned. "Where are you?"

"I'm at home. Can you come over? Please?"

She could hear a rustling in the background, like newspaper. "Yes. I'll be there in just a few minutes."

Jessica blinked back tears, distantly surprised that they were there. She was falling apart. "Thank you. I really appreciate this."

"No problem. Just sit tight."

"Bye…"

She closed the phone and leaned down to kiss the cat's head. It purred in response, as if it was trying to tell her that everything was going to be okay. She hoped the cat was right.

Below and Between

Rick caught up with him halfway to the subway station. He grabbed his son's arm and said, "Hey, wait up. Hold on a minute." Alexander turned to face him, freeing his elbow from his grip, the look in his eyes veiled but hurt. Rick sighed. "I'm sorry I upset you. I didn't mean to. I'm not… I'm not very good at this kind of thing."

"What kind of thing?"

"*Family* kinds of things. I just… I don't know how to react, and I said the wrong thing. Okay? You probably shouldn't go off like this. Your mom will wonder where you are. You should wait for her at my place."

Alexander's voice was tight. "I have a place of my own. She knows where to find me."

"Where are you staying?"

"Why do you care?"

Rick sighed. "Because I do. I'm trying to."

He set his jaw. "Well, you have my e-mail. Let me know when you figure it out."

Alexander turned and walked away, his shoulders hunched in anger. All of the people he passed on the sidewalk stepped out of his way, some of them deliberately, some of them acting on pure instinct. Waves of intensity emanated from him like ripples on a pond, driven harder by his innate incubus charisma, currently turned on its aggressive edge. Rick muttered invectives under his breath and followed.

"Hey!" he called. "Wait up!"

His son ignored him and kept walking, heading down the steps to the subway station below. Rick trotted after him. He barely noticed that the average humans he was passing gave him the same respectful distance they'd given his quarry.

He jumped the last three steps and landed just behind Alexander, who whirled to face him with a set jaw and fists at the ready. Rick held his hands up in a show of harmlessness.

"I just want to talk."

"I think I've heard everything you have to say," Alexander spat.

"No, you haven't."

He glared. "So what else is there?"

Rick hesitated. "I… I don't really know…"

His son huffed a humorless laugh of exasperation and turned away, stalking down the platform. He followed, not even sure why he was doing it. It was clear that Alexander had had enough of him, but he wanted – no, needed – to say something else. The words were caught in his throat, a log jam of intent with no conscious meaning, and he wasn't even certain what those words were going to be. He only knew that there was something he had to get out.

He reached out for his son's arm again but before he could reach him, another hand, big, meaty and covered in grime, grabbed his wrist and wrenched him away. Rick turned on his assailant, a derelict mountain of a man who had clearly been living on the streets for too long. The man growled at him, his broken, pitted teeth blackened and strangely sharp. He pulled back his free hand to deliver a punch into those teeth when Alexander barked an order.

"Ulug! Enough."

The man released Rick abruptly, and he stumbled in the abrupt shift of balance. Ulug stepped back, glaring fiercely, as Alexander walked up slowly.

"This is Ulug. He's my bodyguard. Maybe I should let him beat you to a pulp, but that wouldn't serve any real purpose. Just take this as a hint that maybe you should leave me alone."

Rick looked from his son to the hulking bodyguard and back again. "He's a meat suit."

"He's an Utukku possessing a human, yes," Alexander nodded. "And he's my friend. I don't want to shock you, but demons have feelings for friends, too, as well as for their families."

"Look, Alex…"

"Don't call me that." He pulled himself up taller. "You haven't earned that right."

"I just want to get to know you."

"Why? What are you planning?" he mocked, parroting Rick's earlier words. "You're a partial demon, and demons always have a plan. Isn't that right?"

He groaned. "Look, I'm sorry I said that."

"So am I." He shook his head. "I spent my whole life wanting to meet you. I listened to my mother's stories about what a good person you are, what a good man you are, and I thought you'd be so much more than this. I thought you'd welcome me. Obviously, I was wrong."

"What was I supposed to do? Give you a kiss?"

"That *is* the standard incubus and succubus greeting."

"Well, pardon me, but I was raised on the surface, and that's not how we do things here."

Alexander's eyes narrowed. "Are you so content to live as a human being, to deny the power that you have, to deny your destiny?"

"My destiny is to win the Harper Cup," he snapped.

"Your destiny is wrapped up in the End Times, but, oh yes, you don't want to be bothered with something as inconvenient as all that."

"I'm just a hockey player!"

"No!" He stabbed his father's chest with an accusing finger. "You're half incubus, blessed with abilities and powers that the sheep around you can only dream of. You have the opportunity to do something special, to *be* something special, but all you want to do is masquerade as a normal man. Is that what you're using your human free will for? To hide?"

Rick knocked Alexander's hand away. "Not to hide! To fit in! You have no idea what it's like to be...*this*... here on the surface!"

"So I'm supposed to feel sorry for you now?"

He shook his head, his anger beginning to burn dangerously hot. "You know what? Fuck you, Alexander. Fuck your mother, fuck the Apocalypse, fuck my father, fuck this whole situation."

"Coward."

"*You're* calling *me* a coward? You're the one who's a grown man hiding behind your *mother*."

He never saw the right cross coming until it had knocked him to the pavement. He blinked up at Alexander in surprise, feeling the sting of a split lip and tasting blood. His son loomed over him, fists clenched, and Rick slowly became aware that this had all transpired on a public train station, in view and earshot of a dozen people. He prayed nothing showed up on YouTube.

Alexander growled, "I'm sorry I ever met you."

The train arrived with a whoosh and a rattle, and then Alexander and Ulug were gone, leaving Rick still lying on the platform, wondering how things had gone so wrong so quickly.

Above and Between

She was still shaking when Li arrived on her doorstep, his forehead creased with concern. He watched Jessica as she locked and double-locked the door behind him then saw the apartment's new occupant watching him quietly from the arm of the couch.

"You have a cat," he said.

"I think the cat has me." She wrapped her arms around herself. "Thank you for coming. I just... I really need to talk about something, and I think everybody else I know would think I'm just crazy."

Li smiled, unable to resist poking gentle fun. "And I'm just crazy enough, myself, to go along with whatever you need to say?"

She managed to smile back, but it was weak and timid and very un-Jessica-like. "Something like that."

He put his hands on her upper arms and held on gently. "What's going on, Jess?"

In a halting voice, she said, "Two different doctors have told me that I'm pregnant."

He could sense that perhaps congratulations were not in order. "Okay..."

"And I think the father is... I think he's..." She shook her head as tears welled in her eyes, one hand pressing to her forehead. "God, Li, you're going to think I'm crazy."

"You've already said that. I don't believe you're crazy, okay? I think there's something going on, maybe something strange...?"

"You have no idea how strange."

"Let's sit down, and I'll make you some tea, and you can tell me how strange it is." He smiled encouragingly. "Jessica, I'm your friend. I will believe you, no matter what you tell me."

She sat on the couch and wrapped her arms around her middle, huddling into a ball. The cat mewed sympathetically and climbed into her lap, rubbing its head against her wrist and purring loudly. Li went into her kitchen and filled her Mrs. Tea with water, preparing two cups with bags of green tea that he hoped would soothe her patently jangled nerves.

"I think the father is a ghost."

Her voice was barely audible to him from where she sat, even though the apartment was small. He was grateful that he had good hearing. "Why do you think that?" he asked, his tone level.

Jessica laughed hollowly. "That's not a conversation stopper?"

"Not at all. I am Buddhist. We believe in ghosts." He poured the hot water over the aromatic bags and carried the cups back into the living room, walking in a cloud of earthy aromas. "They are real. It is only in the supposedly rational West that the supernatural is denied."

She accepted one of the cups with a murmured thank you. "Can a ghost have made me pregnant?"

He considered the question seriously. "It's possible, I suppose, if the ghost you are dealing with is something like a *tulpa*, but it would have had to have been created for that purpose, and by someone with a great deal of power." He sipped his tea. "Why don't you tell me about him?"

"What is a *tulpa*?"

"A thought form made real. It's a spirit that's formed by the thoughts of its creator, and it can eventually become self-aware."

"Weird."

"Maybe, from a certain point of view."

She took a deep breath and put her tea aside. The cat snuggled closer, and while it was comforting, it was also annoying. She picked up the little animal and put it on the floor, where it immediately sat down with a little huff of indignation. She took a deep breath. "Okay, so, this guy. He just... *appears*. Right out of thin air. And he's totally gorgeous, but he really gives me the creeps. He said that he's been with me, and he fathered this kid, but Li... I know I never slept with him. I haven't been with anyone for over a year."

"That you know of."

"That's not very reassuring."

"Sorry. But if two doctors have said you have a baby on the way, then you must have been with someone, somehow, at some time." He smiled with a helpless little shrug. "I'm just saying..."

Jessica curled up further, bringing her knees to her chin and digging her heels into the seat of the couch. She wrapped her arms around her legs and brought them even closer, squeezing herself into an impossibly tight shape.

"So, anyway." She took a breath. "He appeared in the room, right there on the couch. Well, right about where I'm sitting, actually. Okay, that's creepy." She abruptly stood and moved to another seat, perching on one of the bistro stools by the kitchen. "He appeared, and the cat attacked him, and he sort of... ripped. But he was all... glowing inside. Red and glowing. And then he just disappeared."

"Hmm."

"See? You think I'm nuts. I told you."

"No, no. I'm just thinking that it doesn't sound much like a ghost to me." He drank more tea. "Sounds more like a demon."

She gaped at him, and the cat let out a purr-laced trill. They both looked at the monk while he serenely sipped away. "What?" she finally squeaked.

"A demon." He looked into her face and chuckled. "And this is harder to believe than a ghost?"

Jessica shook her head. "No, I just... augh! I feel like I'm living *Rosemary's Baby!*"

"Now who watches too many movies?"

"Li," she said, warningly. "Not helping."

He put his cup aside and crossed the room, stopping to crouch at her feet. He took her hands in his and looked into her eyes. "Jessica, I'm on your side. I will help you figure this out. If it's a demon, or even if it is a ghost – and I'm perfectly willing to admit that it might be a kind of creature I don't recognize – then there has to be a way to deal with it. The first thing we need to do is find a specialist, someone who knows about these things."

She snorted. "Oh, sure. I'll just look in the yellow pages for a demon-be-gone service."

He either misunderstood her sarcasm or ignored it. "Good. I'll check with some of my brothers at the temple." He squeezed her hands. "We will find a way to get you out of whatever trouble you've gotten yourself into."

She stood and pulled him to his feet, too, then wrapped him in a tight hug. "Thanks, Li. You're the best."

He smiled into her hair. "We Tsungs never turn our backs on our friends." He stepped back. "See you at the dojo tomorrow?"

"Yeah." She shook her head. "You really take everything in stride, don't you?"

"It's one of my strengths." Li kissed her forehead. "I'll call if I learn anything interesting before karate practice."

She walked him to the door, escorted by her cat, which clung to her ankles with a persistent purr. As he was leaving, she said softly, "Thanks, Li. You're a life saver."

He turned back to her with another beatific smile. "No. I'm just a friend." He reached down and gave the cat a parting scratch behind the ear, then trotted down the hallway to the elevators. She closed her door and slid the chain into place, wondering when her life had taken that fateful left turn at Albuquerque.

CHAPTER FIVE

elow and Between

B　　Alexander got off of the subway at the fourth stop, followed closely by Ulug. He was in unfamiliar territory in many ways. Just as this area of New York City was completely unknown to him, so his emotional responses to his father were a mystery, as well.

Rachel had always told him about his destiny, that he was descended from the line from which the Anti-Christ would be born. He always thought that his father was aware of that destiny, too, and that he would be somehow majestic, grand– maybe even holy in an unholy way. He thought his father would be special. Now that he had met him, he felt disappointed and betrayed by the reality of Rick Buchanan, by the very real mortal man he'd encountered after so many years of imagining a hero.

He went into the first bar that he came to, his sorrow making him hungry for life. Gathering places were good hunting grounds, especially when there were intoxicants involved. He had learned quickly under Lily's tutelage how to draw energy from the crowd and how to select an evening's prey. He yearned for the comfort of a sexual touch.

When they went inside, the early hour was reflected in the very few people perched on stools around the counter. Only two people were there to greet them, and one of them was an employee. The solitary patron sitting at the corner beside the Keno machine looked up, his dark eyes hooded as he sipped clear liquid from a grimy shot glass. He was huge, the largest human male that Alexander had ever seen, and his bald head and eagle-like nose made him even more imposing. He sat far away from the other man and ordered a drink.

Ulug started to sit beside him, but the stench from his meat suit, which was both unwashed and beginning to decay, made Alexander cough. "Ugh! Please, sit a little farther away." He shook his head as his bodyguard slid to another stool further down the bar. "You've just about outlasted that suit."

"I know," the Utukku said, grumpy. "Flimsy."

"It wouldn't be if you treated it better." His drink arrived, and he smiled his thanks to the bartender. "I'd hate to know what you get up to when you go out at night."

"Hate to tell you."

Alexander laughed. "Did you just make a joke?"

"Why so strange? Ulug very funny."

"I have to give you that." He gestured to the barkeeper. "One for my friend, here, and one for the fellow at the end of the bar."

The man snorted. "Feeling generous, huh? You got something to celebrate?"

"I'm young and alive. What better reason to be happy?" He put a pair of twenty-dollar bills onto the counter top. "Keep the change."

The drinks were poured and delivered, and the bartender turned his attention to cleaning up the bar. In the sudden near-privacy, the other patron rose to his full height and drained the glass that Alexander had bought for him. He went to an antiquated juke box that stood in the corner and selected something loud and raucous, then came and sat on the stool beside the young incubus.

"Thanks for the drink," he said. His voice was deep and rumbling.

"You're welcome." He held out his hand. "I'm Alexander Buchanan."

The man looked at his hand but did not shake it. Instead, he fixed a cold, steady gaze onto his eyes. "I know what you are."

Alexander's smile faltered and he said, "Uh... pardon?"

In a move that was almost too fast to see, the man leaped to his feet and pulled a long dagger out of a pocket scabbard stitched into the inside of his tan trench coat. The blade whistled toward Alexander's face, and he grabbed his assailant's wrist to try to stop the attack. Ulug fell on the attacker from behind, wrapping his arms around him and trying to pin him. The man was as immense in strength as he was in size, though, and combined with the deteriorated state of the Utukku's borrowed body, that made it easy for him to throw Ulug aside.

Behind the bar, the bartender watched dispassionately, wiping a glass with a filthy towel. Alexander cried out to him, "Help me!"

"No chance, devil boy."

The huge man knocked him to the floor and straddled him, preparing to bring the dagger down into his throat. Alexander did the only thing he could think of to do, and he played the only trump card he had. He grabbed the man by the ears and kissed him.

As soon as his lips met the attacker's, he connected with the soul inside and started to pull. The man struggled in his grip, but an incubus kiss, even an unwanted one, was a compelling thing, and he soon stopped fighting. Ulug plucked the dagger out of his limp hand as Alexander continued the kiss, drawing the man's life force out in a rush. The bartender cried out in alarm and vaulted over the bar, a short Roman sword in his hand, and Ulug decapitated him in mid-leap. His body fell aside with a clatter as the huge man, shuddering in his last throes of ecstasy, succumbed to orgasm and gave up the last dredges of his soul in the same instant.

Alexander released the kiss and fell back against the floor, the man's heavy body sprawled on top of him. Ulug pulled the corpse aside and gave his master a hand up.

"Not a man," Ulug said.

His mouth felt like he'd been kissing a live wire, stinging painfully. He touched his lips and was mildly surprised that there was no blood. "I don't know what he was. He was part human, but not all." He doubled over, his midsection gripped with agonizing cramps. "Oh, shit..."

Ulug looked from Alexander to the dead bodies on the floor, then gave a shuddering sigh and abandoned his meat suit, which collapsed to the floor in a messy heap. He shrugged into the fallen giant instead, seating himself comfortably in the hollow where the man's soul had been. He rose in his new body, shaking arms and legs and getting the feel of how it moved and felt.

"I like," he said, smiling. "Stronger than the others." He looked on curiously as a tattoo on the left wrist, shaped like wings, sparked and then disappeared. "Part angel, I think."

"What? No..." He held out a hand to Ulug, asking silently for support. The Utukku, not given to things like compassion, stepped out of the way, letting Alexander fall. He watched his master struggling with the after-effects of his meal.

"Too strong for you," his bodyguard told him helpfully. "Too big for you."

The incubus gasped, "Just get me home!"

Ulug grappled his master into something like a fireman's carry and hauled him out into the street, where he waved for a taxi. "Should have waited. Ulug would have killed. Happy to kill." He considered his own words. "Of course, then meat suit already broken. Hmph."

A cab pulled up to the curb, and Ulug deposited him in the back seat. He handed the driver one of the pre-printed address cards that Lily had made up for him, along with more than enough money to pay the fare.

"Take him," he ordered the driver. "Drop him here."

"You got it, buddy."

The Utukku watched the taxi pull away. Once he was sure it was safely en route, he returned to the bar to deal with the mess.

It was his custom, as with most hockey players, to take a nap on the afternoon of a game. Today, though, Rick failed to get anything like sleep and found himself spending the time laying on his back and staring at the ceiling, wracking his brain for something, anything, he could have done differently today.

He hadn't meant to have his first meeting with Alexander – with his *son* – go so badly. He had really stuck his foot in it, and now he was having a hard time getting rid of the smell. He didn't blame the kid for being so upset with him. Hell, if he'd been Alexander, he'd have been pretty pissed, too. Rick had offered him a pretty lame welcome to the family.

Family. He supposed that he finally had one, such as it was. He'd been on his own for so long, he had no idea what family was supposed to feel like. The last time he'd seen his grandparents was when he was moving away for junior hockey, back when he was fourteen. He'd seen enough of families over the years with his teammates and on television to know how families were supposed to look, and how they were supposed to act. He just didn't know how he was supposed to be part of one.

He should really have been angry with Rachel for springing this on him this way. She was always spontaneous, but this was taking things just a bit too far in his mind. Spontaneous surprises that he could deal with were things like tickets to a Yankees game or a weekend in a luxury hotel in the Hamptons. A twenty-something man was not the sort of surprise that Rick could ever see himself happy to receive.

Alexander curled up on his side, his arms clutched across his cramp-pained belly. He was sweating from the pain and swore to himself that he would never, under any circumstances, ever eat a part-angel soul again. He wondered if he was dying from some sort of poisoning and was in nearly enough agony to wish that he might.

Lily crept into the bed and wrapped herself around him from behind, her arms draped over his. She laced their fingers together and kissed his ear.

"Poor baby," she cooed. "Don't worry. It will pass."

He groaned. "I hope so..."

"I'll teach you to tell the angels from the humans. I'm surprised you couldn't tell before you hunted."

"I wasn't hunting. I was... *augh!*... defending myself." He tried to breathe as his insides twisted into sailors' knots. "I didn't have my dagger with me. Stupid."

Lily kissed his temple. "Let me help you," she purred. "I can take some of that energy away from you so you aren't in so much discomfort."

"Anything..."

The succubus pulled him onto his back and straddled him, her hands on his shoulders. He opened his mouth to speak, but she silenced him with a deep kiss. He could feel her tongue probing into his mouth, could feel her reaching out to connect with all of that excess energy inside of him that was making him so ill. He opened his mouth for her and tried to push the energy toward her. Lily moaned happily and sucked it down, greedy for what he offered. He gladly fed soul shards into her hungry need.

His mother had fed him this way when he was a child in the Abyss, back before he was old enough to have sex and feed himself. He had been like a baby bird, accepting the regurgitations of his parent. He had never expected to be on this side of the exchange, but he found that he rather liked it.

The pain in his midsection was letting loose, and other feelings began to take its place. He flipped Lily over onto her back, and she laughed huskily as he let those "other feelings" have sway.

Rick finally gave up on the nap and got up, dressing in his favorite Hugo Boss suit and making sure he looked presentable for the press and fans that always crowded around, watching for a glimpse of the players on their way into the game. Since the Devil Rays' top defenseman had lipped off about the league's poster boy, Chris Michaels, the media circus had been particularly galling, hunting for the next inflammatory sound bite in the war of words between his team and their chief conference rivals, the Boston Rippers. Rick tried to stay out of it. He didn't need to add to the cracktastic sideshow.

He made it past the cameras and fans with a minimum of fuss, then made his way into the changing room. It took no time and less thought for him to change out of his suit and into his UnderArmor, which was good, because his mind was still full of pointless agonizing. He went into the locker room and sat heavily on the stool in front of his stall, dropping his skates to the floor between his feet. Beside him, busy with his own pre-game preparations, his teammate Andrew Kozlarek looked over at him, one eyebrow arching quizzically.

"Bad day?"

"You could say that." He ran a hand over his carefully-coiffed hair. Rick had been a confirmed metrosexual before anybody had even thought of the term. "I, uh... I found out today that I have a kid."

Andrew whistled. "Dude," he said, his Czech accent making the California surfer lingo sound doubly ridiculous. "That sucks."

"Yeah. Big time." They fell silent and busied themselves with their equipment. Rick could feel his friend watching him, and it was beginning to annoy him. He was about to say something when Andrew spoke again.

"You happy? You know what you gonna do?"

He admitted, "No and no."

"It's okay. Same thing happened in Boston to Ipatinev, I hear."

He chuckled in spite of himself. "You always have the gossip, don't you?"

Andrew nodded. "I have *connections*."

"Mafia?"

"Girlfriends."

"You have a girlfriend?" Rick challenged. "Since when?"

Kozlarek shrugged almost defensively. "Not anymore. She's with Ipatinev now. But I still hear things."

"You stay in touch with your ex?"

The Czech hockey player had the good graces to look embarrassed as he admitted, "No... with her mother."

It was the best laugh Rick had had all day.

After the game, after the reporters had finished asking the same three questions in not-new and infinitely boring ways, and after he'd had his post-game work-out and pizza slice, Rick made his way out to the players' parking lot to face the fans. He wasn't alone, for which he was infinitely grateful. He walked out with Andrew, his line mate on the ice and his wingman off of it. They were two of the most popular Devil Rays, and the screams that met them when they emerged from the arena served notice that the puck bunnies were there.

Rick went to the kids first, kneeling down and posing for pictures with a trio of excited little boys, grinning up at their mother while the oldest of the three rattled on about his peewee hockey team. He said something vanilla and encouraging to the kid, signed his jersey, and moved down the line, signing jerseys and other memorabilia that people shoved at him. *This is all gonna end up on eBay,* he thought.

Nina bounced up to him, her cleavage ridiculous. She was easily the most determined and experienced of the player groupies, and she had probably slept with every member of the team at least once. He considered her the captain of the puck bunny team. He smiled to her as she pressed a slip of paper into his hand. He knew from their past history that she was passing him her hotel name and room number, and probably her phone number, too, even though he had her cell number programmed into his Blackberry. It was always good to know where to find a willing slam piece on short notice.

"Great game, Rick," she purred, leaning forward to kiss him on the cheek. She was wearing the perfume he had given her for Christmas last year.

"Thanks, babe." He handed the paper back to her. "Can't tonight. We're jetting out for Calgary. I have to go straight to the airport from here."

She pouted prettily. "Will you call me when you get back?"

"Probably." He gave her his brightest smile. "Take care of yourself until then, eh?"

"For sure."

He heard Andy laughing, dark and dirty, and he shook his head. "I'd better grab Stretch and get him to the airport, or GM's gonna have our heads."

Nina put the tip of a finger into her mouth, puckering her scarlet lips around it for a moment while he caught her drift. "When you come back, maybe I can have your heads, instead."

He chuckled. "I think that can probably be arranged." He stepped back. "Andy! Car!" Kozlarek acknowledged him with a floppy hand wave, and Rick shook his head. "You don't want to be late. You know that makes McMillan insane."

Reluctantly, his friend stepped away from Nina's companions, each of whom had been making the same offers as their "captain." Andy and Rick said good bye to the last of the fans, signed a few more autographs, then made their way to Rick's SUV for the drive to the airport. As they got inside and buckled themselves in, Andy said, "I wish we could have taken just an hour..."

"Be my guest," he shrugged, "but you'll have to drive yourself to the plane. I'm not sitting through another one of coach's lectures about propriety."

The Czech player watched the girls as Rick pulled away. "Might be worth it."

"Nothing is worth one of McMillan's lectures."

"Just ignore him. Keep one ear bud in. Is what I do."

"Yeah, and that's why you still don't know if you have a contract after this season." Rick hit the turn signal with possibly a bit more emphasis that he needed to. "And I'm a good boy, which is why I'm already sewn up for the next five."

Andy shrugged and slumped down into the seat, splaying his long legs out in front of him. "Yeah, yeah, yeah. Well, when we get back, I'm calling Stephanie."

"Feel free. I'm calling Nina."

"She has crabs."

"She does not!"

"You sure?"

"I'm sure."

"When you last with her?" Andy challenged.

"Tuesday, if you must know," Rick responded. "And trust me – she's clean."

"Well, that's different than last time I was with her."

"Maybe the crabs came from you."

Andy glowered. "Not funny."

"Ooh, truth hurts." He nosed the SUV out into traffic and headed toward the highway. "If anybody's dirty, it's Stephanie."

The Czech smiled. "I know. That's why I like her best."

CHAPTER SIX

*B*elow and Between

Being on the top line of a professional hockey team had its perks, including trips on a private plane with pretty flight attendants, a cushy bus waiting at the airport to take them to their hotel well after midnight, and a plush room with a pillow-top king-sized bed. Rick sank gratefully into that bed, weary from the lingering effects of a hard game and a long flight. He closed his eyes and shoved the stiff hotel bedspread down toward his ankles, ready for rest.

He had just begun to doze when a slender feminine form appeared behind him in the bed, literally taking form out of the space between his back and the bed sheet. She pressed against him and snaked her arm out around his waist, snuggling close. Soft lips pressed a tiny kiss between his bare shoulder blades, and he smiled in spite of himself.

"Rachel," he said, identifying his late-night caller. He was rewarded with a tightening of her embrace and a barely-audible hum. He laced his fingers with hers and sighed. "I thought you were out hunting somebody down."

"I was," she whispered, her breath tickling the hairs on the back of his neck. "I got tired."

"Here for a fill-up?" he teased, rolling over and facing her.

The succubus propped herself up on her elbow and looked down at him, affection shining on her face. "I didn't come to feed from you."

"Liar."

She smiled. "All right, then... I didn't come *just* to feed from you."

Rick chuckled. "That sounds closer to the truth." She bent to kiss him, and he returned the little tenderness. "Speaking of truth, you know, I have a bone to pick with you."

"Alexander?" she guessed.

"Give the lady a kewpie doll."

"Ugh. No thank you. Hideous things." She moved closer, and he put his left arm out so that she could snuggle into his side. She happily accepted the silent offer and pillowed her head on his chest, her hand running along the peaks and valleys of his muscular abdomen. "I thought you'd be happy that I gave you a son. I could have forced a daughter, you know. Most succubi do."

He kissed her hair, wondering why he could never stay annoyed with her. "I'm flattered, yes. But it was just... such a shock to have a grown-up son all of a sudden, you know?"

Rachel sighed. "If you want me to say I'm sorry, I'm not going to, because I'm never going to be ashamed of my son...our son."

"I'm not ashamed of him. I'm just... not good at this whole family thing." He gestured helplessly, then rested his hand on her bare shoulder again. "Not a whole lot of practice, I guess. I really screwed things up with him after you left."

"How so?"

"He thinks I'm the biggest loser he's ever met. I made him feel unwelcome, and I can see where he got that idea."

"Is he unwelcome?"

He thought for a moment, trying to be honest with himself. "A little," he finally admitted. "But I just need some time to get used to the idea of him. He's had a lifetime to get used to the idea that I'm out here. I've had about a day and a half." He shook his head. "He's really disappointed that I turned out to be a normal guy and not whatever dragon slayer he'd imagined."

She moved so she could look into his face, her eyes glittering in the partial light from the window. "You are a dragon slayer. You're everything a hero is supposed to be."

"Except heroic."

Rachel sighed. "My darling Richard, you are so impatient. You haven't had a need to be heroic in your life yet. That time will come, and you will rise to the occasion. I've seen it. I've seen the strength in you." She kissed him. "Alexander will see that strength in you, too, in time."

"I'm pretty sure he doesn't give a rat's ass what I am at this point. I doubt he'll ever talk to me again. When I screw things up, I do a really thorough job."

"I'll talk to him," she reassured him.

Her hand on his stomach curled slightly, and he could feel her tugging at the little knot of life force that curled in his solar plexus. His body responded to the pull, and he chuckled again. "So, it's that time, is it?"

She stretched out on top of him and grinned. "Dinner is served."

Between

Tsung Li rose long before dawn was even a hint in the eastern sky. He could hear the rustling sleep sounds of the other monks who lived with him. The walls were thin in the little suburban house on Long Island that they had converted into a Buddhist monastery. He sometimes thought that they should just take the walls down and live together in one large room. They had no need for privacy, and the walls did nothing to stop noise, anyway.

He put on flip flops and pulled his robe on over his sleeping clothes – a very Westernized ensemble of boxer shorts and a New York Mets T-shirt – and headed out toward the shrine. It stood in what had once been the living room of this house, the statue of the Buddha taking pride of place where the fireplace had once stood. In front of that statue, his master sat in prayerful meditation, eyes closed, a look of absolute serenity on his ageless face. Li sat on his own mat, behind and to the right of his master, and waited.

After a few silent minutes, his master spoke. "You are worried."

It wasn't a question. It didn't have to be. His master could have read his very soul from where he sat, his face turned toward the wall and away from Li. "Yes, Master."

"Come, sit by me."

He moved to the front of the room and sat on the mat beside his master, who shifted slightly to face the younger monk. Master Yu Kun was a Caucasian man, born in England but raised in Tibet, where he had shed his Western name. They had come to America together when Li was just a child, and there was no one that Li trusted more.

"I have a friend who says she has been made pregnant by a spirit." He felt ridiculous now that he had said it. He was almost embarrassed, but he put the emotion aside. Emotions were barriers to the truth. Yu Kun watched him quietly, so he continued. "She's not a crazy sort of girl. She's very smart, and not the kind of person to claim something like this without having a reason to believe it."

"Perhaps she is ashamed of her pregnancy and tries to conceal the true father."

"No," Li said, shaking his head. "I know Jessica better than that. She's not that sort of person. If she said that's what happened, then that's exactly what happened. But I believe her for more than that. Master… she said that the spirit that made her pregnant came to her in her apartment and claimed to be a demon. Her cat attacked it to protect her, and where its claws scratched it, it glowed with a strange light. That can't be a natural man. I had thought at first that it was a *tulpa*, but that doesn't make any sense. Who would create a thought-form to disrupt her life so completely?"

"Does she have any enemies?"

"Not that I know of."

"And you know her well?"

"Very well."

Yu Kun raised an eyebrow. "Could you be the father?"

Li laughed. "Oh, no. I don't know her that well, Master. If I were the father, I would admit it."

"That's good. I would hate to think that I had misjudged you after all this time." He smiled to the younger man. "Did this spirit give her any other information during his visitation?"

"No. Not that she said."

He pondered the situation for a moment, and Li waited for his master's wisdom. Finally, Yu Kun asked, "Did she say whether this spirit man was extremely handsome?"

He blinked. "Uh... yes, now that you mention it, she did."

His master sighed. "That's what I feared. So it's come to that, has it? Well, it can't be helped, I suppose. It was bound to happen eventually."

He knew he sounded stupid, but he had to admit his ignorance. "Master, what are you talking about?"

Not uncharacteristically, Yu Kun answered his question with a question of his own. "Li, what do you know about something called an incubus?"

Again, the young monk blinked, inwardly suspecting that he looked not too unlike a perplexed ox. "I think that's the name of a rock band..."

His master smirked. "And? What does the name mean?"

"I think it's a kind of western demon."

"Correct. It's a sexual predator, a male demon that is said to lie with mortal women and beget half-breed children called cambions. The women sometimes know, and sometimes they don't. These creatures are the source of lust and disorder in this world."

Li shifted uncomfortably, a creeping uneasiness tickling his spine. "You're talking like they're real." A sexual demon would explain Jessica's situation more than any of the other explanations he had considered. Somehow, he was not comforted.

"That's because they are."

Yu Kun rose smoothly and gestured for Li to follow. He led him out to the garage, where the community's sole automobile quietly sat and rusted. Today, though, Master was calling the vehicle into service. He opened the garage door and unlocked the aging Chevrolet. Still speaking only with hand motions, he indicated that Li should get into the passenger seat. Obediently, he did, watching his master's face with growing alarm while the Englishman fastened his seat belt and threw the car into reverse.

Above and Between

Jessica stood with the phone in her hand, unable to decide what to do. Her head still felt heavy with confusion after a long and sleepless night, and all she could muster was a vague hope that Li had been able to find someone to help her. She put the phone back into the charger and decided that dealing with the asshat attorney she called "boss" could wait until another day. She left a voice mail for him, calling in sick, and put him out of her mind.

Her cat rubbed against her ankles, its loving eyes turned up toward her face. She crouched down and gave it a scratch behind the ears, then a gentle stroke along the spine. It responded with an arched back and a loud purr.

"Everything is so easy for you," she told the cat. "You just eat, sleep, eat, sleep, repeat. Wow... what a racket."

The cat blinked at her, looking for all the world as if it would have argued with her if it could use a human voice. Jessica sighed and gave the cat one more pat on the side before she rose and walked into the bathroom. It was a strange hour for it, but all she really wanted to do was take a long soak.

She indulged in her rarely exercised girliness by pouring fragrant bath salts into the hot water as it filled the tub. She added to the ambiance by settling her iPod into its dock, the music on her current playlist rising like the steam that clouded the mirror.

Satisfied, she slid into the welcoming heat with a sigh. The cat looked on from its perch on the clothes hamper, silently standing guard.

The song that was playing took her back to the last days of her undergraduate career. "When I'm Gone" by Three Doors Down had been playing in the background on the night she told Evan that she was leaving, going to law school hundreds of miles away. She hadn't realized at the time how appropriate a soundtrack the song had made. Evan had been disappointed, but not angry; if anything, she thought now that he had looked a little relieved. That night had been the last time they'd made love, a good-bye for the ages. It was last time she'd felt a man's touch.

Jessica moved her hand to rest lightly on her lower abdomen, over the spot where she supposed her little unwelcome passenger was growing into a giant life complication. She wondered how she would feel if she had conceived that night with Evan, or if Evan was still a part of her life. She had seen on Facebook that he was dating someone named Lisa now.

Tears rose in her eyes, stinging and hot. With a stifled sob, she slouched deeper into the tub, letting the scented water rise to her chin.

Between

They drove for a long time in utter silence. Li waited for Yu Kun to speak first, out of both respect and bafflement. He had never seen his master behave in this way. For the first time in his life, Li saw tension around Yu Kun's eyes, and it made him afraid.

After an hour of what seemed like pointless driving, the old car chugged and huffed its way into a parking spot outside a grimy little diner not far from a city park. The two men went inside and found a spot in a corner booth, far away from the service counter and the smattering of other diners in the restaurant. A middle-aged waitress with bottle-red hair brought them menus, which Yu Kun directed Li to take with a nod, and offered coffee, which the Englishman politely declined. Once they were alone, his master finally spoke, but in a hushed whisper.

"There is something that I need to tell you, and I'm uncertain how to begin. It has to do with your friend's problem, and with the incubus who impregnated her." He glanced toward the door. "I asked someone to come and help me explain, but he's not here yet."

Li looked down at the menu, not really seeing the faded photographs and smeared print. "Are you in some sort of trouble, Master?"

"In all honesty? Yes. We all are."

The little bell above the diner's sole entryway jangled discordantly, announcing the arrival of another patron. A tall man in a white trench coat walked into view, heading straight to their table. Yu Kun rose as the man approached. Li stood, too.

"Michael," he greeted, something like reverence in his voice.

"Andrew." The newcomer smiled benignly and took a seat across from Li. The monk's senses hummed in the man's presence, something he had never felt before. It was like leaning against a transformer for a city block. Yu Kun sat, too, and once again Li echoed his motions.

"Have you told him?" Michael asked.

"Not yet."

Li looked from his master to the blond stranger. "Tell me what?"

Yu Kun pushed his sleeve up his arm, revealing the aged tattoo on his wrist. "What do you think this is?"

He was getting more confused by the moment. His master had worn the tattoo for Li's entire life; he had never seen him without it. In all that time, Li had never given it the least bit of thought. He finally ventured, "Angel wings?"

"Exactly, but what does it mean?"

"That you like angels?"

Michael smiled at the young monk's bewildered innocence. "It's an emblem. Think of it as a regimental patch."

He looked askance at his master. "You were in the army?"

"I still am. But this is no normal, mortal army." Yu Kun took a deep breath. "Years ago, I was enrolled in a Catholic seminary in England."

"Saint Cuthbert's at Ushaw College in Durham," their trench-coated companion said helpfully.

"Yes, Saint Cuthbert's. I was entering my third year of study when Michael approached me." He took a deep breath, as uncomfortable as Li had ever seen him. It was alarming. "He told me certain truths...."

"Truth," Li said. "I can get behind that."

Michael smirked. "Andrew, allow me." He folded his hands – big, meaty hands with surprisingly well-manicured fingers – on the table and fixed Li with a steady gaze. His ice blue eyes seemed to shimmer for a moment, and Li again had the unpleasant sensation of touching a live wire. "I approached Andrew many years ago to invite him to join our cause. You see, the world has long been locked in a battle between the forces of Light and the forces of Darkness. I am the commander of one regiment in the forces of Light. Andrew was recruited to join me, to help in the fight. Do you understand?"

Li lied, "Yes."

"First, let me tell you that God is real. I don't mean a divine spark, or an ethereal higher consciousness, although He is all that and more. I mean God. Jehovah, Yahweh, Allah, Ahura Mazda, known by many names. But there is no God but God." His gaze seemed to penetrate into Li's mind, and the monk found that he could not look away. He was pinned as surely as a butterfly in a collector's box. "And where there is God, there is also the Adversary, known by nearly as many names, none of which I will speak here. The old adage is true: speak of the devil and he will come. Or at least, speak of the devil and he will hear."

He could not tear his eyes away from Michael's gaze, but he could shake his head. "I don't believe in a Creator-God. I believe in angels and devas and higher spirits, ascended masters, but not a Creator-God."

Michael smiled again, not mockingly, but amused by Li nonetheless. "And what if I told you that I am one of those angels?"

"I would say that I need proof."

The waitress came to their table at that moment, her arrival shattering the strange hold that their visitor had on Li's mind. The monk sat back and blinked, feeling dizzy. Yu Kun ordered breakfast for all three of them, then waited for the woman to walk away. Once she was gone, he said, "Li, you cannot ask for proof. That is disrespectful."

Li blushed in shame. "I know, Master, but this is difficult. I'm sorry."

"It's all right," Michael said calmly. "If you want proof, then I can provide it."

He held up his right hand in a slow, gentle motion, not quite a wave. Abruptly, all sound and motion in the diner ceased. The other diners, the waitress, the short-order cook – all of them froze in their tracks, forks halfway to mouths, conversations stilled. Li looked out the window, and the traffic in the street was static as well, as if all of reality was a DVD and someone had hit the pause button. The only sound was Li's startled breathing.

"Do you believe?" the stranger asked.

He could not wrap his mind around the things he was being asked to accept. He shook his head and stammered, "I – I can't..."

"Then believe this." Michael rose and cast aside his trench coat. In its place he wore shimmering golden armor, almost painfully bright to look upon, and from his back two giant wings with snow-white feathers grew. He stepped into the aisle between the booths and the counter and turned to the side, then spread those wings so wide that the pin feathers touched both the front and back doors at the same time. In his hand, he held a broadsword made not of steel but of brilliant light, and it flashed as he held it up.

Li's eyes watered against the brightness, and he tried to look away, but he found that once again his gaze was riveted. Beside him, Yu Kun said, "Allow me to introduce Saint Michael the Archangel, Prince of the Seraphim, general of the armies of Heaven."

Michael stood in his full glory for a long moment, then folded his wings and once again appeared as a Nordic-looking human in a white coat. He sat, and all around them the world sprang back into motion.

"Do you believe now?" the angel asked.

He could only nod.

CHAPTER SEVEN

*B*elow & Between

    The archangel's revelation went unnoticed by the human population, but for those with demonic blood, it was a literal thunder clap. In Winnipeg, Rachel shrieked and clambered out of bed, covering herself beneath the bed sheet and trying unsuccessfully to gather herself enough to flee. Rick was startled awake by the massive booming in his head, and he leaped to his feet, instinctively ready to fight.

    "What the hell was that?" he demanded. Rachel only whimpered, too terrified to do anything else. He went to the window and parted the curtains, peering out into the pre-dawn darkness for any sign of what had happened. Nothing was apparent, so he returned to his companion.

    Rachel clung to him desperately, her fingers digging into his biceps as she babbled, "He's here. He's here. Oh, hide me, please! Hide me!"

He had never seen a succubus be so afraid. It was contagious, and he felt fear tickle the back of his neck. "Who's here? Rachel, talk to me!"

Tears welled in her eyes, and she whispered, "The Viceroy of Heaven." She pulled him closer, pressing her forehead into his naked chest. "If he's on the surface, then it's happened."

His confusion was threatening to become angry frustration. "What's happened?"

Rick pushed her away and lifted her chin, forcing her to look at him. She was weeping. He had never seen her cry before.

"They've found the Anti-Christ."

Above and Between

The waitress brought their breakfast with a smile, the left the two men and their angelic companion to sit in silence. Yu Kun began to eat, but Li could only stare down at his plate, his mind whirling. Michael watched him with a look of compassion and understanding on his angular face. Finally, the angel spoke. "Your beliefs are not wrong," he told the young monk gently. "I have not revealed myself to you to shake your faith. I have come to extend it." He nodded to the Englishman. "Andrew has known about this for many years. He has had time to adjust his thinking, and he is comfortable with this truth. This is shocking to you. I do not expect you to accept everything at once. The Most High provided humanity with questing minds because He wanted them to be used."

It took more time, but Li finally found his voice. "Wh-why now? Why do you show yourself?"

Yu Kun answered. "There is a terrible battle coming. We need to have men of good heart and good character standing with us. Normally we wait until a human being has had direct contact with the other side, but I think what your friend is going through is contact enough."

"This is a recruitment, to put it in terms you may understand," Michael said, his voice soft. "The armies of Hell are rising, preparing to invade this world. Everything that mankind is, was, and will become hangs in the balance. All of God's creation is at risk, but we still have the chance to stem the tide. Will you stand with us against the forces of evil?"

His stomach tightened, and he pushed his plate away. Food was nauseating him. "How is Jessica involved?"

His Master answered. "I told you that demons are real, specifically the incubi. I believe that your friend was impregnated by an incubus."

"Which could mean that she is carrying the Anti-Christ."

The archangel's words fell onto the table like cold, wet towels. Li could practically feel the thud as they landed in his world. "The Anti-Christ," he echoed. He closed his eyes and took a deep breath. "Tell me what that means, really. I've seen it in movies, and I know it's evil, but I really don't understand. Is it the one true son of the devil? Is that what you mean?"

Yu Kun took a sip of his orange juice, maddeningly unaffected by it all. "Not exactly. The Anti-Christ is a demon-human hybrid, as Christ Himself was a blend of human and divine."

"I don't believe in Christ," Li whispered.

"You'd better start, because He'll be one of your best allies in the days to come."

Michael held up a hand, and Yu Kun fell silent. "I do not ask you to worship, Tsung Li, son of Tsung Tsu. I ask you to believe that what we say is true. Let me ask this: have you heard that Jesus and Mary Magdalene had children?"

Li blinked and looked at the angel, confusion clear on his face. "What?" He shook his head to clear the remnants of his shock. "I've seen *The Da Vinci Code*, if that's what you're asking."

His Master chuckled and Michael nodded. "Yes, something like that. The premise of that film is not fiction. Jesus of Nazareth and Miriam of Magdala were wed, and she bore him a daughter. From her a bloodline of the blessed has sprung." He gave Li a moment to digest this new detail before continuing. "At the same time, another woman bore a son to a fallen angel once called The Son of the Morning."

He had seen enough horror films to know that name. "Lucifer," he whispered.

"Yes." Michael nodded his blond head. "There is a cursed bloodline, as well. Several of them, in fact. Every five hundred years, one of those cursed bloodlines throws out a potential challenger for the throne of God, and they again assail Heaven in their pride and anger. They seek to overthrow the Mighty One and take His power for themselves."

Li leaned his elbows on the table and put his face into his hands. He was feeling a strange urge to laugh. "I feel like I'm caught in a bad movie." He scrubbed the heels of his hands into his eyes, then dropped his arms back to his sides. "I'm listening."

"There is a prophecy that the ultimate Anti-Christ, the one who will finally storm the gates of Heaven and allow the fallen angels to take control of the Kingdom, will be born from a different line of demons. Many have come to believe that this line began with the Watchers."

Yu Kun watched his student to see if he recognized the term; Li's face remained blank, so he explained. "The Watchers were angels who fell from grace and were condemned because of their love for human women. They and their progeny were cursed."

The young man spoke quietly. "That's not very fair. It wasn't the children's fault."

"The sins of the fathers rest heavily upon the sons," Michael responded.

"Still…"

Yu Kun jumped in. "We don't question God's judgment. This was before Covenant, anyway."

"You keep throwing all these Christian terms around. I don't understand." Li looked to his Master. "You know I don't know that religion. You know that the Buddha is all I've ever known. This is contrary to everything I've ever been taught. You're asking me to believe in fairy tales."

Michael scowled, and the air around him crackled. "Be careful with your words. They could be taken as disrespect." His blue eyes were cold as ice chips. "You do not want to disrespect God, and you do not want to disrespect me."

"I don't understand!"

His Master put a hand on his shoulder. "Li, we know this is hard for you. Try to put your questions aside for a little while, though, and listen to what we have to say. This is important for you to hear. The believing part can come later." He took a deep breath. "I tell you this about the Watchers because when they fell and were cursed, they became demons – demons of pride, of lust, of war and of malice. One of them became the first incubus." He nodded when he saw Li make the connection. "Yes. Your friend Jessica may have been impregnated by a demon in the line from which the Anti-Christ is expected to arise. She may be carrying the end of the world within her womb."

Li wanted to vomit. He clenched his teeth on the images that rose in his mind. "Tell me what I have to do."

"Do you want to protect her?" Michael asked him. "Do you want to keep her safe and in the process defend the innocent souls in the world from the power of the Master of Evil?"

"Yes." He looked the angel in the eye, his jaw set. He gathered his courage and it steadied him. "I will stand with you."

A sudden heat spread over the inside of his left wrist, just shy of pain, and he looked down, startled. The outline of angel wings was appearing as he watched, a dark line running around the outside of the figure, then racing in to describe the details. It was like watching computer animation, but it was in his skin. When the last line was drawn, the tattoo glowed gold for a moment, sending a tingling sensation running up his arm all the way to his brain. His head throbbed with it, and he could sense that tingling running down the inside of his spine. He shuddered at the feeling.

Michael and his Master were smiling at him when he looked up. They looked proud. He swallowed a lump in his throat. "Does Jessica know?"

"No," the angel said quietly. "Not yet."

"Should I tell her?"

"No," he said again. "Someone else will do that duty." Michael stood and nodded to them. "I will come for you when you are needed."

Li looked at Yu Kun, who was busy pulling money out of his wallet to pay for their meal. When he looked back, Michael was gone.

Below and Between

Alexander tumbled out of bed when he felt the thunder clap of the archangel's presence. He crouched against the wall, shaking, overcome with the sort of fear he had only known in the Abyss. On the other side of the lair, Ulug was howling like a terrified dog, doing his best to cram his oversized borrowed body underneath the coffee table and succeeding only in toppling it onto its side. Lily was nowhere to be seen.

He cried out mentally. *Mother! What is happening?*

He could sense that his mother was out there somewhere, and that she was as terrified as he, which made everything so much worse. He pressed his trembling hands over his ears to block out Ulug's noise and tried to be as small as he could, hoping against hope that he would not be dying today.

As suddenly as the maelstrom had begun, it subsided, leaving only an unsteady silence in its wake. Ulug finally stopped shrieking. Alexander tentatively rose to his feet and looked around.

"Where is Lily?" he asked the Utukku.

"Don't know! Don't care! Big angel on surface. Fuck!"

"Which angel? What's happening?"

Ulug strode over and bent so that his face was only inches away from the young incubus nose. "Michael," he spat. "Fucking *Michael!*"

He shrank back. "How do you know?"

"You stupid? You feel that? Only Michael that big!" He flapped his big arms like a giant aggrieved chicken. "Only Michael come and go, top to between to top!"

Alexander went to his closet and grabbed a duffel bag, then started shoving clothes haphazardly inside it. "What's happening? Why is he here?"

His question was answered by an unexpected source. His mother and father appeared beside him suddenly. Rachel's hand was tightly gripping his father's wrist, and Buchanan looked confused and off-balance. Alexander might have laughed at him if circumstances were different. "To kill you," she said. "To kill us all."

"Why does he want to kill me?" the young demon asked. "I haven't done anything to him!"

"You've killed humans and consumed their souls," Rachel said quietly. "That is enough."

Her words snapped Rick out of his stunned state. "Wait, what? You've killed people?"

Alexander threw his bag into his father's chest, the impact making the hockey player take a step backward. "I have to eat, dumb ass."

Rachel scowled. "Be respectful."

He snorted. "Of *him*?"

Rick tossed the bag back. "Look, kid…"

"STOP IT!" The familial bickering fell silent as the three of them turned to Ulug, who was holding the outside door open. "Let's go! He comes!"

They followed the Utukku out into the alley, abandoning Alexander's lair. His slender powers were not enough to protect them from the searching eyes of an angel, let alone an archangel, and they all knew it. If Michael and his army were truly on the hunt for them, there was precious little they could do about it.

Rachel took the lead as they exited the hidden apartment, still holding Rick's wrist and dragging him along behind her. In the distance, competing with the golden rays of the morning sun, a strange light was growing brighter.

Alexander and Rick both looked at the approaching illumination, and the younger man spoke for them both. "That can't be good."

Rachel said something to Ulug in the guttural, ugly language of the Abyss, and he handed her a switch-blade knife from his pants pocket. She slashed her palm, then coated her fingertip in the blood. As the light in the sky grew closer and began to hum, she described a strange, twisting symbol in the air with her bloody finger, opening another wormhole like the one she had used to bring her son to the surface. The air wavered like heat distortion in a large oval that hovered before her. On the other side, Alexander could see a wizened old man dressed like a medieval monk, hunched over a writing desk and looking more irritated than surprised by the magical door opening beside him.

The succubus grabbed Alexander and threw him through the opening, then jumped through with Rick in tow right afterward. Ulug, starting to wibble, brought up the rear. Once they were all safely through the portal, Rachel closed the opening and dismissed the power she had called.

The monk looked up, perturbed. "You are not welcome here, demon."

"I wouldn't have come if it wasn't vital," she replied.

It dawned on Rick that he and Rachel were still as naked as they had been when they'd sprung out of bed, and he covered himself self-consciously. Alexander, who was also nude but cared much less, snorted at his sire's discomfort.

The monk snarled, "Clothe yourselves." He gestured toward a closet full of brown cassocks like the one he wore.

Rachel turned up her pretty nose. "I'm not wearing *that*." She made a gesture of her own, and immediately the three were clad in blue jeans and T-shirts. Even Ulug's ratty wardrobe was replaced with new apparel. Once she was satisfied with the changes her demonic powers had made, she turned on the charm and sidled up to the monk. "I'm sure you noticed..."

"... the arrival of the archangel on the surface," he finished for her. "I am aware. What does that have to do with me?"

"I was hoping that you would be willing to help protect us."

Alexander gaped. "From *Michael*?"

The monk dipped his anachronistic quill pen into a short, stained ink pot. "Keep speaking his name, devil child, and he will hear you. Is that what you want?"

His acidic tone burned the young demon into silence. Rick scowled. "Now, look. I don't know what your beef is – hell, I'm not even certain what's going on – but there's no call to be so snippy. Sorry we interrupted...whatever it is that you're doing... but we need help. Rachel wouldn't have brought us here if she didn't think she could depend on you."

He thought he had made an impact when the monk lifted his pen from the parchment and looked at them. That illusion was shattered when the oldster said, "Who's the ape?"

"Where are my manners?" Rachel cooed. "This is my son, Alexander, and his father, Rick Buchanan. This is..." She hesitated, looking at Ulug, who was trying to peek into the closet of clothing without being noticed. He felt her gaze and snapped to attention. "This is Ulug, an Utukku and my son's bodyguard."

He made a dismissive gesture, and the Utukku and his meat suit disappeared in a blurry flash. "And Rachel is the name you're using these days, eh?" he sniffed.

"It is," she said, her voice light. "Gentlemen, allow me to present –"

"Use my actual name and I will burn you," the monk snapped.

"Now, here!" Rick took another step forward. "You don't talk to a lady like that."

The succubus held up a hand and stopped him in his tracks. Her look warned him to rein in his aggression, and he sullenly obeyed. "This," she continued carefully, "is a very old and powerful friend."

The monk finally abandoned his work. "You may call me Peter."

"Peter," she said, rolling the name on her tongue almost obscenely, "we need to talk."

"About what?"

"About the Anti-Christ."

His wrinkled face lost a few lines as his eyes grew wide. "Apes back to the jungle," he said, waving his hand. "The grown-ups need to chat." The heat-shimmer blur reappeared, wrapping around both Rick and Alexander, and before they had time to react, they were tumbling onto the dirty alley pavement outside the younger man's lair.

⚜

Rick rolled with the fall, leaping to his feet and ready for a fight. "What the hell was that?"

Alexander, much to his father's dismay, did not recover as well from their precipitous return to New York. He rolled onto his hands and knees and heaved, his stomach contents splattering onto the asphalt. Rick hurried to his side, but his son waved him away. The athlete stood guard over him while he was sick, watching the sky for the threatening brightness that they had fled before, but it was nowhere to be seen.

When his body was no longer rebelling against him, the young incubus struggled to his feet. His father looked anxiously up at the sky, which was now quiet and showed no sign of the threat they had run from before. "Is it safe to be here?" Rick asked.

Alexander took a breath and nodded. "I think he's passed us by, so it's safe for now. Let's get inside."

He led the way back into the lair, then locked the door behind them. He went to the bathroom to brush his teeth while Rick, uncertain what else to do, sat on the couch. He saw the collection of sports magazines on the floor near the up-ended coffee table, and after he righted the table, he gathered the magazines together into a neat pile and put them down. All of the issues had articles about him, and he was weirdly touched to think that his son had been researching him.

Alexander came back out and went to the refrigerator. "Beer?"

"Love one."

He came to where his father sat on the couch and handed him a cold bottle, then sat beside him. They popped the tops at nearly the same instant, the twin hisses of escaping gas sounding like dissatisfied sighs. Rick gestured with his drink a little helplessly and let out a humorless chuckle.

"I haven't even eaten anything yet today."

"Me, neither. Cheers." He clicked his bottle against Rick's. They drank for a while in silence until Alexander asked quietly, "Were you really getting in that man's face to defend my mother?"

"And you, yeah." He shrugged. "I don't like anybody talking to my family like that."

He hesitated. "Your family?" he asked, his voice even softer than before.

Rick looked into his son's eyes, and he recognized himself in the younger man. He knew what he should say, and now, maybe saying it wouldn't be so difficult. He smiled. "Well, you're my kid, aren't you?"

"Biologically."

He sighed. "I know I didn't give you much of a welcome, but... maybe we can try and start over?" He offered his hand. "Welcome to Earth, son."

Alexander smiled and grasped his hand. "Thanks."

Above and Between

Jessica jolted awake as she started to slide beneath the water. Her stomach was pitching a violent fit, and on the hamper, her cat was crying to her piteously. She lurched out of the tub and barely made it to the toilet in time to be noisily sick.

"Great," she moaned to herself, kneeling on the water-slick floor. "Morning sickness."

Beside her, her cat meowed sympathetically, its large eyes full of compassion. Another wave of nausea swept over her, and she repeated her undignified performance, then sat on the bathroom floor, her knees pulled up to her chest.

She leaned her forehead against her arm and groaned, "Oh... God help me..."

It was nearly a prayer, and close enough to count as far as Ariel was concerned. The angel shook himself and cast aside his feline disguise, rising to his feet and standing before his startled charge.

"He will always help His children," he said, his voice sonorous and loud in the tiny room.

Jessica leaped to her feet and fell into a fighting crouch, ready to defend herself with every karate skill she'd ever learned. "Who the hell are you?!"

Ariel smiled gently. "I am Ariel, an angel of the Lord, sent to protect and guide you in your hour of need."

"Angel?" She shook her head. "No way. Prove it."

"You have already seen a demon, and yet you doubt an angel? Ye of little faith." He spread his hands out to the sides, palms held up in a show of harmlessness. "What proof would you demand?"

"Let me see your wings. Let me see your *halo*."

"This room is too small for me to unfold my wings for you, but if you wish to see my true countenance, then you shall."

To her dismay, the man before her began to glow, surrounded by a dim white luminescence that danced along his skin. The glow grew stronger, the light more intense, until it was too bright to look upon. She turned her eyes away, spots dancing in her vision, as the rest of the bathroom disappeared into the brightness. There was no wallpaper, no floor tile, no towel bar only brilliant whiteness remained, tingling around her like ozone after a lightning strike. She covered her eyes with a shaking hand.

"All right," she said quietly. "Please, no more."

The light disappeared completely, the sudden change making something in her eyes jerk and cramp. She sat on the edge of the tub and put her face in her hands.

"I don't understand what's happening..."

Ariel crouched before her, his face turned up to her and his eyes filled with the same loving understanding she had come to expect from her cat. The thought that her cat had been an angel all along, and the thought of everything the cat had seen, made her embarrassed. *Great*, she thought, shock and giddiness making her irreverent. *An angel has seen me naked.*

"I have no sexual desire for mortal flesh," Ariel told her. "I am not tempted by your nakedness."

"So you can read minds, too." She straightened, looking into the angel's eyes. "That's rude. You could at least knock first."

He nodded gravely. "I understand. I will 'knock', as you say, before I read your thoughts in the future."

"Thanks." She laughed hollowly. "I can't believe this."

Ariel took her hands. "There is much you do not know, much that I need to tell you. Will you listen, Jessica? Will you hear?"

She pulled her hands away slowly. "I don't have a choice, do I?"

His smile turned a shade regretful. "No, I'm afraid you don't." He stood and offered her his hand. "Your world will never be the same."

Jessica stood shakily and, after a brief hesitation, took his hand in her own. His skin was surprisingly cool to the touch, like marble or glass. She shook her head.

"I think I knew that."

CHAPTER EIGHT

*B*elow and Between

After the sudden departure of her son and her mate, Rachel pouted at the being who now called himself Peter. "That was rude."

"I don't have to be polite to apes."

"As I recall, that attitude got you in trouble once before."

His face puckered in irritation. "You are not endearing yourself to me, succubus. You said you needed to speak about *him*. So speak."

Rachel walked to him slowly, one hand gliding along his shoulders, feeling the tension in the muscles beneath the rough fabric. The old stumps of his wings quivered beneath her touch, the nerves still sensitive all these years after his self-mutilation. "The Anti-Christ has been conceived."

Peter pulled away from her touch and moved so his writing desk was between them like a shield. "Another one? How tedious.

Every five hundred years they try the same thing, and every five hundred years the angels and their armies put him down. Why should you be so excited this time? It will go as it always goes."

She shook her head. "No, this time is different."

"Why?"

"Because the sire is your dear brother Yeter'el. This time, the prophecy is coming true."

He snorted. "Demonic prophecies are poppycock, Rachel. You should know that by now."

She was insulted. Crossing her arms, she tossed her hair and said, "Not this time. This one is true. This one came from an angel, not a demon."

"An angel?" He squinted at her. Though he knew the answer, he asked, "What angel?"

"Gabriel's little assistant, Harahel. He was captured in one of the skirmishes in purgatory and brought low for some spirited conversation."

"Torture, you mean."

"Tomayto, tomahto." She shrugged. "He sang like a canary. If you hadn't spent the last two centuries hiding here, you'd know that."

"Who has him?"

Rachel sat on Peter's bench and examined her immaculate manicure. "He's free. The archangel came to rescue him, of course. Left a scorch mark three leagues wide doing it, too. Ugly business." She smiled at him, all beauty and bile. "Not the sort of place for a lady like me."

He turned away and began shuffling through one of the piles of parchment that littered his cell. "You are many things, Rachel, but you are no lady."

"No, but I'm very good at pretending." She watched him while he fidgeted, knowing his discomfort for what it was. It had probably been decades, maybe more, since he had been in a room alone with a female. She could smell his yearning from where she sat. "Harahel said that when the Anti-Christ is born, the *real* Anti-Christ, it will be from the loins of a Watcher. Only an angel who has turned against

85

God can sire the Son's equal and opposite. A king of Hell will rise from his line, and I intend for that king to be my son. Any actual Anti-Christ will be an impediment to that." She leaned forward, her eyes burning into the back of Peter's head. "I went out of my way to find a suitable father for my child. I have mated with every one of Yeter'el's bastards, and only Rick had the qualities that I needed."

"What qualities?"

"That's my little secret." His hands continued scrabbling in the aged documents, scurrying like frightened mice. She tilted her head and smiled to herself. "Tell me... did you know Harahel when you were in Heaven?"

As she knew they would, the words stilled him. Beneath his robe, she could see his wing stumps beat once, the again, like the final spasming of a dying heart. He sighed. "It was a long time ago. I cannot remember Heaven now."

"If you help me to find and end the Anti-Christ, you might find a way back in..."

He straightened but did not turn back to her. "I believe that there are other pathways to salvation."

The succubus laughed. "You think that recopying the same book a thousand times will earn your Father's forgiveness?"

In less than a blink, Peter lurched over the desk and grabbed her by the throat. She cried out as she fell backward, his heavier body bearing them down to the floor with a thud. He knelt above her, his hands choking her, and he hissed, "Do not mock me, demon!"

She gathered up a handful of his energy and used it to teleport across the room, freeing herself from his grasp. Rachel put a hand to her throat, cradling the bruises that were beginning to bloom there.

Peter rose and glared at her. "I have served God as a priest for five hundred years! I am doing my penance for my rebellion. Someday I will be forgiven, and not because I help you with some infantile grudge match!"

"You're a fine one to talk about grudge matches, Pinem'e!" she spat, using his true name. He flinched at the sound of it. "You've been holding a grudge against your brothers since Constantinople, haven't you? You can talk all you like about seeking salvation, but I know that you're just looking for a way to spit in your brothers' faces!"

The Watcher threw a book at her. "Get out!"

Rachel could see that aggression would never win his assistance. She softened her face, let the hard anger in her eyes melt into something like pity. He saw the shift in her attitude, felt the change in her energy. He watched her warily.

"My friend, my friend," she cooed. "I'm sorry. Let's not argue. We've known each other for fifteen hundred years, and we've never argued before. I don't want to fight with you now. I believe that we can help each other in this situation."

"I know the prophecy you're so obsessed with," he said softly. "I know it word for word, exactly as it was ripped from Harahel's mouth. I do not believe you understand."

She crossed the room and took his hands in hers. "Then *help* me understand. I am concerned for the well-being of my son, and of my mate. They will be lost if the Anti-Christ truly comes and brings about the destruction that's been foretold." She made him meet her eyes, and when he did, she smiled gently, like one of the Madonnas hanging on the church walls. "If you help me, then you will be rescuing humanity, your Father's chosen children. He will reward you for your faithfulness."

He knew that he was sliding into the same tender trap that had cost him a place in paradise. It seemed to be his fate to be weak before a beautiful woman. He sighed. "You want me to find the child and help you slay him."

"Yes," she said, drawing out the sound like a lover's whisper. "Please, my love, my darling scribe… can you help me do this thing?"

"And what if he is protected?"

She shook her head. "Why would He protect His sworn enemy?"

"Why did He allow his Son to be killed?" he countered. "His prophecies have to be fulfilled."

"Why, that's silly," she objected mildly. "He's the author of His own word – He can change it any time He likes. He's not bound to things like that, not the way we are." She caressed the Watcher's wrist with one delicate fingertip, smiling into his uncomfortable gaze. "We are slaves to our natures, are we not? But your Father… He is the slave master."

"That is blasphemy." His voice was soft, barely more than a sigh. She was moving him, she knew. "I can help you to find the child, but I cannot help you slay him. Thou shalt not kill."

Rachel pulled him into her embrace. "That's all I ask."

Above and Between

Jessica sat on the couch, now fully dressed but still feeling naked. She had her knees drawn up to her chin and her hands clasped around her ankles and was doing her best to resist the urge to rock. Ariel sat on the edge of the chair, his wings folded but awkwardly positioned. He was watching her with his careful, golden eyes, and she wondered what he was thinking.

"Okay," she finally said. "What's going on?"

The angel put his hands on his knees and took a breath before speaking. "You are a very important person. You don't even begin to understand the meaning of your role in this."

She waited for him to continue, and he looked at her as if he had just told her everything she needed to know. Frustrated, she prompted, "What is 'this'?"

His eyebrows rose in a look of genuine surprise. "Why, the End of Days, of course."

"Of course. How foolish of me." He did not react to her sarcasm. She sighed. *This is going to be like pulling teeth.* Pointing to her abdomen, she said, "This isn't a child, is it? It's a monster."

"It is both."

"How comforting." Her stomach twisted, and she thought for a moment that she would have to run for the bathroom again. The nausea settled into her gut and seethed. She put her head back against the couch and spoke toward the ceiling. "This is like a real-life version of *Rosemary's Baby*, isn't it? At what point in pregnancy do I start listening to LP's with my fingers?" Ariel gave her the same blank expression that she usually gave Li when he went off of one of his pop culture sprees. She smiled to herself when she remembered that Li was the reason she had ever seen that movie at all. *How ironic.*

"*Rosemary's Baby.* It's an old movie about a woman who's pregnant with Satan's child. I'm guessing that's sort of what's happening here."

"Ah. There are similarities, but the father of your child is not the Adversary. You would not have survived such a mating."

The images that rose in her imagination dissuaded her from asking any questions along that line. "So who is the father? I get that he's not human. He's a demon, right?"

"Yes. He was once an angel, centuries ago."

"How does an angel turn into a demon?"

"By being very, very bad."

She laughed, and Ariel smiled. He looked completely harmless in that moment, almost gentle. She found herself warming to him, even while her head still struggled to come to terms with the fact that just this morning, she'd been feeding him Friskies. She put a palm to her forehead and sighed. "Wow. This day just gets weirder and weirder."

The angel nodded. "Wait for it. It has some weirdness still to go."

"Could you give me a hint? I'm not sure how much more weird I can take today."

"Your cell phone," he said. "It's ringing."

She heard nothing and was about to say so when the ringtone assigned to Li began to play. She was surprised, but knew she probably shouldn't have been. Giving the angel the one-finger "one minute/stay there" sign, she picked up the phone. "Hello?"

"Jess? How are you doing today?"

There was something in Li's voice that made her hesitate, an uncertainty she'd never heard before. "You wouldn't believe the day I'm having."

"Ditto." There was a shuffling sound on the other end of the line, and she thought she heard another man's voice speaking to her friend in the background. Li spoke again. "I'm at your apartment building. Can we come up?"

She frowned, wary. "Who's *we*?"

"There's someone that you need to meet."

Ariel nodded to her, encouraging her to assent. Grudgingly, she did. "Okay."

The phone went silent in her hand, and she put it back on the end table. Ariel rose and stood behind her like a huge feathered bodyguard and waited while she went to let Li in.

"Shouldn't you, you know, kitty-ize yourself again?"

Ariel shook his head. "No."

"Okay. Great. Suit yourself." *How am I going to explain this?*

She could hear at least two people climbing the stairs to her apartment, both light-footed and nimble, moving quickly. Jessica opened the door at the first knock. Li was standing there with another man, a Caucasian with grey-peppered blond hair and an unreadable expression. Li, though, looked both tired and anxious, which she had never seen before. He led the way into the apartment when she stepped aside.

"This is Yu Kun, my master at the monastery. Master, this is Jessica Norgren, my friend." He suddenly realized that they were not alone, and he stopped to stare at the angel standing in the living room. "Oh. You have one, too."

Yu Kun chuckled and put a hand on Li's shoulder, then went to the angel and offered his hand, speaking in a cultured English voice. "Ariel," he said. They clasped each other's wrists like actors in a costume drama. "So good to see you. It's been too long." He then nodded to her amiably. "Hello, Miss Norgren. I hope you're feeling well today."

Jessica reached out to Li, and he responded by lacing his fingers with hers. They had never held hands before; she found that she liked the feeling then kicked herself for noticing something so trivial at a time like this.

The young monk squeezed her palm gently and said, "Master Yu Kun is a servant of the Archangel Michael, and he told me about the Apocalypse. I guess I have to learn a little more about being Christian now."

"You don't need to convert," his master reminded him, knowing

90

that the question was still heavy in Tsung Li's head. "Just gain in knowledge, and the rest will come."

They stood awkwardly for a moment, then Jessica let go of Li's hand. "Okay, then. Why don't you guys make yourselves at home, and I'll go make some tea." She shook her head as she walked to the kitchen. "I think we might need something stronger, though."

Below

The Abyss looked just the same as it always had. She found that being back home made her miss the surface. Lily strolled down the street of the infernal city, stepping out of the way of the larger and more powerful demons as they passed. A lump-like mass that had at one time been a human soul reached out to her, wheedling a pathetic plea for mercy. She kicked it in the face and kept walking.

Ahead, behind a swaying board reminiscent of the signboards of English pubs, was her destination. It was a busy little establishment, selling the distilled liquor of souls stolen from limbo and boiled down in the fires of Hell. She had been without the taste for too long, and she wanted to feel the tingle on her tongue as she swallowed someone's life force down. The bartender would give her a double for free, as he always did; if there was one thing the males in the Abyss had learned, it was that the succubi had many creative ways to show their gratitude.

A pile of human astral bodies lay outside the door, and she stepped over them, knowing that in Hell nobody was out of their misery forever. Sooner or later, those bodies would re-animate and start to drag on again, doing whatever their personal brand of damnation required. She couldn't be bothered to deal with the riff-raff.

Mitchell, the bartender, broke into a wide smile when she entered the room. "Lily!" She went to the bar and leaned closer so that he could kiss her on each cheek. "So, back from the material plane, eh? How was it?"

"Delicious," she purred, sliding onto a stool. "Too bad you can't come up and see for yourself. Things have changed a lot since you were walking and talking among the living."

He chuckled. "I have no doubt." He reached below the bar and pulled out a carved granite tumbler, then filled it with the softly-glowing liquid she had been craving. He put the drink down on the bartop in front of her and smiled. "On the house, sweetheart."

"Oh, Mitchell, you're too kind." She slammed the double shot, shivering as the energy of what had once been a human soul slid down into her demonic gut. She licked her lips, her heavy-lidded eyes locked on the bartender's face. "Mmmm. That felt *good*."

"That's what I like to hear. Another?"

"Yes, thank you." She watched as he refilled the glass. "Not many patrons here today."

"Well, I've got a pretty heavy client in the back room. Don't tell me you can't sense it." She shrugged, noncommittal, and he continued. "All the lesser folk sense it, and they're too afraid to come in when *he's* here." He leaned on his elbows and smiled, only a few inches away from her face. "I don't mind, though. It gives me more time to pay attention to you."

Lily kissed him, deep and open-mouthed, then sat back with a flirtatious smile. "I'm not afraid of a little fallen angel. Are you?"

He sighed contentedly. "No, not as long as I keep his drinks coming. He's hitting the hard stuff today – straight from the Wall – so he's either celebrating or grieving. It's hard to tell the difference."

She pursed her lips. "The Wall," she cooed. "Yummy. There's nothing like the taste of a baby's soul."

"So I'm told." A bell behind the bar rang, jingling where it hung from a sconce made of bone. He straightened. "Speak of the devil," he said, then laughed at his own pun while he snatched up another bottle of the wine of the Wall. "Duty calls, love."

The succubus sipped her drink and watched Mitchell carry his precious cargo into the back room. She couldn't see the entity waiting inside, and the smell of soot and sulfur and the reddish glow emanating from the back corner convinced her that she didn't really want to. She cast her eyes down to the bartop and started idly counting the claw marks in the petrified wood.

The door opened and a blast of hot, stinking air announced a new arrival. She could feel the power rolling off of him in waves, and she resisted the urge to turn around and look. She did permit herself a smile, though, when the newcomer came and sat on the stool beside hers.

"I'm surprised," he said, his voice the smoothest and most musical she had ever heard in the Pit. "A succubus who isn't fashionably late."

She took another sip. "Hello, Asb'el. Thank you for coming."

He chuckled and let his black-feathered wings beat lazily, like the tail of a contented cat. "You knew I would. I can't resist your kind and your little plots."

Lily pouted. "It's not a little plot. Really, I should be hurt. You don't give me enough credit."

The Watcher gestured to Mitchell's assistant, a one-armed Utukku with a bad attitude, and laughed to himself. "I give credit where credit is due, my dear, and until I am convinced by your latest scheme, there is no credit to be had."

"Let's go somewhere more private to discuss this, then." She put her hand on his forearm, her thumb caressing the firm muscles beneath his ivory-white skin. "I'll make it worth your time."

The Utukku brought him a glass, and he sniffed at it before drinking. "But I just got here." He nodded toward the back room. "What is it that has my elder brother so intense back there?"

She removed her hand from his arm. "That's above my pay grade," she said. "I don't question the First Fallen."

"Probably wise."

Mitchell returned to the bar with an empty bottle, which he placed in a pit in the floor. It would be refilled later, when he made his next trip to the Wall. In the meantime, he hovered by the tap, trying to hear what his guests were saying at the bar without looking like he was listening. Lily almost laughed at how obvious he was.

Asb'el shared her mirth. "Former humans always think they're so smart, don't they?"

"It's cute."

They sat together quietly for a moment, then finally he asked, "So...what's going on Between these days?"

She gave her glass a half-hearted spin. "Oh, you know. Same

old, same old. There's a new Anti-Christ brewing. The top archangel himself came to the surface to have a look. Must be an important new happening."

"It's rare for Michael to become personally involved, I'll grant," he said, signaling for another drink. Soul wine was thin food. "What makes you think that this go-round will be any different than any of the others?"

"Well, to start with... they're looking at the wrong baby."

"How do you know?"

She met his eyes and slowly, deliberately patted her abdomen. "Because I'm carrying the real one, right here. His grandsire is the pick of Yeter'el's litter, and Rachel is his granddam. His sire has been broken out of the Abyss and brought to the surface, just a little bit before Michael chose to return to the scene. I find the timing...interesting."

Asb'el's cool disinterest showed a crack. "Why should I care about another whelp from Yeter'el's line?"

"Because his line is the one that will give forth the real contender. You know the prophecies."

He drew his finger across the bar, leaving a long scorch mark behind. "I tire of prophecy. I'm tired of the whole rotten game."

Lily patted his arm. "I know. It has become tiresome, hasn't it? Every five centuries, another kerfuffle." She leaned closer to the Watcher and whispered to him, "If the archangels are assembling, then that means that the One has been found, and I believe that is my child's sire. That means that this child will have what it takes to be the Lord of Destruction...and possibly even the pretender to the highest throne in the Abyss."

He was unable to stop himself from looking toward the back room. She followed his gaze and watched as the closed door heaved, a beleaguered chest laboring for air. Smoke and red haze surrounded it and seeped out through the cracks. It was clear that the entity behind that door was terrifying and powerful. She was thrilled to be so close to it.

She whispered again into Asb'el's ear. "Is that... is that *him*? *The First Fallen*?"

Slowly, he nodded. "The Light-Bringer. He will want to hear

this news."

He stood and folded his wings tightly to his back, and they betrayed his anxiety with their shivering. Asb'el took her hand and pulled her after him as he walked to that pulsating door.

Mitchell called out from behind the bar, "I wouldn't, if I were you."

The Watcher's voice was barely a whisper. "Quiet, ape."

The thrill she had felt from the mere proximity of the Evil One suddenly turned into complete panic. Lily tried to pull out of his grasp. "No, I don't want to go in there." His grip did not falter; she pulled harder, fear creeping up her spine. "No! Asb'el, let me go!"

The door before them swung open of its own accord. The ghastly red light poured out onto their faces, and Lily held up her hand to shield her eyes from the sight of the demon sitting there. Asb'el pulled her into the room despite all her protestations. When they had crossed the threshold, stepping over the lines of the warding sigil drawn in blood upon the floor, the door slammed shut behind them. The succubus whimpered and pressed her face against Asb'el's shoulder.

Against the far wall, occupying a throne forged in black metal and barely large enough to hold him, he sat. His face was painfully beautiful to look upon, and his body was a vision of masculine perfection. Only his wings, huge and black, with bat-like membranes stretched over a delicate tracery of bones, betrayed that he was no longer the angel he once had been. His eyes glowed a solid, lurid red, no trace of pupil or iris. Those eyes were the source of the light that suffused through the room like contagion. He sat in the center of undulating waves of evil, power flowing and ebbing all around him. Lily dropped to her knees and pressed her forehead into the floor at his feet.

She had never thought the she would live to see the face of Lucifer.

"What do you bring me, little brother?" he asked of Asb'el, casting those glowing eyes upon the supplicating form of the succubus. "A treat?"

The Watcher hesitated, then said, "I bring you a gift. This demon female has conceived a child from the bloodline of the One.

She carries your possible successor."

Lucifer's hands clenched on the arms of his throne, and the metal groaned. "The One? Can you be so sure that he has been born?"

"The son of Yeter'el's son rose to the surface, and not long after, the archangels began to appear Between. They would not have come for just another Anti-Christ. The timing shows that the One has come, and that they mean to use him to destroy you." He dared to look directly into the face of the First Fallen. "The One is either her child or his sire. Either way, the last battle may well be upon us."

Lucifer studied the succubus' prostrate form. "Get up, woman. Let me look at you." Lily rose, standing nervously in her king's examining gaze. "You chose to conceive this child. Why?"

She licked her lips. "As Asb'el said, I believe his sire is the true Pretender. I wanted to bring his child to the Abyss... to you."

He rose from the throne and approached her. His robes parted as he walked, revealing the twisted claws where his feet had once been, clicking against the floor. He took her chin in his hand and forced her to meet his gaze. When she did, he tore through her mind, reading everything she had to tell and leaving her gasping in pain. He released her.

"I will have no successor! Find these pretenders, these whelps of Yeter'el," he ordered. "Destroy them."

From the shadows of the room, shapes emerged, melting out of the darkness and taking form as something less physical than flesh but more solid than smoke. The tizalem were Lucifer's personal assassins. At his bidding, they swirled into a spiral and blinked out of existence, heading toward the surface.

Lucifer looked at Asb'el and smiled, exquisitely dangerous. "And you, little brother." He held out a hand to him, his black curved nails glistening. "Come to me..."

CHAPTER NINE

B elow and Between

Jessica handed mugs of tea to her two human guests and offered one to Ariel, who politely declined. The two monks were occupying the couch, so she perched in the armchair, crossing her legs and sipping her own tea like a reasonable adult. It was funny how appearances could be so deceiving.

Li looked at Yu Kun, who took it as a signal to begin. "I'm told that you've been visited by an incubus, and that you are carrying his child."

She looked down into her cup. "I was visited by an incubus. I guess that's what he was. That's what I'm told, and since there are obviously angels and no better explanation, I'll accept that. And, yes, I'm pregnant. But I'm not so sure the baby is his."

The angel frowned. "Why?"

"Because he told me it was, and demons lie. Isn't that what we're told? Demons lie. So I'm not going to believe anything he tells me."

Ariel looked flummoxed, which was an odd look for an angel to wear. It clashed with his wings. "But... *I* told you this, as well. Do you doubt me?"

She could feel a burning in her lower body, an angry heat where her menstrual cramps usually sat. She answered, "How do I know where you get your information?"

Li turned to his master, who calmly asked, "If the child is not the demon's, then whose could it be?"

"I don't know." She ran her thumb along the lip of the cup, keeping her fingers interlaced around the china. The burning seethed. "I guess I don't want to believe it. You have to admit that it's a little much."

Yu Kun nodded. "It must be very hard to understand."

"Understanding isn't my problem," she said a trifle more harshly than she had intended. "Believing, though? That's entirely different."

Her friend put his tea, largely untouched, onto the coffee table. "They told me a lot of things, and I understand what they said, but I'm not sure I believe it, either."

She smiled at him, grateful to him for trying to make her feel less alone. Ariel, though, was unimpressed. "You have been spoken to by my commander, and you have yet to believe? What more do you require?"

"I don't know," the monk said quietly. "When I figure it out, I'll get back to you."

Jessica searched Li's face. "What commander did you speak to?"

His master answered for him. "Today he met the Archangel Michael."

"Archangel." Her tone was flat, more an echo than a question.

"Yes." They were silent for a moment, then Yu Kun continued. "You have to realize that this is a very serious situation, and that time is of the essence. I don't wish to push you, and I don't mean to be insensitive, but... have you decided what to do?"

Irritation began to blossom in her like a rash, spreading up her spine from the burning in her belly. She narrowed her eyes. "Do about what?"

"The baby."

"You want me to kill it."

"It would be the best course of action for the world."

Her narrowed eyes were joined by a furrowed brow. "Well, what if I don't want to?"

"You must."

"Don't tell me what to do."

If there was one thing that Jessica hated, it was being pushed. She didn't care if Yu Kun had the best of intentions, or if common sense seemed to be backing him up. Li, who knew her very well, just leaned back and put his face in his hand.

Yu Kun, for his part, looked confused. "But... that child is the Anti-Christ. He could bring the end of the world."

"You don't know that."

"The prophecy says..."

"Prophecy?" she interrupted. "You're coming in here and giving me orders over a *prophecy*?"

Ariel looked confused. "Prophecy is a time-honored and ancient form of God's will being revealed to the people of the earth. Prophecy has always been used, and heeded. Do you not know the Bible?"

She stood up. "I've read a little of it, yes."

"Then you know that Jesus Christ Himself was prophesied."

"As I recall, Jesus' mother was in the same boat I'm in... pregnant without having sex and not really knowing who the father was."

"This is different," Ariel objected. "The Archangel Gabriel came to her and sought her agreement before it ever happened, and she agreed. She was told that it would be God Himself who would sire her child, and she was willing."

"So, she believed that God was his father because some angel told her so?"

99

"Of course," Yu Kun said, annoyed. "Angels don't lie."

"Didn't Satan start out as an angel?"

Yu Kun looked to Ariel, and the angel only looked back helplessly. She had a point. The English monk said reluctantly, "Well, yes."

"Then angels can lie, just like demons can lie."

Ariel said, "Mary knew it to be true because she had faith. She knew the Word when she heard it from the Messenger of God, and she willingly submitted. 'I am the handmaid of the Lord; let it be done unto me according to his word.'"

Jessica went to the door and opened it. "Mary was a fucking doormat. Li, you can stay. The rest of you, though – get out."

The angel bowed his head. "The Lord granted humans free will, and I must obey His chosen children." He looked to Yu Kun, then back to Jessica. "If you need me, call for me, and I will hear."

"Don't hold your breath."

Ariel faded from view, and the energy level in the room dimmed. Yu Kun rose and put his tea cup on the coffee table. "I am sorry that you feel this way," he said. "I hope that you will do the right thing."

"Right or not, what I do is my business, not yours." She gestured toward the open door. "Goodbye."

He turned to Li. "Find me when you return to the house."

"Yes, Master."

Jessica glared at him as he made his way out into the hallway. He turned to say one last thing, and she slammed the door shut in his face, sliding the chain into place. Crossing her arms, she leaned against the door and waited until she heard his footsteps retreating down the stairs.

Li looked up at her from where he sat on the couch, hunched and feeling very, very small. "Now what?"

"I'm not mad at you, Li."

"I'm glad."

She came to the couch and sat beside him, her elbows on her knees. "Hell of a morning, huh?"

"You can say that again."

"An archangel? Really?" She looked at him with reluctant curiosity. "What was he like?"

Li considered his words, then answered honestly. "Scary. Blond. Big, big wings. And he kind of... shone. Really bright."

"Wow."

"Yeah."

She sat back. "So... what's your part in this?"

He turned to her. "I... I promised to help them. I promised to protect you, and to protect innocent people from whatever happens."

"You didn't promise to make me abort my baby?"

"No." He showed her the angel-wing tattoo on his left wrist. "This appeared when I said I'd help."

She took his hand and examined the mark. "Nice. They branded you."

"I guess."

The burning in her gut twisted, and she felt a hiss in the back of her mind like static on a radio. "Assholes."

He made no effort to take his hand back, and she made no move to let it go. Quietly, he said, "I guess maybe you should watch out for any mystery tats that show up on you."

"That would really, really piss me off."

He smiled. "I can imagine."

They sat in silence for a long minute, then another. He finally took the hand that was interlaced with his and pulled her gently toward him until she was nestled against his chest, his strong arm safe around her shoulders. She could feel the anger in the pit of her stomach melting away, and she put her arms around his waist in a loose embrace. He leaned his head against hers and just held her – no advice, no wasted words, no aphorisms. She listened to the steady rhythm of his heartbeat, the even cadence of his breathing, and the tension in her neck and back began to melt away.

Her cellphone shrilled suddenly, startling them both out of the brief wordless reverie. She grabbed the offending thing off of the table and flipped it open to see who was calling. Her jaw set.

"Caller unknown," she told him.

Li took the phone away from her and answered the call. "Hello?"

She could hear the familiar self-satisfied tone of the demon on the other end of the line. "Put Jessica on the phone."

He looked at her and mouthed, *Is that him?* She nodded. He said, "She not here. Just cleaning man. Call back later." His put-on pidgin English was jarring, his normally smooth voice raised to a scratchy yelp. She smiled in spite of herself.

The demon was neither fooled nor amused. "Put her on the phone, Tsung Li. Now."

Busted. He changed his voice back to normal. "If you know who I am, then you know that I won't do that." He ended the call and turned off the phone. "You didn't want to talk to him, right?"

She chuckled. "Now you ask? Fine timing."

"Of course."

"No, I didn't want to speak to him."

"Didn't think so."

They were quiet for a moment longer, then Li asked her, "Are you scared?"

Nodding, she admitted, "Yes."

Li pulled her close. "Me, too."

After two bottles of beer, Rick realized that he was nowhere close to where he was supposed to be. A glance at the wall clock confirmed that it was well past noon now in New York, which meant that it was after 9 in Winnipeg, and he was late for morning practice and had missed the team breakfast.

"Shit," he grumbled, patting stupidly at his conjured clothes, looking for the cellphone that he had left back in his hotel room.

Alexander raised an eyebrow. "Problem?"

"Yeah, huge. I'm gonna get my ass handed to me by my coach." He gave up his search. "I have to get back to Canada."

"Mother can take you when she gets back."

"Okay... any idea when that might be?"

His son thought, then took another sip of beer. "None at all."

"Can I use your phone?"

Alexander found his own cell and handed it to his father, getting a perverse amusement from the look of panic that was starting to gleam in the older man's eyes. "Here."

"Thanks." He punched in the only number he had memorized and waited through the ring tones. "Come on, pick up," he urged. "Don't let me go to voice mail..."

To his relief, his best friend picked up. "Hello?"

"Koz, thank God. Please tell me McMillen hasn't noticed that I'm not there."

The agitation in his friend's voice killed that hope rapidly. "Rick, you had better get to the arena now or he's going to bench you for the game. He's really pissed that you didn't show and busted curfew."

"I'm really pissed that we have a curfew." He put a hand to his forehead. "Okay, I'll figure out a way to get there. I don't know when I'll be there, though."

"Where the hell are you?" Koz's Czech accent was thicker than normal, his voice a little louder. He must have been worried.

"I'm with my kid," he said, glancing at Alexander, who raised his beer bottle in salute. "I'm back in New York."

"*New York*?" The other man was nearly shouting now, and Rick could imagine the veins in his neck throbbing. "What the fuck, man?"

"Look, it's a long story, like, the longest ever. Just tell McMillen that a family emergency came up, and I had to take care of it, and that I'll meet up with the team as soon as I can."

Koz whistled, the sound exceptionally loud over the telephone. "You're in so much trouble, dude."

"Don't I know it."

He ended the call and tossed the phone back to Alexander, who caught it out of the air with a one-handed flourish. Rick sat down again to wait for Rachel to reappear. He rapidly discovered that his new case of the nerves was demanding something more active, and he rose to his feet again.

"Problem?"

He laughed with no mirth at all. "I'm probably going to get fired for being AWOL."

"AWOL?"

"Absent without leave. It's a military term, I guess. Sort of mainstream now, though." He began pacing, his hands on his hips. "I can't believe it took me so long to think about the game tonight. Gah... there goes my career."

"Cat on a hot tin roof," his son said quietly.

"Pardon?"

"That's an expression I heard the other day. 'Cat on a hot tin roof.' I guess it means that you're acting really nervous." He shrugged. "It's just a job. Can't you find another one if this one goes bad?"

"I wish." Rick could see that Alexander just didn't understand. Gesturing vaguely, he explained, "See, there are only 15 teams in the whole league, and only 22 spots for players on those teams. I play left wing – that means that there are only 4 positions per team for someone like me."

"Okay..." He did some fast calculations. "Well, that means that you have 59 other positions that you could fill, right? No problem."

"Yeah, well, those positions are filled, and coaches and team owners talk, and, well... I'm about to become *persona non grata* in hockey circles."

The younger man finished his beer and put his bottle aside. "Then do something else, or do nothing. I mean, it's the end of the world. You won't be needing paychecks soon."

"That has to be one of the most depressing things I've ever heard."

Alexander looked confused. "Really? I thought it would be comforting."

He stopped pacing and leaned on his fists, pushing dimples into the cushions on the arm of the couch. "What would be comforting would be knowing where your mother is."

"Yes," the incubus allowed, "that would be very nice."

Rick looked again at the clock on the wall, then shook his head. "Look, I've got to at least hit the gym if I'm not going to practice. Do you want to come with me?"

His son smirked. "I prefer to get my exercise in other ways." He rose. "Besides, I need to go get something to eat."

"I could eat. You want to go to a deli or something?"

Alexander fixed him with a strange look. "I need...*something*...to eat..."

He understood then and responded, "Oh... eat, like incubus eating. Got it. Do you, uh... do you even eat regular food?"

"I eat some. It's not the majority of my diet, though."

The hockey player's gaze dropped toward his shoes. "Oh," he said again, impressing himself with his intellectual conversation. "Do you always kill the people you feed from?"

"Don't you?"

He looked up into his son's face, seeing honest confusion there, not a challenge or some sort of cynical game-playing. He usually tried not to think about the needs of his dark half, but he knew that whenever he was with a woman, he left her exhausted the next morning. He was aware that his incubus part needed to feed on human energy. He also knew that the thought of existing like some sort of battery-charged vampire made his stomach turn.

"No," he finally answered quietly. "I only take energy, not souls."

Alexander looked fascinated, like a scientist who had just discovered a new kind of bug. "Have you ever taken a soul?"

"I..." Visions and memories swirled in his mind, and he shuddered almost as a reflex. When he spoke again, it was in a very small voice. "Once."

His son recognized his distress but had no idea how to react to it. Quietly, he asked, "Did the person die?"

Rick ran a hand over his hair, still messy from bed. He felt so dirty. "It's complicated."

"Death isn't complicated. It happens, or it doesn't. It's a yes/no question."

"Not really, no." He shook his head. "Look, can I borrow your phone to call a cab? I need to get to my apartment and get some gear. This isn't my usual exercise wardrobe, you know?"

The younger man chuckled and went the nameless space between the living room and the kitchen. He opened an ornately carved wooden box sitting on a built-in shelf and extracted some cash, which he brought to his father.

"Unless you're planning on walking to Manhattan, you'll need this for the fare."

He accepted the offering. "Thanks. I'll pay you back."

Alexander smirked. "No need. What are sons for?"

Rick borrowed the phone again and called a taxi company to send a driver. He took a breath before saying, "Have you ever tried, you know, feeding on just energy? Not taking souls, not killing people?"

He blinked, surprised by the question. "I don't know how. You think I should learn?"

"It might make life a little safer for you, if you intend to stay here on the surface. The police take a dim view of people who kill and eat other people."

He chuckled, and for a moment, Rick felt like he was looking in a mirror. "I can see how they might."

He picked up a pen and a scrap of paper from the coffee table and wrote down the numbers of his land line. "Here. Call me when your mom shows up, or if you need anything before then."

Alexander accepted the digits and followed him to the door, which he held open as Rick prepared to leave. They looked at one another wordlessly, and the athlete smiled wanly. His son returned the same unenthusiastic expression.

"I'll just wait out on the corner for the cab."

"Okay. See you."

The incubus closed the door and slid the lock into place. Rick turned toward the street and waited for the cab to arrive.

Between

The precinct was humming with the usual daytime assortment of pickpockets, shoplifters and vagrants. Detective Lloyd Herman sipped his cold coffee, wondering why his coffee was always cold when he wanted to drink it, and flipped through the witness statements he'd taken that day.

Alan Brooker, his sometime-partner, sat at the desk across from him, scanning mug shots in the computer and comparing them to the artist rendering of a witness description. The woman who spoke to them this morning had seen a big man dumping a lifeless body onto the subway tracks not far from Christopher Street, in the same place where other bodies had been left. The press was starting to call him "the Subway Killer," and the last thing the city needed was a sensationalized serial killer to add to their other concerns. Lloyd knew that it was an important case, and he wanted to solve it.

"Any luck?" he asked Alan, putting his paperwork aside.

"Not really." The other detective sighed and rubbed his eyes. "Man, after a while they all start looking alike."

"It's the eyes." He sat back. "Take a break, get some water or something."

"And what about you?" He indicated the break area with a jerk of his head. "You should try to walk a little, too. Old people like you need to worry about blood clots when you sit for too long."

"Fuck you, Brooker."

"You should be so lucky."

Lloyd shook his head and pointedly ignored his younger colleague, who gave his shoulder a companionable smack as he took the advice and went to the water cooler. He had run out of things that he could do at his desk. The only thing left to do was to set up a stakeout of the subway station and hope that the killer showed himself, or to start canvasing the area for other witnesses. He knew that he had a better chance success with the stakeout; New Yorkers were notorious for their selective inability to remember anything they'd seen. It would be easier to find someone who'd step over a dead body than someone who'd get involved and try to stop a murderer.

He took the asylum case file out of his drawer and looked through it again, as if it would tell him something different on the hundredth viewing than on the first. Brooker came back to their area and snorted.

"I'm beginning to think you just get off looking at the gore. What is it with you and that crime scene?"

Lloyd paused, looking into a photograph of what had been left of the young woman's face. He felt that same twisting ache in his chest when he looked at her.

"I don't know," he admitted. "I don't know."

Below and Between

Rachel rose slowly from the cot, stretching like a cat. Beside her, Pinem'e lay in a sullen afterglow, his eyes screwed shut. He seemed upset, but she couldn't bring herself to care. If he was so bothered by having sex with her, then he could just go to confession or something. It wasn't as if she had forced him.

She still had the clothing that she had created, but she wanted a souvenir. She pulled a robe out of the vestment closet in the fallen angel's cell and pulled it over her naked body. The rough weave of the fabric was harsh against her skin, but in this moment, it felt good. She could enjoy anything while her body was still tingling.

"I will search for original documents about these prophecies," he whispered to her. His eyes were still closed, as if looking at her would somehow make the shattering of his priestly vows more real.

"Thank you, Peter," she purred. "I'll be very grateful if you can come up with any new information. And I think we both know how much you like it when I'm grateful."

He turned his face toward the wall, and she teleported back to her son's lair.

Alexander finished dressing and checked his appearance in the mirror. If he was going to go hunting, he had to look his best. A pretty package made his brand of poison much more palatable to his victims.

He had just put the finishing touches on his hair when he saw it. On the outer edges of his lair, pressing against the invisible force field that marked the delineation between his space and the outside world, there was a shadow. No, not a shadow – an opposing force, a non-corporeal entity made of darkness and hatred that pushed its long fingers through the fabric of his wards and shredded them to bits. He turned to face the thing as it shoved its way into his home, his hands balling into useless fists.

He never even had time to scream.

Rick paid the cab driver and hurried into his apartment building, barely nodding at Bill's surprised greeting. The elevator sped him to his floor, and he was grateful that he was able to avoid running into any of his neighbors. He realized as soon as he reached his door that his keys, his clothes, his wallet and his dignity were all back in the hotel in Winnipeg. He kicked the door and succeeded only in jamming a toe, which sent him hopping on his good foot and swearing with gusto. He was so angry that he didn't see the shadows move until it was too late.

A black cloud, roughly man-shaped and disconcertingly solid, darted between him and the door to his apartment. Two spots of glowing orange light appeared where a human face would have been, and then the mouth opened. Black teeth, inches long and jagged, framed a writhing mass of tentacles where there should have been a tongue. It uttered a low growl that changed into a laugh, and two pairs of hands wrapped around his arms and started to pull.

His first instinct was to attack. He delivered a head butt into the thing's glowing eyes and was pleased to feel his forehead connect with something rubbery instead of the door behind his attacker. The pulling stopped for just a moment, long enough for him to stomp down on the shadow's foot and drive his other knee up into what he hoped was a sensitive spot. He was rewarded with a roar that was simultaneously a hiss and a howl, but his satisfaction was short-lived. The creature resumed trying to pull his shoulders out of their sockets, this time with a little more enthusiasm.

He could feel something ripping. The pain was white-hot and sudden, and he threw his head back with a garbled cry. The attacking demon laughed at the sound, and another hand extended from its body like a pseudopod, gripping his jaw and trying to pull it away from his skull. Rick screamed in pain and rage, struggling against the thing holding him. He managed to vocalize only one word.

"God!"

Instantly, a white flash blinded him. The shadow screamed like a banshee, deafening him, and its hold on him was abruptly released. Rick fell to the floor in a crumpled heap, hunched in the agony of his dislocated shoulders, and looked up. The flash was resolving into a brilliant line of light that dimmed until he could see that the light was really the blade of a sword. The hand holding the blade belonged to a tall, blond man in a white trench coat who looked at him patiently. Beyond his appearance, there was nothing human about the man. Rick tried to scoot away from him, trying to raise arms that could not obey.

The man spoke in his mind. *Be not afraid, for I mean you no harm.*

He couldn't gather himself enough to respond in kind, so he whispered, "You saved me."

You called for aid, and I was sent.

"Thanks..." He gathered his legs beneath him and managed to stand, although he wavered on his feet. He felt like he'd just been hit by a freight train. His rescuer extended a hand to steady him, and the gentle grip on his bicep sent lancing pain through his ruined joint. He hissed and pulled away, falling against the wall but remaining upright.

The man spoke aloud. "Do you need help?"

"No, I'm just dandy," he said sarcastically. "Does that pig sticker of yours open locks?"

"No." The blond man touched the doorknob, and the lock clicked open. The door swung open. "May I enter?"

Rick staggered into his apartment and mumbled something like permission. His rescuer came inside and closed the door behind them, locking it again. The lights came up automatically, something that they were not designed to do. Rick chose not to contemplate that right now. Instead he managed to sit on his couch and nod toward the telephone.

"Could you dial 911? I need to get to a hospital."

"Would you like healing?"

He took a deep breath. "You're an angel, aren't you?"

The blond nodded. "I am."

"You know what I am."

"You are human."

"Half human," he corrected.

"It is enough." The angel extended his hand to him again. "Will you accept the grace of God?"

Images of surgery and rehab haunted his imagination, and he nodded. "Yes, please."

Pinkish-white light surrounded him, warm and soothing. He was encased in a sleeve of pure energy that danced along his skin and sank down into his offended ligaments and tendons. The warmth suffused through him, radiating like the light itself, and the pain passed completely. He felt the energy filling him up, quenching the fire in his demon half for the first time since he had entered puberty. It made him feel a peace he had never thought he would ever feel.

The healing light dimmed, then vanished, absorbed into his very soul. He slid from the couch and knelt at the angel's feet, compelled by his long-forgotten catechism into a posture of gratitude.

"Thank you," he breathed, overwhelmed.

"No," the angel corrected, not unkindly. "Thank God."

Rachel stepped back into the material plane, appearing in Alexander's lair, and found herself in the center of a scene of horror.

The room had been torn to pieces. Bits of stuffing and ragged pieces of wood were all that remained of the sofa. The coffee table had been reduced to kindling. Every electronic piece was smashed into piles of splintered plastic and torn wires. Nothing had survived the destruction.

There was no life in the room, but she knew he had been here. She could smell his blood long before she found what was left of him on the bathroom floor, and in the bath tub, and in tiny pieces in the sink. There was not enough left of Alexander to call a body. Clearly, whatever had done this had come with an appetite.

She sank to her knees in the puddles of gore and gathered the bloody shreds together in her hands. Cradling what was left of her boy, she began to sob.

CHAPTER TEN

B*elow and Between*

Jessica blinked awake and sat up, extricating herself from Li's patient embrace. She looked at him in embarrassment. "Did I fall asleep on you?"

"Yeah, more or less literally." He smiled. "Feeling better?"

She put a hand on her stomach, which she was pleased to find was no longer twisting. "Yeah, a lot better." She straightened her legs out of the curled-up position she had been lying in. Li's chest had apparently been a comfortable pillow. He was watching her with a warm expression in his eyes, a tenderness that she quite liked. Her cheeks felt hot suddenly, and she looked away, standing up and using the motion to hide her awkwardness.

Li either didn't notice or was kind enough not to comment on it. Instead, he asked, "Do you want to go and get some lunch or something? You probably should get some food in you."

"Yeah... let me just go comb my hair and try to make myself presentable."

"You look fine."

She raised an eyebrow. "That just goes to show what low standards you have."

Once she had closed the door, Li picked up her cell phone and turned it back on. There was a voice mail from Caller Unknown, and he wished he knew Jessica's password so he could screen it for her. He looked at the missed call menu, then called the number that Caller Unknown had used.

He wasn't expecting anyone to answer, but to his surprise, the same urbane voice came on the line. "Hello, Tsung Li. That was very rude of you to hang up on me earlier."

"I'd say I'm sorry, but I don't want to lie," he replied. "What do you want from Jessica?"

The demon chuckled. "I thought that would be obvious."

"Pretend I'm stupid."

"That should be simple enough." The tone in his voice hardened. "She is the perfect vessel for my child. He will grow and flourish from her strength."

Li walked into the kitchen, just in case Jessica could hear him from the other room. "And after the baby is born, what then?"

Again he heard that chuckle, obscene and oily and just a little appealing. He didn't like the way the demon's voice affected him. "You're assuming that she'll survive the birth."

"Won't she?"

"That all depends on how difficult she makes things."

He set his jaw. "Difficult for herself? Or difficult for you?"

The demon said, "In this case, it's all the same."

"And what if we find and destroy you before the baby's born? What then? Won't he just be a baby then?"

The only answer he received was hearty laughter and dead air after the demon ended the call. Li looked at the phone in disgust and headed back into the living room.

Jessica was waiting for him when he came in. She was sitting on the couch, her legs crossed. She gestured toward the phone in his hand. "So... you called him back?"

It was Li's turn to blush. "Uh...yeah. I guess I wanted to be macho and get up in his grill."

"Li!" She tossed her head back and laughed. "My God, now you think you're gangsta!"

He shrugged and grinned crookedly. "What?"

"You're too much."

"I'm too hungry," he corrected. "Let's go eat, huh?"

He held out his hand to her, and she took it, letting him pull her up to her feet. She snagged her jacket and her purse on the way out the door, noticing that he was holding her hand again. She really didn't mind.

***

Ulug raced down the sidewalk, knocking other pedestrians out of his way, his ungainly meat suit cutting a wide swath through the complaining crowd. His feet pounded into the pavement, forcing grunts from his chest that sounded almost like crying. The Utukku knew that it was only noise. Demons didn't cry.

High above his head, bouncing along in the air stream between the tall New York buildings, was a glowing ball of light. It twinkled and drifted like animated snow, and he was having difficulty keeping up with it. He had to grab it, had to bring it back to the lair. It was important. It was all that was left of Alexander.

He had been brought up to the surface to be the boy's protector, and when the monk sent Ulug away, he'd spent the rest of the afternoon trying to get back to his side. He had finally reached the lair just a heartbeat behind the tizalem.

Ulug was strong and smart for an Utukku. There were only a few fights that he couldn't win, and he would give those his best attempt, but against the tizalem, there was nothing he could have done. Not even the princes of hell could stand against them, which was precisely why they had been made. If they had come for

115

Alexander, well, they were going to have Alexander. Ulug certainly wouldn't be able to stop them.

He had done the next best thing. When they had torn out the little glowing light that was his master's soul, he had followed it out into the world. It was only a blue dot, a tiny glowing thing that the humans who impeded his path could never see. He had to catch it.

As he watched, the blue wisp began to climb upward, drifting up along the side of a glass-walled high-rise, bouncing and bumping along as if it knew where it was going. The horrible thought occurred to him that the soul was trying to make its way Above, and Ulug knew that could never be allowed to happen. He hesitated at the base of the building, looking up at the ascending soul-light.

Rachel was going to kill him.

Michael sat and watched quietly as Rick begged his coach for mercy over the phone. "Fine," McMillen's voice thundered through the speaker, "that's just fucking fine. You think it's all okay for you to just run off and leave town on a game day? You think that's all right? Well, you're fucking wrong, okay? You stupid bastard! You better find a way to get your ass back to this arena before the puck drops in three hours, or you'll be up shit's creek, you hear me? You get back here and on this ice or I'm gonna send your ass back to the minors where you belong!"

Rick hung his head and listened to the diatribe, then said, "You know I can't get back to the arena in three hours."

"Well, you shoulda fucking thought of that before you fucking took fucking off!"

His coach's clumsy use of profanity shouldn't have been funny, but it made him smirk anyway. He nodded. "Yes, sir. I'll rejoin the team as soon as I can. I'm sorry, it's just... something came up."

"They let me into your hotel room, you know," McMillen raged on. "I've got your wallet, your credit card, your car keys, your *everything*. Who runs out and leaves all that shit behind? What's really going on, Buchanan? Is it the drugs?" He made an alarming choking noise. "You know, I don't fucking care what's going on.

You're my top fucking scorer on my top fucking line, and I need you on the fucking ice in this fucking game! I don't care what you have to do to get back here. Just fucking do it!"

The phone went quiet in his hand. Rick turned to his angelic visitor. "Well," he said drily, "he took that better than I thought he would."

"His speech patterns leave much to be desired," Michael opined.

"You should hear him during a game." He hung the receiver back into its cradle. "Do you know how long it's been since I actually used my land line? Actually, I don't think I've used it once since I moved in here. I bought that phone as a conversation piece and just hooked it up because... well, because it's what you do." He ran a hand over his head. "But you're not still sitting here because you want to talk to me about my phone choices."

Michael smiled. "No."

"Well, I'm listening."

The angel leaned forward and put his elbows on his knees, his hands clasped loosely before him in an echo of Rick's posture. Their positions reminded the hockey player of an opening face-off, and he facetiously wondered who was going to come in and drop the puck.

Rachel suddenly appeared between them, streaked with blood and tears. Scarlet droplets escaped between her trembling fingers and dropped onto his white carpeting. She was keening, a high-pitched, frightening sound, and he was convinced that she had somehow lost her mind.

Michael rose and drew his sword, and Rick hurried to grab his wrist. "Don't," he begged. He released his grip suddenly, wondering if it was sin to touch an archangel. The blond relaxed marginally, his sword hand lowering just enough to show that he was standing down, at least for the moment. Rick turned to his lover.

"Rach," he said, grasping her biceps gently. "What is it?"

She held out her hands to him then, showing him a glistening chunk of flesh. His stomach lurched. He knew that scent. Through her sobs, she managed to gasp, "They killed him."

Bile flooded his mouth, and he staggered back. "Oh, God."

"They... *killed*... him."

Michael's jaw set. "Who?"

The succubus turned to the angel as if seeing him for the first time. She shook, her grief now laced with terror, and sank to her knees on the soiled rug. She held her gore-laden hands up to Michael and cried, "My baby! They killed my baby!"

The angel grabbed her face in his hand, forcing her to look up at him. *"Who killed him?"*

Rick punched at Michael's arm, trying to break his grip on Rachel's face. "Leave her alone!" he barked. He pulled her up and into his arms, sheltering her from the anger on the angel's face. He petted her hair, trying to soothe her while trying not to vomit. *That's my son in her hands*, he thought. His heart ached. *That was my son.*

"Your son was not meant to die," the angel pronounced. "His destiny was different."

The succubus raised her tear-stained face to him. "Then *change it.*"

"Where is his soul?"

"I don't know."

"Did you consume it?" he accused.

She gasped at the audacity of the thought. "No! I would never harm my child!" Rick tightened his embrace around her shoulders, and she sagged back into him. "He was gone when I found him. His soul... I don't know where it went."

Rick could not stop staring at her bloody hands. "Who... who did this?"

"The tizalem."

Her answer made no sense to him, but Michael apparently was familiar with the word. For an instant, white fire flared around him, brilliant and painfully bright. Rick closed his eyes against the sudden explosion of light. The outward display of the archangel's inner fury was short-lived, though, and soon he looked like a man again, albeit an enraged man holding a very large sword.

"The Adversary is active, then. This is more serious than we had believed." He turned his face to them, and the intensity of his gaze made the athlete want to turn away. An invisible force held him, though, and made him meet Michael's eyes. "You are needed,

Richard Buchanan," he intoned. "You must join this fight if your world is to survive."

"But – the Apocalypse? That fight? I'm just a hockey player. How can I –"

"No," the angel interrupted. "You are more than that. Demon, did you not tell him the truth?"

Rachel shook her head and tried to bury her face in Rick's neck. He pulled her closer. "What truth?" When his lover could only weep, he looked at Michael and repeated, "*What truth?*"

"You and your son are instruments of salvation."

A short, harsh laugh of disbelief erupted from his lips, and he objected, "That's ridiculous!"

"I speak truth, and there is no time to argue." He gave a little shrug, and his trench coat disappeared, replaced by a suit of silver-white armor and a huge pair of snow-white wings. "The Lord our God is gracious and forgiving. At the End of All Things, He will offer salvation to all of his children through the one that some have called the Messiah. The humans have had many Messiahs, and nearly all of humanity knows the way to Grace. Your son was meant to be a Messiah, as were you."

Rachel leaned heavily against him. Rick gave himself a merciless pinch, leaving a bruise and no doubt whatsoever that he was not dreaming. "Damn," he whispered. "What are you talking about? Messiah?"

"God wants all of his children to be redeemed. *All of them.*" He looked pointedly at Rachel. "Even those who rebelled against him and chose exile in the Pit."

She whispered, "Alexander was the One."

"The One?" he echoed, feeling stupid.

"The Devil's Messiah," Michael said. "You and Alexander and his son are destined to bring the light of forgiveness and mercy to the demons of hell."

Rick shook his head again. "No, no, no... that's too much... that is *way* above my pay grade."

"Who ever said you were going to be paid?"

It was a stranger's voice behind him, and he and Rachel were startled by the sudden newcomer. Another angel stood in the apartment foyer, his black skin gleaming, his soft white wings brushing the floor and walls as they slowly beat like a soothing heartbeat. He nodded to Michael, who returned the wordless greeting.

Rachel's shaking grew to nearly seismic levels. The new arrival stepped forward. "I am Gabriel, Messenger of God. I brought God's will to Mary of Nazareth, and gave the Word of God to Mohammed. You know me."

"I don't know you," the athlete rasped.

Gabriel smiled gently. "You will remember in time." He turned to Rachel. "Do not fear me, child. Though you were born a demon and have committed a thousand sins, repentance can still bring you mercy."

He held out a hand to her, and she shrank away, trying to retreat into Rick's side. "Don't," she pleaded. "Please don't."

Another angel materialized in the living room, standing with his back to them, facing the huge picture window that looked out over Manhattan. This angel, brown-skinned with rose-tinged white wings, spread his hands toward the glass, and a tiny blue spark appeared, pushing into the apartment from outside. The angel held his palm up, and the glowing dot sank down to rest there, feather-light and pulsating gently.

Gabriel said, "This is Raphael, our brother. He can heal your son."

Rick looked down at the remains that Rachel still clutched in her hands. "But... how?"

"The Lord works in mysterious ways," Michael said.

His brother added, "Allah will turn in mercy to whom He will."

In a deeply musical voice, Raphael said, "'I will have compassion upon you, says the Lord your Redeemer.'" He nodded to Rachel encouragingly. "Hold out your hands."

She held out the sodden remains of her son to the angel, turning her eyes up to him in silent supplication. He gently took the remains and cradled them to his own chest, folding his wings around himself. His wings were so large and the feathers so densely interwoven that they were completely unable to see his body or anything he was doing. A soft pink glow emerged from behind the rose-white screen, and the other archangels bowed their heads in prayer, emitting a soft hum. Rick pulled Rachel closer, and they clung to one another in the shadow of the mystery before them.

A feeling of purity descended into the room, an unseen presence of boundless love and peace filling the space around them. The angels' humming grew louder, becoming a wordless song of praise. Rick felt Rachel cower in his arms, and he suddenly felt both incredibly comforted and incredibly small. The presence came with the slight scent of incense, heady and exotic, and his head swam with it. The room was becoming brighter, and he squinted to see in the radiance. Behind Raphael, forming in the pink light, he thought that he could see a distant luminous stairway lined with winged beings, but when he tried to look closer, it was gone.

The glow in the room gently faded, and the presence and scent disappeared slowly. Finally the light from within Raphael's wings vanished like mist in the morning sun, leaving just the flesh-and-feather screen of his wings between them and the archangel. Those wings gently parted, and Rachel let out a cry when she saw within that protective circle.

Alexander stood there, whole and alive.

He was naked as a newborn and blinking in wonder. His mother rushed to him, and Rick was right behind her. They embraced their son, who wordlessly hugged them back.

Michael spoke first. "Thanks be to God."

CHAPTER ELEVEN

*B*elow and Between

Ulug was halfway up the building's stairs when he sensed the power, and it terrified him. He flattened himself against the stairwell wall, hugging the painted "35" floor number. The glowing presence above him paid no attention to him, though, and the Utukku stayed motionless but whimpering until it was gone.

When he finally felt the Spirit depart, leaving behind the three archangels he had already steeled himself to face, he began racing up the stairs again.

He burst out of the stairwell on the top floor then pelted down the hallway until he got to the room where the angels were standing. He wasted no time on civility, choosing instead to simply kick the door from its hinges. He threw himself into the room and onto his knees.

"What the hell?!" Rick exploded. "Man, don't you knock?"

"Tizalem," he panted, desperate to avoid looking at Rachel or the angels. He was going to be destroyed, he knew it. "Couldn't stop them. They came..."

"Ulug," the succubus said quietly, "hush."

The Utukku looked up then, surprised by the almost beatific tone of her voice. The angels were still there, and they glowed painfully in his sight, but the most riveting thing he saw was his master. Alexander offered him an off-kilter smile, and the demon in the massive meatsuit lurched at him for an enthusiastic embrace.

Michael's sword hand tightened. "Possessing spirit," he growled. "You are unclean."

Raphael shook his head slightly, and Michael fell silent, albeit a little sullenly. Gabriel looked to his brothers, shared some sort of wordless communication with them, and vanished from sight. Rick went into his bedroom and retrieved a robe for his son to wear while Rachel stood beside Alexander, her hand on his shoulder as if she was trying to prove to herself that he was real.

Ulug squeezed Alexander until the young incubus begged, "Air!"

The Utukku released him immediately and stepped back, awkwardly bumping into Rick's couch and nearly overturning it. The hockey player returned to the room with the robe and steadied the furniture before it could topple.

"Easy, Moose," he said. "Here, Alex. You don't want to catch cold."

Raphael smiled and faded from view, leaving only Michael to witness the rest of the demonic family reunion. Rachel turned to the blond angel and raised her chin.

"Are you going to kill me, now?"

"Those are not my orders."

Rick said, "Nobody's going to kill anybody, all right? There's been entirely too much dying here already today."

Alexander pulled on the fuzzy garment and tied it around his waist. "Stylish," he teased.

"Shut up, kid. It's warm." The affection in his eyes countered the harshness of the words, and he smiled at his son. *Nothing like losing a kid to make you really want him*, he thought.

His lover seemed to hear his thoughts. She reached out and squeezed his hand, giving him a serene smile. He gently pressed her fingers in his palm, returning the touch.

The mood was perilously close to veering into the realm of the Hallmark commercial. Michael sheathed his sword, extinguishing the flames that wreathed the blade. He nodded to Rick.

"Sit down, all of you. We need to talk. There are things you need to know." He included Alexander in his gaze. "You *all* have things you need to know."

Ulug went to the door and tried unsuccessfully to put it back onto its hinges while Rick, Rachel and Alexander settled into seats on the couch. The door fell onto the floor with a bang, and Michael waved a hand impatiently. Ulug skittered aside, afraid of what the archangel might do, but the gesture was just accompaniment to the unseen power that lifted and repaired the door as if it had never been broken.

"Nice trick," the Canadian said. "Can you do that with hockey sticks, too?"

Rachel shushed him. "Don't be disrespectful."

Michael said, "He has no reason to fear me. As long as he and your son have human blood flowing in their veins, they are God's children, and I will never harm them."

The Utukku muttered, "But me? You kill."

"Not yet." The angel regarded the body-snatching demon with a jaundiced eye. "Not until you give me reason."

"Won't do that, then."

Rick smirked. "Probably a good idea." He put his arm around Rachel, who was already nestled into Alexander's side, and the three of them found comfort in the huddle. Ulug sat on the kitchen floor, waiting quietly to die. Everyone ignored him.

Their son spoke first. "Please, let me start with a question. What were the things that... that killed me?"

"Tizalem," Ulug answered, shuddering. "Nasty."

"I think that's an understatement."

Rachel squeezed her son's hand. "Do you remember it, darling?"

His hazel eyes were haunted as he nodded. "All of it."

"I am sorry for your suffering, truly. The memories will pass in time," Michael assured him. "For now, you must be strong. You are needed."

Rick asked, "Needed for what? You said something about the Devil's Messiah. I don't understand how that can be us. I mean, doesn't the Messiah have to be the son of God? And anyway, as I recall, the last time there was a Messiah, the gig came with a crucifixion, and I would really like to avoid that."

The archangel looked stern. "The time for cowardice is past, Richard."

"My name is *Rick*. Only my grandmother calls me Richard. And why is wanting to stay alive suddenly the same as cowardice?"

"It is... complicated."

"We have time."

Rachel's face went white, her eyes pinned to the far corner of the room. Her grip on Alexander's hand was tight as a vise, and she whispered, "No, we don't."

The shadows in the corner lurched into form, and three moving blots of utter lightlessness surged into the apartment. Ulug uttered a high-pitched scream and scrambled across the kitchen floor as one of the tizalem streaked through the air toward him. The other two headed straight toward the couch, intent upon repeating their attack on Alexander.

Michael's sword reappeared in his hand, the fire that raced along the blade arcing and sparking. He cut through the first tizalem, which sizzled where the weapon touched its incorporeal form. A guttural shriek split their ears. Rachel reached out and grabbed Rick with her other hand and, in a purely instinctual move, teleported the family away from the source of danger. The archangel battled the attacking assassin demons while Ulug screamed, terrified into uselessness.

A slashing claw raked through Michael's face, splitting the skin and letting white light pour out of him. The wound was superficial, and it could be nothing else, for the angel was only energy and will encased in a thin wrapper of flesh. He shook off the mortal disguise and transformed along with his weapon into a single entity of light. The three tizalem converged on him, but their shadows could not withstand his brilliance. He struck them down, and they fell to the ground as ashes.

In the sudden quiet of the aftermath, Ulug gasped for air to fill his borrowed lungs, finally done shrilling like a frightened cow. Michael spared him one glance before he vanished into the ether, searching out his vanished charges.

The Utukku managed to rise to his feet despite the way his body shook, and he hunted through the kitchen cupboards until he found a single canister of salt. It was not enough, but it was something. Gritting his meat suit's teeth, he set about pouring lines of protection across the door jambs and window sills until the canister was empty.

Jessica and Li ate lunch in the corner deli, stuffing themselves on corned beef sandwiches and Matzo ball soup. Since the monk never carried any money and had no funds anyway, she picked up the tab. Unlike some men she'd known, he showed no embarrassment at having a woman pay for his meal. It was endearing.

After lunch, they strolled down the street, window shopping to take their minds off of the bizarre world their lives had become. Li once again took her hand, and once again she let him, lacing her fingers with his as they walked.

"Those shoes," he said, pointing through a store window, "are awful."

She laughed. "What do you know about shoes? Are you a secret foot fetishist?"

"I watch the Style Channel," he defended mildly. "Seriously... would you wear those?"

"Uh, no."

"I rest my case."

The next store had even more questionable sartorial choices, and Jessica was going to make a crack about the selection when she saw three people suddenly appear in the middle of the room beyond the glass. A woman and two men, one of them dressed only in a robe, simply materialized out of thin air, their eyes wide and expressions of fear on their faces.

Li blinked. "That's different."

The shop clerk was in a state of apoplexy, unable to comprehend what she had just seen. She began screeching and flailing for the panic button under the counter. Out on the sidewalk, Jessica knew that they couldn't allow the authorities to get involved in this. She grabbed her friend's hand and hauled him into the store behind her.

They had barely crossed the threshold when the store clerk, still trying to put her hand on the alarm button, suddenly switched from screeching to gurgling. The three new arrivals backed away from her, the woman clinging to the man in the robe, and Jessica and Li stopped short to stare as the clerk's head toppled onto the floor, severed from behind. A human-sized and -shaped form of black mist and cloud bolted into the center of the room, and three more just like it oozed out of the walls and merchandise cupboards to join the attack.

One of the shadow beings raced toward Jessica, and Li stepped between them, dropping into his fighting crouch and gathering his *chi*. The tattoo on his wrist began to glow, bluish light racing like a strobe along the outlines of the wings. The shadow creature hesitated at the sight.

In the center of the room, the two men and the woman were hemmed in by the other monsters. Jessica dropped her purse and raced into the fray, wondering as she did whether her karate would be any good against a creature made of shadow. Her first flying kick connected with something solid, much to her surprise and gratification. Li and the fully-clothed man saw her success and swung into action themselves, the monk with the grace and elegance of his lifetime of kung fu practice, the other man with the bullishness of a bar fighter.

It was effective, but not nearly enough. Shadow fingers like knives cut furrows into their limbs and torsos as they battled, and although it was clear that all of the flesh-and-blood contenders knew their way around a fight, it was equally clear that they were outmatched. These opponents were fueled by the very fear that they inspired, soaking in the negative energy of the aggression and anger of the mortal warriors, growing stronger with each exchange of blows.

A high-pitched scream lanced through the air, murderous and agonizing. The material denizens of the room crumpled beneath the sonic onslaught, and even the shadow creatures seemed to be knocked off balance by the noise. Jessica staggered back from the monster she had been fighting, bumping into the fully-clothed man as she did. They huddled together behind an upended mannequin and pressed their hands over their ears, searching for any kind of relief from the sound.

The shadow creatures began to vibrate, and so did the glass in the display cases and in the front window. Li, the woman and the man in the robe joined Jessica and her companion behind the store dummy, the five of them crouching together in common agony. The glass all around them shattered, sending shards and splinters flying into the center of the room. The shadow creatures were pierced by a thousand projectiles, and they, too, exploded into tiny wisps of disjointed smoke.

As suddenly as it had begun, the noise stopped, and the five people hiding behind the mannequin found themselves stooped together in the silence. Their ears were ringing, and they still had their wounds from the fight, but not one of them had so much as a scratch from the shattered glass.

Jessica looked around, trying to identify the source of the screaming that had saved them, hoping that it hadn't been the start of a new attack. In the doorway stood Yu Kun, flanked by the angel Ariel, his face utterly calm.

"It's all right," he said. "They're gone."

Ariel fixed Jessica with a strange, almost hurt look. "You shouldn't have sent me away."

"Sorry. I didn't know they were coming."

Yu Kun said, "They're likely not the only ones. There are more where these came from. We should get everyone to someplace safe."

Rick straightened. "I have to get back to Winnipeg. I've got a game tonight, and a team that needs me."

As soon as he finished speaking, he knew he had somehow crossed the line. The angel glared at him. "Wherever you go, the tizalem will follow. They will slaughter your team and everyone who has assembled to watch that game. Do you want that to happen?"

"Of course not," he replied quickly, stung.

"There are things more important that sport now." Yu Kun glanced over his shoulder. "Come, quickly, before someone notices the clerk…poor woman."

Rachel finally found her voice. "Where are we going?"

Ariel took them into the ether as he echoed the senior monk's words. "Someplace safe."

Above, Below and Between

Yu Kun's haven turned out to be a house on Long Island across from the Buddhist monastery. The English monk unlocked the door and ushered everyone inside.

"There are two bedrooms, so we'll have to share," their host explained. "The pantry is fully stocked, and there are more than enough toiletries and such to last us for a while."

Jessica looked around the front room and its modest middle-class furnishings then asked, "So how long do we have to stay here? I have classes and a job, and I know that Butch here has some team or other to get to."

"Rick," he told her. "My name is Rick Buchanan."

"Jessica Norgren. This is Tsung Li. The angel is called Ariel, and the other fella is Yu Kun, Li's master at the monastery on the other side of the yard."

The hockey player responded, "This is Rachel, and our son Alexander."

"Your son? He looks maybe two days younger than you. Either you're extremely well-preserved, or there's something else going on here."

"I was born in Hell," Alexander said quietly. "Time passes differently there."

Jessica raised an eyebrow. "In *Hell*?"

"Open your ears," Rachel said testily. "That is what he said."

"Well, pardon me," the other woman snapped back. "I'm used to people saying they're from Jersey, not Hell."

Li interjected, "There's a difference?"

Yu Kun held up his hands in an appeasing gesture. "Please, ladies and gentlemen. We are going to be sharing close quarters until the tizalem are no longer on the case, or until Michael comes to us with other orders." His words were met with varying degrees of displeasure from nearly all of those assembled, with the exception of Li, who was placid and unreadable, keeping his feelings strictly internal. The senior monk seemed satisfied with that reaction, and so he continued speaking. "As I said, there are two bedrooms. That couch also folds out into a bed, but it's rather uncomfortable. We should post a watch to be sure that no attackers catch us unawares."

Rachel hugged herself. "It'll take more than salt lines and good intentions to keep the tizalem away. It'll take wards, and strong ones at that. I can build a pretty good barrier, but not against the tizalem."

Alexander sat on the couch and took a deep breath. "Where is Ulug?"

"Back in Manhattan," Ariel answered. "He is not needed now."

The succubus huffed, "He did a piss-poor job as a bodyguard, anyway. The only thing he was good for was disposing the empties."

Yu Kun's mouth pressed into a thin line. "The empties," he echoed. "What a cavalier way to talk about the dead."

"Sorry to offend your delicate sensibilities," she said, clearly not sorry in the least.

Jessica looked at her, taking an all new dislike to the other woman. "The dead?"

"I am a succubus," she replied, proudly raising her chin. "When I feed, people die. It happens. There is no other way."

"Then you're as bad as those things that are hunting us."

Rachel's face set into a smile, both lovely and dangerous. "Be respectful, ape. You are nothing but fodder to me."

Li stepped between the two of them, his face still passive, his manner composed. "If you lay one hand on her," he told the female demon, "I will end you."

Rachel laughed at him, and Rick growled, "Easy, there, buddy. I didn't threaten your girlfriend. Don't you start threatening mine."

I'm not his girlfriend, she started to correct him, but it seemed like such an unimportant thing to argue about that she left it alone. Li glanced at her, unreadable again, and kept his silence on the point.

"Nobody is going to hurt anybody else," Yu Kun chided. "We are all needed, and we must learn to work together."

Rick took Rachel's hand and gently pulled her away from her face-off with Jessica. She looked up at him through her dark lashes, flirtatious as always, and he gave her a little smile. She put a hand on his chest and snuggled up under his arm, turning to look back at the others.

"Michael was going to tell us what this was all about," Alexander said, his voice small and distant even though he was only a few feet away. There was a haunted look in his eyes that made Rick's heart ache. "Do either one of you know what he was going to say?"

"Let's at least all sit down so we can talk about it," Li said.

Ariel looked over his shoulder toward the door, his face troubled. "A demon is coming."

"The tizalem?"

"No," he said. "A succubus."

The door burst open, and a terrified and bedraggled Lily fell into view, slamming the door behind her. She was bloody and torn, her clothes ripped to ribbons. Rachel rushed to her, taking Lily into her arms before she collapsed from fear and blood loss.

"Looks like we have mutual enemies," Li observed. "Is she all right?"

Rachel did not answer him. Instead, she gathered up her fallen sister in her arms and carried her to the couch. Alexander obediently scooted out of the way to let his mother work. She put Lily down on the cushions and bent over her, pressing their lips together. Energy surged out of Rachel and into the other succubus, and in its wake, her wounds began to heal. The supine demon began to gain color and health, but her benefactress grew paler as she poured out the saving life force.

"Mother, no," Alexander whispered, pulling her away. "Too much."

The elder succubus sank down to sit on the floor beside the couch, one hand resting lightly on Lily's lower abdomen. She smiled.

"The baby lives," she said.

"Baby?"

She looked up into her son's confused expression. "My grandson."

"Your... oh...."

Jessica folded her arms. "So, she's pregnant, too? Regular demonic baby boom, isn't it?"

Rick smirked despite the lack of humor in the situation. "So it seems."

Ariel was standing by the door, his hands flush against the wood, his trembling wings spread out to the sides. He closed his eyes and began to hum, the sound quiet at first, but building in intensity.

"Please tell me he's not going to start screaming again."

Yu Kun chuckled at the hockey player's words. "He is warding the house. He is making it so that the tizalem cannot sense any of us in here. You might say it's spiritual camouflage."

A vibrating light appeared around Ariel's hands, spreading rapidly to cover the door and the wall that held it. As they watched, the white glow spread over the entire house, blanketing the structure completely, encasing the walls, floors, ceilings, roof and basement in the same protection. When the encapsulation was complete, the light brightened and pulsed once, then again, before receding into the fabric of the building.

Rick shook his head, something that he could tell was going to become a habit. "Wow," he said stupidly. "That was... wow."

Li looked to his Master. "Now what?"

"Now we wait."

It wasn't often that Yeter'el was nervous, but receiving a summons from the Throne of Hell was enough to rattle anyone's cage. He stood in the barroom that Lucifer had chosen to use as his newest meeting place, waiting to be brought before his king. Behind him, his pet imp picked at the human soul tending bar, keeping himself occupied while his master stewed and worried. The imp was safe in the knowledge that whatever the Prince of Lies wanted, it had nothing to do with him.

Yeter'el could guess what this was about. Someone had come and told their master about the child. He should have known better than to let the human woman come to him on her own time; he should have seized her and taken her to the hiding place in limbo he had prepared. Lucifer never would have looked for them there, and the child could have been born in safety and reared by Yeter'el's own hand.

Now that would never be.

Asb'el opened the door to the inner sanctum, and his fellow Watcher could see that something was badly amiss with him. His eyes, normally such a soulful brown, glowed with pinpoints of orange flame, and his face was slack and expressionless. Yeter'el's mouth went dry as he contemplated these hints of pain to come.

His brother beckoned him forward, and so he went, keeping his eyes turned down and his stance as compliant and peaceable as he could make it. Inside the room, on his black throne, Lucifer was staring at him; even though he kept his gaze on the floor, he could feel the weight of that stare and he knew it for what it was.

He was in deep, deep trouble.

As soon as the door closed again behind him, the Watcher fell to his knees and pressed his forehead to the ground at Satan's feet. He hoped that groveling would moderate the punishment he was about to receive. It had always worked in the past.

"You have conceived another child with a mortal woman," the First Fallen intoned.

"Only one of many, Master."

"But this one is different, isn't he?"

Yeter'el's palms began to sweat. "In what way, Master?"

A lash of fire fell across his back, ripping into his wings and rendering them useless. He cried out, and the whip fell once again, the sound of the crack filling the room.

Lucifer growled, "Do not play the fool to *me*, little brother. I know every lie before it's told. Do you not think that I would see through you?" His clawed feet hit the wooden floor with a clack, and he came closer. "You thought to bring the prophecy of my downfall into being, didn't you?"

"No!" Yeter'el wanted to squirm away from the anger of the King of Demons, but he knew better than to move. His wounded wings quivered, the torn flesh dripping hot blood onto his skin. "It was my line's turn to try for the Anti-Christ. That is all!"

"More lies?" Lucifer laughed coldly. "You do not learn, Yeter'el." He stepped onto the Watcher's back, his claws digging deep, his preternaturally heavy weight pushing Yeter'el flat against the floor. He could hear his ribs snapping. "Do you remember when you and your brethren fell? Do you remember what I told you when you came to me, looking for a place to shelter from His anger?" He stomped. "*Do you?*"

Since he had no air for speech, he simply nodded his head as much as he could bear.

"I told you that the only way I would allow you into my domain was if you swore an oath of loyalty to me, on your blood and the blood of all of your descendants, on penalty of total destruction if you ever broke your vow." He stomped again, grinding his massive, clubbed foot into the fallen Watcher. More bones strained and broke. "And did you swear?"

He could only nod again.

"You *made a bargain*. You sealed it with the blood of your first-born infant. And now you have betrayed me." He crouched down, his own bat wings beating a furious rhythm, and sneered into Yeter'el's ear. "You heard the whispered prophecy that was ripped from the mouth of a dying angel and you believed it to be true. You heard Harahel say that one day, a child born of the lustiest Watcher and a woman from the rod of Jesse would take the throne of Hell and bring destruction upon those angels who fell in the first rebellion against Him. You heard this, and you tried to bring it to life. *Didn't you?*"

The Watcher could not respond, not even with a movement of his head. He was slowly being flattened, his bones being ground to dust. Agony burned through him, and for the first time, he regretted that he was immortal.

"Those words were lies," Lucifer told him. "A fever dream of a dying soul, nothing more. Do you think that I would have allowed any of you to remain alive while there was a threat of such a thing? Foolish, foolish boy!" His claw punched through the front of Yeter'el's chest, gouging a deep furrow in the wood below. "Now you will earn the reward of all your sins. Damnation is not only for human souls. Your pain will be eternal and *exquisite.*"

He wanted nothing more than to scream, to relieve the horrible pressure of his king's claws through his body, but he was powerless. His life force, and all of the life force that he had stolen from humans along the way, seeped out and into the Devil's hands, leaving him bereft. When the last jot of energy had been sucked away, Lucifer stepped back, leaving the Watcher's body to shrivel like an earthworm in a frying pan.

CHAPTER TWELVE

*A*bove, Below and Between

Yu Kun stood in the living room, facing the others as they assembled around him like schoolchildren in a class. He folded his hands and began.

"I know that there are some among us – Rachel, Ariel – who are more familiar with these stories than others. I also know that there are some who know nothing of what I am about to relate. I think it's important to start at the beginning so that we all have the same information as we go forward. I ask you all to have patience and to listen mindfully."

Rick looked at Alexander, who was sitting on the couch with Lily's head cradled in his lap. His son looked pale and frightened, and Rick only hoped that whatever was about to be said wouldn't be too hard for him to hear.

Yu Kun cleared his throat then spoke. "In the beginning of the world, before humanity existed, God created the heavens and the earth and filled them with creatures made of light and energy. These creatures were the angels, and they were God's beloved children."

Jessica whispered to Li, who was sitting beside her on the floor, "Great. Fairy tales."

"Shh," her friend responded.

"The first of His children was the very soul of light itself, and he was called the Light Bringer, because everywhere he went, his power and his beauty filled the heavens. He shone almost as bright as His Father, but he was content, because he knew that God loved him best. He is known to us today as Lucifer. His second child was a sterner soul, a warrior at heart, obedient to his Father without question. He accepted his position in God's affections and desired only to please Him. His name is Michael.

"The other beings who have come to be known as archangels were born next – Raphael, the healer; Gabriel, the messenger; Uriel, the fire of God; and Raguel, created to be God's friend. Also created in this time were other beings whose names are known to humankind today: Aniel, Sadaquiel, Metatron, Selaphiel, Remiel, Sammael, Belial, and hundreds more. They numbered in the thousands, and they lived together in harmony. They were powerful, magnificent, and beautiful, and they loved God as their Father. They did not, however, please Him completely. For reasons known only to Himself, He was not satisfied, and so He decided to create man."

Ariel drifted through the living room, walking a slow patrol from window to window, watching for the tizalem to show themselves again. Rick tried not to watch the angel, tried to focus on the things Yu Kun was saying. His mind kept trying to wander, though, because it all seemed so ludicrous. There was a reason he had always slept through catechism.

If the angel's progress through the room was a disruption, the senior monk gave no indication. "When mankind was created – when God started his new children on the path upward from protozoa to amphibian to ape and finally to human being – there was great controversy in the celestial realms. God made it clear that these new children, these imperfect, mortal children, were more beloved to Him than his angels. He bade his angels to love mankind as He loved them, to be obedient to them, and to accept their position behind mankind in God's affection.

"Michael and his brothers, who would become the archangels, obeyed. As long as they still enjoyed their Father's love, they cared little for rankings. They accepted their assignments as mankind's helpers and protectors, and they helped to shepherd the evolutionary process along as God designed.

"Lucifer, though, was bitter. Like any spoiled first-born child, he resented being supplanted in his Father's eyes by these newborn, imperfect creatures. He hated mankind, and he went to His Father to complain. He refused to bow to men, refused to acknowledge mankind's primacy over the angels in God's love. He told God that he would not obey, and one third of all of the angels in heaven joined him in his argument.

"His Father, like many fathers, was angered by the challenge of his son, and so he called on Michael and his army to castigate Lucifer and his angels. To punish them further, God created a place of torment and never-ending darkness far from His light, a place of pain and misery. The angels fought in Heaven and on the earth, causing great destruction and sorrow to their Father and to each other. Finally, Michael's army with God's power prevailed, and Lucifer and his allies were cast down into the Abyss, where they were condemned to live in isolation, out of favor of God and far from His grace for all time."

Rachel leaned her head against Rick's shoulder, her eyes watching the speaker. He kissed her hair, and she smiled. "You know all this already, don't you?" he asked her in a whisper.

"Of course. And so would you, if you'd paid any attention in those CCD classes your grandparents sent you to."

He frowned. "How did you know about that?"

She chuckled. "Oh, honey... I know *everything* about you."

Yu Kun took a sip of water from a cup then glanced at Rachel and Rick, waiting for them to be done. When they fell silent, he continued. "For a time, the heavens and the earth returned to normal. Mankind continued to evolve, and the angels once again stood guard over them, watching them as they grew. The angels were like shepherds, and they loved God's flock as their own.

"This love, though, was foreign to Lucifer and his brothers. The former angel, once called the Light Bringer, embraced the darkness into which he had been cast. If his Father was going to turn His back on him so unjustly, then he would take his hurt and distill it into spite. He would become the darkest force the world had ever known, and he would send evil into the world to plague these new-born sons of man. The angels who had fallen with him became demons, the princes of hell, answering only to Lucifer and hating mankind with a venom exceeded only by their master's own. They took the Abyss and made it from a place of silence and loneliness into a realm of screaming and lamentation.

"Without meaning to, it seems, a young and inexperienced God had taken a formidable ally and turned him into the bitterest of enemies, creating an endless balance. For as God is good and made of love and mercy, so Satan, the Adversary, is bad and made of hatred and cruelty. They continually oppose one another, using angels and men as pawns, tugging first this way, then that, until the entire universe is suspended on a taut line between the two. And so it continues to this day."

Alexander snorted. "Good going."

The interjection was met with a chuckle from Yu Kun. He nodded and shrugged and went on. "But Lucifer and his fellows were not the only angels to fall from grace. When mankind was just beginning to take hold in the world, when the entire population of mankind was barely as large as a large village is today, there came a day of disobedience. The angels who had been assigned to protect the infant human race, known as Grigori, or the Watchers, realized that their love for their human flock was no longer pure. Indeed, these angels looked upon the daughters of men and saw their beauty, and they took them for themselves.

"God had given them charge to watch and protect, but He had strictly forbidden them from directly contacting mankind. These Watchers did just that, and more."

Rachel whispered to Rick, "This is where it gets really interesting."

"The first to come was Yeter'el, who seduced the women of the earth. Then came Pinem'e, who took a wife and made a child, and taught his child everything there was to know about the magic inherent in words. It is said that he taught his child the very Name of God, the Hidden Name that nobody should ever know. Azazel came and taught his children the arts of war. Gadriel taught the use of cosmetics and the ways of hedonism. Shamsiel, Armaros, Araquiel, Bezaliel – they all came and took human wives, siring a race of half-angelic bastards and sharing the secret knowledge of heaven, corrupting the innocence of God's newborns forever.

"God was furious. He raged as He had never raged before. He once again sent Michael and his armies, and once again, his angelic sons were cast out and punished. They were set loose upon the land, cut off from God and from their mortal families, who had been cursed by God in His anger. Their bastard children became not half-angels but half-devils, known as the nephilim, and they were condemned to wander the world for eternity. The Watchers and their half-blood children, and all children born to them, were damned."

Li sighed. "That still doesn't seem fair to me. The kids didn't do anything. Why should they be punished?"

Yu Kun smiled to his young student. "We're coming to that. Patience, my boy.

"So where were these new fallen angels to go? Why, nowhere else but to their older brother, who had already made his kingdom in the Abyss. They crawled to him, and they swore to do him honor and service in the wrecking and destruction of mankind, seeking revenge upon God for His harmful rage. They, too, became demons, and some of them spawned new races of demons and devils who continued the sins that had caused their fathers' fall. Yeter'el, you see, had fallen out of lust, and so his children came to embody that vice, and are today known as the incubus and succubus. Pinem'e's children became enchanters and whisperers of hidden knowledge, and it is they who have emboldened wizards and sorcerers for centuries. So it was with all of the Watchers who fell in those dark days."

"I may not be the godliest or best educated guy around," Rick said, "but this doesn't sound like the God I was taught about. What happened to all that stuff about forgiveness and mercy?"

"This was not the God of the Covenant, not the God who sent Jesus to redeem his sinful mortal family," Yu Kun explained. "This was a young God still devoted to His own power, still harsh and unthinking and elemental as lightning. Rationality and mercy were still part of him, yes, but they were parts that still needed to grow. He had no mercy for the Grigori or for the nephilim."

Rick snorted. "What a guy."

"Now, when God sent Jesus to redeem his human children, the old injustice He had done to the Grigori was brought back to his attention. You see? I said we were getting to this. His beloved soldier Michael came to him and gently, without challenge, asked if perhaps a savior might be sent so that his fallen brothers might return again to heaven and God's light. God thought and thought, and centuries of time passed on, for God is eternal and sees no need to rush.

"Michael was not the only one who thought along those lines. Lucifer too began to think. If God wanted to redeem only his straying mortal men, then it was clear that mortal men's redemption should be tainted. It was a gesture of spite to an unloving and distant father ... something entirely too many mortal sons can understand.

"In this time when He was thinking, when God was distracted and perhaps not as attentive to the mortal world as He should have been, Lucifer decided that he needed a singular son of his own. If God was to have His Christ, then Lucifer would have the Anti-Christ. The vehicle of salvation born to a simple human woman would be countered by a vehicle of damnation, also born to a human woman. It was decided that he would visit his seed upon a woman and bring about the downfall of God's merciful plans."

"Gee," Jessica said drily, feeling a spark of empathy for that distant woman. "Let me guess – she didn't have to be a willing participant, did she?"

"Not at all. Lucifer is cruel, and after all, he is also known as the Father of Lies. If a lady was meant to conceive, then he could come to her in the guise of her husband, or her lover, or just a seducer to woo her. And if that failed, then... there is always rape, which is nothing more than a diversion in Lucifer's world."

"Goody."

"The first Anti-Christ was born in Rome thirty-seven years after Christ's sacrifice. He was meant to bring the mortal world to ruin in flame, and he did his part, but the power of Lucifer's hatred and the

141

weakness of the mortal line to which he was born did not mesh well, and he perished in insanity. The next Anti-Christ was born in China in 537 to the Gao family in Northern Qi province. He, too, was misled by his own debauchery, and he also failed to destroy the world. Lucifer still seeks to create his Anti-Christ. He has refined his plan so that only women who are descendants of holy blood lines will become the vessel of his child. Other Anti-Christs have risen and fallen, roughly every 500 years or so, always destroyed by Michael and his army. And so it goes."

Ariel said softly, "But that is not all that happened." He looked pointedly at Alexander. "Listen well to what you are about to hear."

"Lucifer was not the only resident of the Abyss looking for retaliation," Yu Kun continued. "The Watchers gathered together in Constantinople, just before that great city was sacked in 1204. They agreed among themselves that they had suffered too long under Lucifer's rule, and that the time had come for them to stop being second-class citizens in Hell. They decided that one of them would sire a challenger for Satan's throne, and they took a vote. Because he had been clever in his dealings and had seen to it that many of his brothers owed him favors, Yeter'el was the winner of that election, overturning Pinem'e, whose intelligence and magic would have made him a better choice. In anger, Pinem'e stormed away, and nobody has seen him since."

"Not true," Rachel piped up. "I and Rick and Alexander and Ulug – we really should fetch Ulug, shouldn't we? – we all saw him just yesterday. Or today. Or sometime recently." She shrugged. "Time runs together. Anyway, he's still around, still obsessed with words."

The angel at the window nodded. "Good to know."

Yu Kun could think of nothing to add to that, so he merely returned to his story. "Finally, though, God stopped thinking and decided that the time had come to act. He called His archangels together and decreed that it was time to rectify His impetuous punishment of the Grigori and their children, and that a Messiah would be sent to them, as well. Like the true Messiah and the Anti-Christ alike, this Watchers' Messiah would be born from a Watcher and a woman from the holy line known as the Rod of Jesse, the same family tree from which Jesus Himself arose."

Rick asked, "But what does any of this have to do with us?"

"That takes some explaining, too," the English monk replied.

"Terrific. Why am I not surprised?"

"Because in spite of your behavior, you have wisdom," Yu Kun fired back, cheeky but not harsh. "So, you see, three children are coming into this world, all of whom will bring great changes. One will bring peace and justice at last to those God wounded, one will bring about a war in Hell to echo the war in Heaven, and one will usher in a thousand years of Satan's rule on earth. For obvious reasons, we need to know who and where these children are. We already have some idea.

"In the time of God's distraction, Michael as Viceroy of Heaven took it upon himself to gather to him human beings of distinction. Some human beings, by virtue of their strength of character or their singular blood lines, are a step above other mortals. In the old days, they would be called heroes with a capital 'H', like Hercules or Perseus. Now they are light workers and monks and ministers and nurses and people in all walks of life, different in every way but this: they have been Called. Michael has called them to help him seek out and set right the machinations of the Adversary, and they are part of his army in operation here on Earth, or as the angels and the demons call it, Between."

He held up his left arm, displaying the skin on the inner side of his wrist. There was a tattoo there, small and discreet and shaped like angel wings. Rick couldn't be certain whether it was a trick of the light or something that he had really seen, but it seemed that those wings shimmered a bit as he showed them off.

"These wings on my wrist and there on Li's are the insignia of our battallion. We are directly under the command of Michael himself, and it is our duty to oppose the Adversary and his minions with old-fashioned battle skills. We are the fighters in Michael's mortal army. There are other insignias, as well – crosses for Raphael's healers' corps, horns for Gabriel's communications regiment, and for the few who bear the right qualities, there is the flame of Uriel. Each battalion has its own function and duties, and sometimes within each battalion, there are specialist soldiers.

"You are all in this fight for a reason. Some of you, like Jessica and Lily, are here because you were chosen to bear the children at the center of this tale. Others, like Li and myself, are chosen to fight to protect mankind against the snares of the devil. The rest of you will be approached by the angels as they deem it appropriate, either to ask you to join the army or to offer you more explanation.

"These are dangerous and precarious times. It may be that none of us assembled here will survive the battle to come. I cannot ask you to sacrifice your lives, but you must know that the Adversary and his minions sense your importance, too. The tizalem were sent because Lucifer believes that the Pretender, the child who will one day take his throne in Hell, is one of the fetuses here with us today. The tizalem will not stop until they are destroyed, recalled, or successful in their duty. If Satan of all demons believes in the validity of what I've told you, then you can rest assured that others will, as well.

"We are stronger together than apart. I ask only that you think on this."

With that, he gathered up his water cup and went into the kitchen for a refill. Rick twisted to watch him go while Jessica said, "Wow. Talk about your data dumps."

Li smiled at her ruefully. "My head is spinning."

"So, best guess?" Rick prompted. "Who's got which kid?"

From the couch, Lily weakly said, "My son is the Watcher's Messiah. I'm sure of it."

"I hate to break it to you, dearest, but you're not a woman from the Rod of Jesse," the hockey player pointed out.

"But that blood is in this child's veins, courtesy of your mother," she said. She sat up slowly, and Alexander gently supported her back while she got her bearings. "She was descended from Jesus and a British woman..."

Jessica laughed. "*What*? That's the most preposterous thing I've ever heard! When was he ever in Britain?"

Lily glared at her. "His uncle, Joseph of Arimathea, was a successful tin merchant, and he had holdings in Cornwall. Jesus came there with his uncle when he was fourteen and found a local lass very much to his liking."

"Oh, honestly... how would you know?"

"Because, bitch," she said acidly, "I was there."

144

Rachel waved her hand dismissively. "It's an old story. What do you think that old hymn 'Jersualem' is on about? Anyway, Rick, darling, yes, your mother was descended from a holy bloodline. That's why you were such a stand-out choice to be Alexander's father."

The color in Jessica's face turned suspiciously grayish, but she said nothing further. Li squeezed her hand and wordlessly asked if she was all right, but she only shook her head and offered a brave smile. He could see that she had something to say, but he knew that this was not the time. He nodded his understanding.

"Okay, then," Rick said slowly. "Wow. So, that explains that... doesn't that mean that my part is done, here? I mean, Alexander's baby is the Watcher's Messiah, and I guess that means that Jessica here is carrying the Anti-Christ –"

"Because I'm just that lucky," she said, mostly to herself.

"So now we just have to find the third baby and we're done, right? I mean, I'm done. Right? I have to get back to my team..."

Ariel shook his head. "Your sport career is over. The only team that remains to you is here in this room." He sighed. "And we don't know that Jessica's baby is the Anti-Christ. It may well be the Pretender."

Yu Kun sipped more water and leaned against the wall. "She can't be carrying the Anti-Christ, not if Yeter'el is the father. The father of the Anti-Christ is Satan himself."

Lily shuddered. "I saw him."

Rachel looked at her, thunderstruck. "The First Fallen? When?"

"Today. Before I came back Between. I was there when he ordered out the tizalem." She looked at Alexander. "I was coming to warn you. I'm so sorry I was too late."

Jessica narrowed her eyes, watching the interplay between the two. "That's funny timing," she said.

"It was just coincidence. That happens to demons, too, you know." The younger succubus shook her head. "I was having a drink with Mitchell – you remember Mitchell, don't you, Rachel?" When her sister nodded, she continued. "The First Fallen happened to be in the back room, having a meeting with Asb'el."

"Asb'el?" Jessica repeated. "Who is that?"

"Another of the Grigori," Yu Kun answered. "He was the one who convinced Yeter'el to take a mortal woman as his wife." He drained his cup. "If the Watchers have any leader, it is him."

"So Asb'el told Satan about what Yeter'el's been up to, and so Satan sent his assassins to clean up the neighborhood," Jessica said slowly. "Am I keeping up here?"

"So far, so good," the English monk agreed.

"So where's the Anti-Christ?"

Ariel sighed. "That is what everyone wants to know."

CHAPTER THIRTEEN

elow and Between

B

Changing his appearance was an easy thing; a simple flicker of a thought, and it was done. His chosen face was young and attractive, but not too much so. His hair was blond, his eyes blue, his body fit and athletic. It would suffice for the job he meant to do.

Lucifer sat in a street cafe in Selçuk, sipping dark Turkish coffee and watching the tourists boarding a bus to Ephesus. They were Americans – a Baptist church group from some little burg in Texas – and had no idea that they were so close to the being that their preacher vilified every Sunday. There was a young woman among them who had caught his eye, and he watched her as she climbed aboard the rickety old bus with her parents. She was at that delicious age between child and woman, with a simple and innocent mind tied to a body ripe for passion. He loved teenagers.

He tossed some coins onto the table – 30 silver coins, just to amuse himself – and climbed onto the bus with the tourists. He found the girl sitting near her parents, the seat empty beside her as he had willed. She glanced up at him shyly, and he smiled to her with as much friendly warmth as he could. He could display anything when he wanted to. He was, after all, the Father of Lies.

"Is this seat taken?" he asked, his voice a gentle tenor.

"Uh, n-no," she stammered back, tucking her skirt under her leg to give him room to sit. He slid onto the cracked vinyl beside her and held up his ragged, dog-eared copy of the Bible.

"Exciting, isn't it? The chance to walk in the footsteps of the Apostles." She smiled at him again and simply nodded, looking up at him through her eyelashes, speaking the ages-old language of flirtation. "Oh, but where are my manners? My name is Jason."

Finally she spoke in a voice both musical and meek. "My name is Mary."

He could not suppress his grin. "Of course it is."

They divvied up the sleeping accommodations and decided that they would take turns sleeping and keeping watch. Alexander and Lily took the first sleeping shift, disappearing together into one of the little house's bedrooms. Li and his master took the other room, where they did their evening meditations and took the opportunity for a little rest. Rachel and Jessica were given the sofa bed with its pull-out mattress, but only the demon went to sleep.

Rick, who had taken first watch, copied the patrol path that Ariel was still walking, not at all certain what it was he should be watching for. At least he was moving, though, and that was a relief. A whole day of sitting had done nothing but make his legs twitchy and his mood sour. He wished he could go skate.

Jessica made herself a cup of tea and, without asking, poured one for Rick. He accepted it with a nod and whispered, "Thanks."

"Don't mention it."

She leaned her hips against the kitchen sink while he did the same against the island, both of them sipping their drinks in silence. The house was still, almost unnervingly so. For the first time in his life, he quoted an old Western movie cliché and felt that it was totally, unbelievably accurate.

"It's quiet. Too quiet."

Jessica looked up at him, her brows briefly furrowed, and then she erupted into stifled giggles. "You did *not* just say that."

"No, I think I did. Let me check... yep, I definitely did."

"Moron."

"Thank you. It's like you already know me."

The levity helped make both of them slightly more comfortable. After a moment, Jessica said, "So... pretty heavy stuff, huh?"

He ran a hand over his hair. "You can say that again." He put his cup aside and crossed his arms. "I'll be honest. I don't really know how to react."

"I'm not sure any of us do." She looked down into the brown liquid. *Maybe I should ask someone to read my tea leaves*, she thought. *Too bad I made this with a Lipton bag.* She admitted, "I don't know what to do."

"About the baby?"

She dumped the rest of her tea down the drain and put the cup in the sink. "About anything. My job, my school, the baby... my *life*."

"You're in school?"

"Yeah, studying to be a lawyer." She laughed. "I'm pretty sure there are no precedents on the books for the kind of custody battle I'll be facing if I bring this thing to term. And you know, I don't even know if I want to be a lawyer anymore. Everything looks so sideways."

Rick had plenty of concerns of his own, but he opted not to complain and tried to be sympathetic instead. "Well, look at it this way. No matter what happens, you have your angel, and you have your boyfriend."

"He's not my boyfriend, not exactly."

"Not exactly?" he teased. "Isn't that sort of like being pregnant, you are or you're not?"

"It's... complicated." She shrugged. "I don't know if he wants that sort of a relationship. I'm not sure *I* want that. He's my best friend, and I don't want to screw it up by..." Her voice trailed off. "You don't really want to hear this."

Rick smiled. "Sure I do. We're all stuck in here like contestants on *Big Brother*. The least we can do is get to know each other. At least there're no cameras."

"You and Li would get along like gangbusters," she chuckled. "All these media references."

"If you guys are all going to be my new team, like I was told, then it's time for me to get to know him, too."

"So you're an athlete," she said. "Hockey, right?"

"Right."

"I never watched hockey. I don't understand it. I actually think it's pretty boring."

He threw his head back as if she's just slugged him. "Ouch! You can never say that to a Canadian!"

"Oh, I'm sorry," she said, although the smirk on her face said that she clearly wasn't. "I hope I didn't just destroy all of your national pride."

"No, not all of it. Just a little bit. It's got a real bad bruise on the side, there."

"You're crazy."

"It comes with the territory."

"Which territory is that? The being half demon part or the being a hockey player part?"

He smiled. "Well, both, really." He poured his tea out, too. "This has been a really weird day."

"Tell me about it."

They fell silent once more, and Ariel glided through the kitchen, silently keeping his patrol. He glanced at them but said nothing as he skirted around the other side of the kitchen island, turning sideways so that his wings could pass. They watched him as he went into the laundry room to check the back door again.

"So have you always had an angel with you?"

"No, I haven't. He actually was just a new arrival in my life a few days ago. Came in through my apartment window."

"Big window, if there was room for him to fly in."

She smiled. "Well, actually, I sort of picked him up and brought him in." She saw the surprise in Rick's face and explained, "He was a stray cat at the time."

"Interesting..."

From the living room, they heard Rachel shifting in the bed, and they both looked in the direction of the sound. Jessica asked, "So what about you? Have you always had a succubus with you?"

"I just met her last summer while I was on vacation in Maui. Nice resort. Great clientele." He smiled at the memory. "She sure made that week memorable."

"Apparently that's not all she made."

"Yeah... I just found out about Alexander a little while ago. Days ago, sort of when you met your angel."

"Coincidental timing, that."

"I'm beginning to think that there are no such things are coincidences." He scratched his neck. "I'm still not used to the idea of being a father. I'm really not ready to be a grandpa, too."

"I'm not really ready to be a mom." She led the way over to the kitchen table and sat down. He pulled out another chair and joined her.

He folded his hands together and leaned on his forearms, bending a little closer to her. "I'm going to go out on a limb, here. Can I ask you something?"

"Sure."

"Have you thought about an abortion?"

She laughed ruefully. "Oh, I more than thought about it. I actually went to a clinic. The problem was, once I got there, I just couldn't go through with it. I mean, my head just started swimming and I started hallucinating... real serious psychosomatic stuff."

"Either that, or the demon inside you was doing its best to stay alive," he suggested. "Anything is possible."

The thought was disturbing to her. "It's barely bigger than the head of a pin right now," she said. "How could it possibly know what I was planning?"

"The body is small, but the soul is already attached to it, and the demon part of it is very, very aware." He sighed. "If that baby is anything like me – and since he's my half-sibling, apparently, he probably is – he's going to be lucid the moment he's born. I remember being born. I remember the nurses and the doctors and the noises and everything."

She raised an eyebrow, skeptical. "Are you sure? Maybe you've seen births on TV or in movies or something and just convinced yourself that you remember."

"I'm sure. I remember what they said, word for word, and when I was old enough to talk, I repeated it. There were things that happened that day that I was never supposed to be told."

She frowned. "Like what?"

Rick hesitated. "I, uh, I don't want to scare you..."

"Tell me."

He could see from the look in her eye that she wanted to know. He sighed and hoped that she was as tough as she thought she was. "My mother died giving birth to me. My grandparents, who raised me, tried to tell me that she died because of an infection or something that she picked up in the hospital, but that isn't what happened. I remember that she died because of the way I was born."

Her palms began to sweat. "What way were you born? Breach? Turning?"

"No." He looked ashamed. "Biting and scratching."

Her brows shot up toward her hairline. "*What?*"

"Um... yeah. I was a real little monster when I was born. A *real monster*, if you understand. They freaked out." He looked down, unable to look her in the eye. "I heard the doctors say that I had torn chunks out of her uterus on the way out. I apparently didn't want to be born. And my...*deformity*... probably hurt her a lot, too."

"Deformity?" She glanced at his body. "You look fine to me. What deformity?"

He rubbed a hand over his mouth, wondering why he had started telling her any of this at all. "I was born with wings."

She was turning into an echo chamber. "Wings?"

"Yeah. Like, incubus wings. I guess they were pretty spiny or something...they cut them off right away."

"They cut off your wings."

"Yeah."

"That's... wow." She put a hand to her forehead. "Please tell me that you don't remember them doing that."

"Not really, no. I sort of blocked that part out."

"My God! How horrible!"

"It's okay," he shrugged. "Really, it is. If they hadn't done that, I never would have been able to fit in, never would have had any kind of life. It's sort of like when you're born with six fingers, or a tail, y'know? That happens."

Jessica leaned back. "Do you think that'll happen to me?"

"I hope not."

"Yes or no."

"Maybe."

"That's not an answer," she pressed.

"Well, sorry, but I can't tell the future, so I don't know," he said, frustrated. He never should have said anything. "Look, forget I said anything, okay?"

Jessica laughed. "Oh, sure. No problem. You just told me that this thing inside of me might rip me apart when it's born and that I might die, but, sure. I'll just forget it. Why would I remember something as insignificant as that?"

"Geez Louise, you're sarcastic."

She shook her head at him. "'Geez Louise'? Where did you come from, 1952?"

"Brampton, Ontario, actually. But close enough." He stood. "I should probably keep moving. Don't want to be caught unprepared, right?"

"You were a boy scout, weren't you?"

He laughed. "In some ways, I guess I still am."

There was something about Rick that made her want to heckle him. She chose not to give it too much thought and just went with it. "A demonic boy scout," she teased. "Now I've heard everything."

Rick just grinned at her and slipped into the bedroom occupied by his son and Lily. He closed the door as silently as he could, careful not to disturb either sleeper. When he was certain that they were still safely dreaming, he crept across the room and checked the salt lines at the bases of the windows.

The line at the window sill nearest Alexander's head was undisturbed, and a quick peek through the blinds showed him nothing. Given that the tizalem were shadows and it was the middle of the night outside, he wasn't expecting to see anything. Still, the lack of anything visible was reassuring.

He went around the bed to check the window near Lily's head. He was halfway to the window when she stirred and opened her eyes, which were luminescent in the dark. He had never seen a succubus' eyes glow before.

"What are you doing, Rick?" she asked, her voice throaty and oozing with enticement.

"Checking on the salt lines," he whispered back. "I don't want anything to come in and get you while you're sleeping."

She made a little pleasure sound and shifted to lie on her side, propped up on one elbow. "Such a gentleman," she cooed.

"I do my best."

Something in her demeanor was all wrong, and while he wasn't familiar with Lily on a good day, he was suspicious. He started back toward the window, and she put out a hand, gently catching him with one palm on his thigh.

"I can think of so many more interesting things than salt, can't you?"

"Alexander is *right there*."

"I know," she shrugged. Her hand inched a little higher. "He's sleeping. He won't wake up for hours. I made sure of it."

"How?"

She chuckled. "I'm a full succubus, he's a three-quarter demonling. Who do you think has the most power? I took him and drained him down, that's all. He'll recover. But baby..." She patted her flat abdomen. "Baby has to eat."

Rick shook his head and stepped away from her touch. He knew they should have declared the bedrooms sex-free zones. "That's dirty pool."

"Honey, I'm a demon," she said. "Do you really expect me to play by the rules?" He headed back to the window, and again she stopped him, this time putting her hand in the place most guaranteed to get his undivided attention. "Come on," she sing-songed. "Come play with me. All work and no play make Rick a dull, dull boy."

He narrowed his eyes and tried not to react to the things she was doing with her fingers. He pushed her hand away. "Why are you trying to keep me from checking the salt line?"

"I'm not," she pouted. "I'm just trying to get you to come to bed."

"With my son right there? No way. Not gonna happen."

"Then we can roll him out onto the floor," she urged. She was starting to seem a little more assertive than suggestive. "He won't wake up, I promise you."

"I thought you succubi didn't poach in each other's territories," he said, moving closer to the window.

Lily rose up out of bed, letting the sheets fall away to reveal her naked flesh. His body had a predictable and annoying response to the sight, and it was all he could do to take a step backward. He tried not to make eye contact with her, not really knowing why, but convinced that she would own him if he did. He didn't want to give in to whatever tricks she was playing.

"Normally we don't," she said. "Are you referring to yourself? Are you Rachel's territory?"

He took another step. "Well.. yes..."

"I'm not worried about Rachel. If she objects, I can just slap her back into place."

"She's way older than you."

"That doesn't matter anymore." Lily was closer now, and he could feel her body heat through the thin cloth of his shirt. His mouth was watering and he was running out of places to look that didn't involve her eyes. She took his face in her hands and said, "Look at me."

He closed his eyes and tried to back away, but she was physically stronger than him and held him in place by his head.

"*Look at me*," she commanded.

He did. When their eyes met, he felt that he was contacting another being within her. That being, linked now by the line of sight between them, shot through their locked gaze and deep into his soul, burning and shredding its way into the very heart of him. He gasped but could not cry out, and his body, suddenly rigid with the pain, disobeyed him completely.

Lily kept her hands on his face with her intense gaze boring into him until the demon she had been hosting made its way completely into Rick. When the transfer was complete, she released her hold on him and let him fall to the floor. She teleported back into the bed and curled up against her bedmate, closing her eyes and pretending to be asleep.

In the living room, Jessica heard the thud of Rick falling to the floor, and she darted into the bedroom as quickly as she could. She saw Alexander and Lily lying in bed, apparently asleep, and Rick on the bedroom carpet, unconscious. She rushed to him and shouted for Ariel.

Lily stirred, and Jessica could hear Li, Yu Kun and Rachel all responding to her shout, but Alexander never even twitched. Ariel appeared at her side and helped her pick up the hockey player, putting him on the bed when Lily left her spot. Jessica put a finger on Rick's throat.

"He has a pulse," she said. "But I'm not a doctor. I don't even have first aid training."

Rachel shoved her out of the way. "Let me see."

156

Jessica took umbrage but obeyed. She stepped aside and let Rachel kneel and examine Rick while Li turned on the bedroom light.

"What's the matter with Alexander?" Yu Kun asked.

"He's tired," Lily said weakly.

Rachel touched Rick's solar plexus and shook her head. "He's completely drained. He's barely got enough energy left to keep alive. The medical term, I think, is 'coma.'" She reached out and touched her son the same way. "Damn! Him, too. Lily, what have you done?"

"I've done nothing!" she protested. "I was sleeping..."

Yu Kun went to the window nearest Lily's side of the bed. "The salt line is broken. It looks like four claws were dragged right through it." He gathered the salt back together with his hands, repairing the barrier.

Jessica asked, "The tizalem?"

Ariel shook his head. "No. They would have been kept out by my wards. It had to have been done by something that was already in the house when I sealed it. It was probably trying to get out and assaulted Rick when he tried to stop it."

Lily pulled on her tattered clothing. "There was a spy in here?" She sounded suitably frightened.

"Perhaps." Yu Kun looked at her. "Perhaps there still is."

"Take this outside," Rachel commanded, sitting on the foot of the bed between her lover and her son. "I'll stand guard over these two and see about getting them bumped back up."

"Pray for help," Ariel suggested.

Rachel snorted. "Right. You *do* know who listens when demons pray, don't you?"

Jessica took a wild guess. "The devil?"

"I'd say give that woman a prize," the succubus confirmed. "If I pray, I'm only going to be notifying our greatest enemy where we are."

Li noticed her wording. "Our enemy? You're against him now?"

"Darling," Rachel said, shaking her head, "I have been for years."

"Then I will pray," Yu Kun said. "Perhaps some good will come of it."

Ariel nodded. "Good always comes of prayer. He always hears. Help will always come."

Lily shuddered. "I'd feel safer if we were all out in the living room together, anyway."

Her elder sister looked at her with narrowed eyes. "That's an excellent idea. Gentlemen, please help me carry these two out onto the sofa bed. We can all be in the same room while they recover. That was a brilliant idea, Lily."

Yu Kun lifted Alexander while Li bent to pick up Rick. He grunted. "Man, what does this guy eat? Bowling balls?"

"He's an athlete," Rachel smiled. "That's 190 pounds of solid muscle."

"Solid is a good word for it," Li agreed, carrying the heavy man out of the room.

The older succubus held Jessica back as the others left. "I need to know that I can trust you," she said quietly.

"Can we trust each other?"

"We'll have to. I swear that I will do no harm to you if you will swear the same to me."

"Why?"

"Because women are stronger united than apart, and there's something suspicious about Lily."

She hadn't expected that answer, but she nodded. "I was noticing something fishy about her, too. I don't think she's telling us the truth."

"She stinks of lies," Rachel said, "among other things. The smell of the Pit is still rank upon her. I think there may be many reasons for that." She extended her hand. "Pact?"

Jessica shook her hand. "For now."

"Well," the succubus smiled, "nothing is ever permanent, is it? Now... let's keep an eye on that little bitch and see what she's really up to."

Lucifer left Mary unconscious in the back of the bus, limbs akimbo and her skirt hiked up. She had been so easily seduced at first, but she had fought like a wildcat once he'd carried her into the vehicle. He liked that; it meant that she had some fighting spirit that she could impart upon the child. He touched her lips once more, wiping away a little of the blood that stained the skin. She had withstood much. He smiled. The child would be strong.

Humming to himself, he left the bus and strolled away down the rocky path to the ruins of Ephesus, fading into nothingness as he went.

CHAPTER FOURTEEN

*B*elow and Between

The apartment was silent except for the raspy breaths coming from his meat suit. Ulug had not been in a panic like this for longer than he could count, which was not too surprising, considering his limitations with things like numbers. He huddled on the kitchen floor, his long legs drawn up to his chest, spider-like. Around him he had drawn a protective rune using a big black Sharpie he had found in Rick Buchanan's junk drawer. The main entry door had salt all across it, and he had salt strewn all through the entryway. He thought that maybe, just maybe, he would survive the night, or at least until Rachel came and told him what to do next.

He stayed that way, waiting and watching, through the long night and into the day beyond. His meat suit was uncomfortable, and it was starting to get mushy in spots. He was hungry, he was afraid, he was lonely, and he was going to have to find a new host soon. He had almost used up the body he was wearing.

He could no longer sense the tizalem sniffing around the building, watching for Buchanan and his family to return. Perhaps it was safe for him to leave the circle. He stood slowly, his knees cracking, and took one step beyond the protective drawing.

The door shifted under the pressure of a human hand, and a fit young man with a concerned expression pushed it aside. "Rick? You here?"

There was an accent to his speech that Ulug had not heard before, and it was disagreeable. He was certain it meant this newcomer was a threat. He crouched behind the kitchen island and waited like a spider for him to come closer.

"Rick?" the man called, looking around the disheveled living room. "Jesus, what happened here? Rick! It's Koz!"

He stepped further into the apartment and turned his back on the kitchen, looking toward the bedroom and the shattered furniture. He bent to prod at a scorch mark on the carpet, and that was the perfect opportunity for Ulug to move. He sprang forward, grabbed the man's head, and twisted it until he heard and felt the neck bones snap. He dropped the body to the ground and stepped back.

He couldn't wear this one, not with a broken neck. He'd have to find something else. He looked around briefly then decided to simply do what he'd been doing with dead bodies for weeks. He picked the dead man up, slung him over his shoulder, and carried him out to the subway line.

Detective Herman leaned against a support pillar near the trash barrel, his hands in his pockets as he watched the commuters and tourists come and go at the Christopher Street station. Brooker was upstairs on the street fetching them some coffee, and Herman was glad he was gone. The kid was a good enough cop, but he'd found after a few hours of this stakeout that they had absolutely nothing to talk about. Shop talk only lasted so long.

A pretty girl with her hair pulled back into a severe bun hustled past him, a duffel bag on her shoulder. She moved on the balls of her feet, graceful, almost like a deer with her large brown eyes and slender bones. He was certain she was a dancer. There were a lot of dancers in New York. She rushed to an open train door and waited for her chance to climb aboard, and she happened to glance his way. He offered her a smile and a tip of his battered fedora, his one detective affectation.

She frowned. "Creep."

She disappeared onto the train, which barreled away with its load of humanity. He shook his head and looked toward the stairs to the street level, irritably wondering where his coffee was.

Staking out the subway had been a logical thing to do. The bodies had been dumped here fairly regularly, almost exactly 5 days apart, and today was the sixth day since the last corpse had been found clogging up the tracks and smoking on the third rail. He still didn't know how the killer had managed to drag a body all the way through the concourse and down to the rail level, but he had plenty of mangled stiffs in the morgue that proved he'd found a way.

He turned and looked in the opposite direction, peering off down the incoming side of the track. A single figure was walking toward him, barely more than a silhouette in the dim light of the tunnel. She was coming from a place where there was no platform, walking between the rails and risking becoming the next pedestrian incident. He frowned and started to move toward her.

"Hey," he called. She did not react. "Hey! You can't walk there."

She was a slight girl, wearing a sack-like white dress that hung straight down from her shoulders to just below her knees. She was barefoot, which also caused him some concern, given the things that could be lurking on the ground.

"Hey, miss! Can you hear me?"

She looked up at him, and his heart nearly stopped. It was the girl from the asylum. He had stared at her blood-flecked face in the crime scene photographs for hours, and he had memorized her. He knew it was her, just as he knew that he was suddenly unable to hear the noise of the train or the people or the public address system crackling in the air. He slowly approached her, one hand moving toward the pistol he wore in a shoulder holster, as if a gun could do anything against a ghost.

She walked straight up to him, a beatific smile on her face, her eyes soft but sad. There was no sound but his own breathing and the fluttering throb of his own pulse. She put her hand on his wrist and stopped him from pulling his weapon with a simple, gentle but inexorable push downward. He gaped at her. Without a word, she stood on her tiptoes and leaned forward, kissing him on the forehead. It made a memory of his mother and his three-year-old self flash into his mind, and he felt his mouth fall open. He was dazed.

The girl pulled back and smiled at him again. "Your compassion has been noted, and you are blessed. Thank you for the concern you've had for me. I'm no longer in any pain, and I'm back with my Father, now."

"You," he breathed, "you're dead."

"No," she smiled. "Just resting."

Brooker's voice in his ear jolted back to the real world, and he nearly fell from the violence of his startled reaction. "Hey, I've been yelling at you. You all right?"

Herman could feel that he was pale, and when he faced his partner, he was briefly disoriented and confused. He shook his head to clear it. "Yeah," he lied. "Fine. Just daydreaming, I guess. You got the coffee?"

"Yeah, right here."

He gratefully accepted the cardboard cup with it plastic lid and took a hearty swig of the strong liquid inside.

Brooker was still looking at him curiously. "You sure you're all right, man?"

"Fine," he repeated. "You see anybody when you were up in the mezzanine?"

"About three hundred people, yeah, but nobody that looked like they were gonna dump a body."

"Great." He took another sip and sat down on a rust-spotted bench. "Then I guess we're back to waiting."

Brooker sat beside him, a skeptical look cast toward him, and sipped his own coffee, for once keeping his opinions to himself. Herman was grateful for the reprieve

What the hell just happened to me?

Below, Above and Between

Morning sunlight dappled the rumpled linens on the sofa bed, highlighting the hills and valleys of fabric on the lumpy mattress. Rick and Alexander were still locked in a deep, unnatural sleep, and Rachel still stood guard, keeping watch over their recuperation. Jessica, who had taken to pacing, crossed her arms over her chest and glanced at Lily, who was sleeping peacefully in an armchair as if she had never had a worry in her life.

Li watched his friend for a moment then walked to stand in her way, physically blocking her in the path she was wearing into the floor. She normally would have been irritated, but something about the look on his face made her smile. He had such clear and open eyes, she decided. That was what made his expression so endearing.

"You should get some rest," he told her. "You didn't sleep all night, and you have to take care of yourself."

She chuckled. "Thanks for the concern, but I'm fine."

"Nice words for somebody who had morning sickness to beat the band yesterday."

"Don't worry so much." She spontaneously hugged him. "I'm not fragile."

He hesitated then hugged her back, his hands on her waist as light as butterflies. "No," he said, his voice soft in her ear, "but your baby is." She froze, and he pulled away to look into her face. "If you're not going to take care of yourself, then I'll be forced to do it."

She pushed herself to smile at him. "And how are you going to force me to sleep? What if I'm not tired?"

He put an arm around her shoulders and started guiding her to the room he and Yu Kun had claimed the night before. "You'll never be a very good lawyer, Jess."

She turned to him, surprised. "Why would say that?"

"Because you're a terrible liar." He smiled at her. "You've got a complete set of luggage under your eyes this morning, and you've been yawning like crazy. You're tired, and I'm going to put you to bed."

She walked with him into the room, sitting on the bed as he closed the door behind them. "You're avoiding the question. How are you going to make me fall asleep if I don't want to? Some sort of stupid monk trick?"

Li chuckled and turned down the bed. They had never touched it last night. "That's an ancient Chinese secret."

"Bullshit."

He tugged and prodded her, and she did not resist, allowing him to guide her into a supine position with the covers pulled up to her chest. "That's a bad word," he told her, walking around to the other side of the bed. "Are you going to kiss your baby with that mouth?"

"Li," she said, her voice barely more than a whisper, "I don't know if I even want to keep this baby." Tears rose in her eyes, and she struggled not to cry. She hated it when she did something so stereotypically girly. A salt drop leaked out anyway, and she admitted, "I'm afraid."

He got into the bed beside her, and he held out his arm to her. After a moment, she snuggled up to him, her head pillowed on his chest. She rested her hand on his T-shirted sternum and let him rub her arm with a comforting hand. "I'm scared, too," he told her. "I think we'd be really dumb not to be scared right now. But you know what?"

"What?"

He turned her face so that she was looking at him. "We might be scared, but we're together."

She felt a flood of warmth and it cancelled out her ability to speak. Instead, she kissed him. Li returned the kiss gently, almost chastely, his arm around her back pulling her closer to him. When their lips parted, she ducked her head back down onto his chest again, afraid to look into his eyes, afraid she would see some disapproval or regret there. She couldn't bear it if she had just made a mistake.

To her relief, she felt him delicately kiss her hair, the touch feather-light but enough for her to notice. He hugged her again.

"Whatever you want to do," he told her, "I'll help you do it. No matter what."

She was still speechless, and now her fatigue was catching up to her, too. Jessica wrapped her arm around his waist and clung to him, feeling safe for the first time in days.

It was sometime after noon when Alexander finally stirred, lifting his head from where it had been laying in his mother's lap. She stopped stroking his hair and looked down at him in silent, cautious curiosity. He rubbed a hand over his eyes and sat up, looking around.

"How did I get out here?"

"We carried you and your father out here. There was an attack in the night, and you were injured."

He glanced down at his body, then up at her. "I don't have any wounds."

"It wasn't that kind of an attack, darling."

Alexander pushed himself up onto his hands and slid into a sitting position, crumpling the sheets around his waist. He took a moment to look around the house at the other refugees, noting his father sleeping beside him, nuzzled up against Rachel's other hip. "He was hurt, too?"

She looked down at her lover. "Yes."

"Is Lily...?"

"She's fine." She nodded toward the kitchen. "She's in there, with the Englishman."

He nodded and lay back down, still too weak to stand up or walk. His mother put a solicitous hand on his shoulder and pushed some of her own energy into him, infusing it through his skin and into his very being, just as she had done off and on all through the night. He took a contented breath and a modicum of tension seemed to leave him. He put his hand over hers in silent thanks.

Lily came into the room wearing a big, beautiful smile that Rachel trusted not at all. "You're awake!" She rushed to the bed and knelt beside it, touching Alexander's pale face. "How are you feeling?"

"I'm... I'm okay. Did you feed from me?"

She looked stung. "Of course not. You need your strength while we're running from the tizalem. I'd never do that. It would risk you, and I couldn't bear that."

Rachel snorted quietly, and her younger sister looked up at her, perturbed. She spoke in Lily's head. *You're such a liar.*

I'm not lying, sister.

You know as well as I do that when one of us feeds from someone, it leaves a sigil behind. Don't treat me like I'm stupid.

Lily looked surprised. *I...I don't remember doing that. Why would I do that?*

Alexander interrupted them churlishly. "Out loud, please. You're being rude."

"Nonsense," Rachel said with a click of her tongue. "We're being considerate of your father. He's still trying to sleep, after all."

The younger succubus retreated back into the arm chair, wrapping her arms around herself in a show of confused sorrow. The look Alexander was giving her was warm and compassionate, with more than a hint of affection. Sometimes Rachel regretted allowing his human blood to have so much influence over him. If only she had taken the opportunity to design his personality while he was in the womb, the way so many other succubus mothers did, then she wouldn't have to sit and worry that he was going to let his girlfriend lead him into perdition by the short hairs.

Lily was looking at Rick. "I don't think you could wake him right now if you tried."

Yu Kun came into the room and stood behind her. When he spoke, the younger succubus nearly fell out of her chair in surprise. "Perhaps we should call a healer for him."

"Which healer did you have in mind?"

The monk answered, "Raphael."

"Oh, no. Not another archangel."

"Why not?"

Rachel shook her head. "You don't understand, do you? I am a *demon*. That means that archangels scare the living shit out of me. It's like being next to someone who's trying to hold a nuclear fusion reaction steady between their hands. That's what being near their power is like. It's dangerous, and it's harmful, and there's just no way that you'll get out of it without being hurt." She shook her head again. "No. No archangels."

The monk looked amused. "That's probably psychosomatic, you know."

"It is not. It's a very real pain, I'll have you know."

"Maybe it only hurts because you expect it to."

"Maybe you should go away and meditate on the question," she snapped. "At least then you'd be quiet."

Yu Kun laughed, far more amused than annoyed by her pugnacious attitude. He let the matter drop out of respect for her wishes, at least for the moment.

Lily chimed in, "I agree. The angel that's here is hard enough to stomach. An archangel would be absolutely beyond the pale."

"The Pale," Yu Kun repeated. "A ditch in Ireland."

"You are very strange."

He laughed again, amused by Rachel once more. The succubus seemed to dislike being the source of his mirth, though, so he transformed the laugh into a smile. "I think that you only remember to be afraid of angels when you think about it," he said, "and I have proof that out of sight really is out of mind for you. Maybe you and the angels aren't that different after all."

"What are you on about now?"

He smiled at Lily. "Neither of you have noticed, have you?"

Alexander spoke up. "Noticed what?"

"Ariel has been gone for over an hour. He left the house to try and find your friend Ulug, and to check on the status of the tizalem."

He sat down on the arm of the couch. "So much for the pain of their presence, eh?"

Rick could hear the chatter of the people around him, and he could feel the weight of his own body like a prison. He felt small and distant, like a dust mote lying in the far back corner of the closet that was his mind, hidden behind old coats and broken vacuum cleaners. It seemed that the inside of his head was infinite, and that he could keep going back and back and back forever until all the outside noise stopped.

The thought was almost appealing. He was so tired.

Another voice in his head agreed. *Yes,* it seemed to say. *Retreat.*

He stopped in his backward glide down the rabbit hole, considering where that voice was coming from. In the front of his head, the part that controlled the walking and talking, there was another mind. There was an entirely other personality there, another spirit, and it was in control. Someone else was driving the bus.

Now wait a God-damned minute, he thought angrily. *Who the fuck are you?*

The other voice laughed at him and gave him a savage push. Suddenly the impression of walking backward in a big, empty tunnel turned into the feeling of drowning in clammy water, and he fought. The sounds outside were garbled now, cloaked by the interference of the spirit that was shoving him down, drowning him in the depths of his own soul. Rick flared with anger at the gall of the invader, stubbornness and independence and a dose of his well-cultivated hockey mental toughness conspiring to make him powerful. He pushed back, driving at the entity within him the way he drove toward the net. Suddenly he saw himself on the ice in a darkened arena. In his mind's eye, that parasitic being had become a puck, black and rock-hard, and he had his hockey stick in his hand. He could see the tape pattern and the curve of the blade, could feel the weight of it. He could feel the puck skitter and try to slow down against the ruts in the ice.

What are you doing, ape?

He passed the puck from his forehand to his backhand. There were defenseman ahead of him, big, burly demons with bat wings and clawed hands, curved horns growing out of their heads. There was no way they were going to be able to fit helmets on over those things. They weren't even in skates. He saw them slipping and clumsily trying to block his progress, but he could dangle past the best skaters in the business. He wasn't going to let these amateurs stop him now.

Stop! The puck was whining at him, afraid of the wrist shot to come. *I command you to stop!*

Command this, he thought, and in his mind, he flipped the puck up and out of play, twisting and spiraling through the air in slow motion until it disappeared into the darkness on the other side of the glass. Instead of a whistle shutting down the play, he heard the goal buzzer and saw the red light flashing over the net. He turned to celebrate with his teammates, and found that he was alone. Even the awkward defense demons had gone.

The cold, dry air rasped in his throat as he looked around.

"Hello?" he called out. "Is anybody here?"

The answer came in the form of his hockey nemesis, Chris Michaels, the so-called face of the league. The top-line forward for the Boston Rippers appeared in Rick's head, barreling at him at top speed. The open-ice check was brutal and complete, and it sent him flying. He hit the ice with a profound thud and skidded into the boards, where he lay still and unconscious.

Asb'el dropped the disguise and showed himself for who he was, standing over Rick's prone thought-form self in satisfaction. He was amused by the single-mindedness of the world the partial-blood creature had created in his mind. Apparently, hockey was the core of his existence. Still, it had worked to his favor, and he had manipulated things to his satisfaction. The rightful owner of the physical body was down for the count, and now there was nothing to stop the takeover.

Everything was going according to plan.

CHAPTER FIFTEEN

*B*elow and Between

Ulug found that taking a body into the subway in broad daylight in one of the tonier sections of Manhattan was a much different proposition than dumping one at night by Christopher Street. With so many mortals milling about, there was no way that he could offload the refuse in peace. Instead, he carried the corpse down into the basement of the apartment building, past the custodial closets and the elevator machine room, following his nose. He could smell the sewer running underneath the building, filled with the usual excreta of the city, the aroma wafting up through the drains and through the cracks in the concrete slab. When he was confident that he was directly above the pipes, he dumped the body to the ground.

"Wait here," he told it, then laughed at his own joke. He thought he was very funny for an Utukku.

He went back to the custodial closet and tried the door. It was, of course, locked tight. He gripped the knob and used every ounce that he could pour through his borrowed meat suit's sinews. With a satisfying cracking sound, the door jamb splintered, and from there it was a simple thing to disassemble the lock and make his way inside.

There were cleaning supplies, garbage bags, and assorted tools of the clean-up trade. More to his liking was the monkey wrench that he found in the back corner, the heavy metal handle painted bright red. He hefted it in his hand, decided that it would do the job, and then went back out to the basement.

As he turned around, he did not look up. If he had, he would have seen the camera pointed down from the ceiling, aiming into the room from above the door. He walked through the machine's field of vision and left it behind, the little red light above the lens flashing like a lonely Christmas light.

He returned to the man's body and shoved it slightly aside. It was time to get to work. With a massive crash, he brought the wrench down like a sledgehammer, pounding his way through the floor and into the pipes below.

Between

The subway stake-out, as Brooker delighted in repeating, had been a waste of time. There had been no bodies found, which of course was a good thing. There had also been no sightings of anyone matching the description provided by their one and only witness.

Herman should have been more disappointed than he was. He was an old pro at these things, and he'd been a detective for longer than Brooker had been a legal adult. He knew that stakeouts rarely if ever turned something up on the first day. Still, he had been relieved when the second shift had arrived, freeing him and his partner to return to the station house to work on their endless paperwork and to try to give their other cases a little love.

He found his mind turning back time and again to the young woman he had seen, the one who had died so bloodily in the asylum. Nothing about the encounter made sense to him, and no matter how many times he went over it in his head, he could get no closer to understanding what it all meant. Maybe he just needed to take a vacation and forget about murder for a while.

He almost laughed at the thought. His last vacation had been years ago, back when he'd still had a life. A lot had changed since then, himself included. He was older now, and grayer, and he knew that in his heart he was a lot angrier. Cynicism was the burden of disappointed old age, and he carried it like a compulsion.

She had said that he was blessed. He could certainly use a few blessings right about now.

He sat heavily at his desk and started flipping through his mail, barely taking interest in the vast majority of it. One envelope caught his attention, though. It was postmarked from the Archdiocese of New York, the return address and crown-and-shield seal on the envelope heavily gilded and embossed. Curious, he gave a quick slash with his letter opener and pulled out the piece of paper inside.

The single page was typewritten on an old-fashioned typewriter. Its message was simple and to the point:

"Detective Herman,

I have learned of your involvement with the recent mysterious and horrible murders that occurred at the Saint Martha Medical Center mental health facility. I have information that could be of use to you.

Please call for me at the rectory of St. Benedict's Church on 61st Street in the Woodside area of Queens.

Yours,
Rev. Thomas Fitzpatrick, DD, SJ."

Herman had been raised Lutheran, so he was unfamiliar with the hierarchy of the Catholic Church. He Googled the acronym "S.J." and found that it stood for Society of Jesus, the order better known as the Jesuits. He was familiar with Jesuits from having seen *The Exorcist*, where the title character had been a Jesuit priest.

His frown attracted the attention of his partner. Brooker asked him, "What do you have there?"

Herman handed the letter over. "What do you make of this?"

"Maybe he heard something in a confession."

He scratched his head. "I thought priests were forbidden to discuss that sort of thing."

"Well, he can't give you specifics, but he can tell you to watch out using generalities." He shook his head. "Jesuits, though. They're a pretty intense bunch. God's Marines, they call themselves, or The Company. They think they're like a military unit in God's army."

The older detective chuckled. "You sound like an ex-altar boy."

"Guilty as charged."

"You got any stories about any handsy priests you'd like to tell me?"

Brooker cast him a scathing look. "Fuck you, Herman."

"You'd never be so lucky."

He took the page back from his partner, noticing as he did that there was a very faint line drawing on the back. There was a squiggly line, irregular and bumpy as if it had been drawn by someone with a few too many Red Bulls in their system. Off to the right of the line was a large circle with an "x" drawn inside it. It looked for like a treasure map and begged the question of what treasure a Catholic priest would be interested in finding.

"Now what are you glaring at?" the younger detective asked.

Herman showed him the drawing. "Does this look like a map to you?"

"It looks like scribbling." He shook his head. "It's probably nothing, but I guess it could be a map. I don't know you'd ever be able to figure out where it's supposed to be, though. Is it a street map? A train track? A path through Central Park? I don't know."

"I guess we'd better get to Queens."

Ulug finally succeeded in stuffing the body into the sewer line, creating the mother of all back-ups in the building's plumbing system. He was coated in filth, which would make it difficult for him to disappear back into the world without being noticed. It would, however, keep people away from him, which he liked.

A tap on his mind alerted him to the telepathic presence of another demon. *Ulug,* Rachel's voice called, *are you well?*

He nodded, even though she could not see him. *Yes. Not hurt. Where are you?*

In a house on Long Island, in lockdown. Are you at the flat?

No. I go there, though.

Good. She told him, *Sit tight. There's an angel named Ariel who's looking to bring you here. Don't hide when you see him, and don't run away.*

He kill me?

No, she answered, *not unless you give him a reason.*

A man came. I killed him.

Her furrowed brow was palpable over their connection. *A man came where?*

To the room I was in. Rick's place. I killed him. Will angel be mad?

Probably, but there's nothing we can do about it now. What did you do with the body?

He glanced down into the plugged-up sewer pipe, which was leaking brackish, reeking water. *I flushed him.*

She sighed. *Well, I guess it's better than the subway.*

Above, Below and Between

Jessica and Li emerged from the bedroom a few hours into the afternoon. The young monk sought out his master immediately, and she went to the couch, looking down at Rick's sleeping face.

"Have you noticed," she said to Rachel, "that when men sleep, they look really innocent? Like they couldn't hurt a fly."

The succubus replied, "That's so we don't choke them to death before they wake up. It's the same reason babies are always cute. It's to keep women from killing them."

Jessica chuckled. "You do have a unique viewpoint."

"I certainly do."

She looked around and noticed Lily dozing near one of the windows, sitting in an armchair and curled up in a sunbeam like a cat. In the kitchen, she could hear Yu Kun and Li talking quietly. Her head count was coming up a few refugees short.

"Where are Ariel and Alexander?"

Rachel shifted slightly, her long vigil starting to bore her. She ran her fingers over Rick's close-cropped hair to occupy herself. "Ariel has gone looking for Ulug, and Alexander is in the bathroom taking a shower."

"Who is Ulug?"

"He's a servant, Alexander's bodyguard."

"Hmm. Another demon?"

Rachel nodded. "He's more of a possessing spirit than a physical presence, though."

Jessica's raised an eyebrow. "So he's running around wearing some poor schmuck like a bad suit?"

"That's a very apt way to describe it."

She got an unpleasant tickle in her stomach. "I, uh, I hate to ask this, but what happens to the owner of the body?"

The demon shrugged. "Oh, he's very dead. Ulug casts out the soul when he takes the body, so it goes to wherever it was going to go – Above, Below, or Sideways."

She sat in a chair near the sofa. "Okay, so Above is Heaven, and Below is Hell. What's Sideways?"

"Limbo."

"Not purgatory?"

"No, not at all. Purgatory doesn't actually exist. What people call purgatory is really just a nice neighborhood of the Abyss."

Jessica shook her head. "Just when I thought things couldn't get any trippier..."

Rick stirred, and both women looked down at him, waiting. He did not disappoint, opening his eyes and looking up into Rachel's face with dazed partial recognition. She smiled to him.

"Good morning, handsome. How do you feel?"

He looked around the room, mostly by moving his eyes. Physical motion was something he wanted to put off. "Weird. I had the dumbest dreams..." He hesitated. He had the feeling that he was supposed to be relaying some vital piece of information, but he just couldn't remember what it was.

Jessica said, "No big surprise. If these last few days haven't been nightmare fuel, I don't know what would be."

Rachel was looking at him, and he found that he suddenly didn't want her to look into his eyes. The thought made him nervous. He looked away from her hurriedly when she established eye contact.

He'd never looked away from her before, and it added to her suspicions. "What's the matter?" she asked, keeping her voice light.

Rick searched for an answer without success. Finally, he lamely answered, "Headache."

"Again, I'm not surprised." Jessica stood up. "I'm going to see if there's anything to eat in this place. We'd probably all feel a lot better with food in our stomachs."

Alexander emerged from the bathroom with damp hair, feeling much more like himself. He smiled when he saw that his father was awake.

"Hey!" he greeted. "How are you feeling?"

"Like somebody hip checked me from Philly to Denver," he replied. He wondered why that sounded vaguely true.

"Do you know what attacked you?"

The Canadian blinked stupidly. Perhaps that was the information he had misplaced. He finally said, "I don't remember."

Part of his brain felt dull, fuzzy, almost like his lip had felt the last time he'd had novocaine. He knew it was there, could feel the weight of it in his head, but everything about it was completely inaccessible to him. He prodded and tried to push through to the memories that were locked inside, but he was unable. Frustrated, he slapped his hand against the bed.

Jessica returned with a plate stacked with peanut butter and jelly sandwiches. "Okay, before you guys make any cracks, I know I'm not the best cook in the world. The selections were limited, and if you think you can do better, the kitchen's right over there." She distributed the food to the three of them, keeping a sandwich for herself. "It'll do for now."

Li followed her into the room with a stack of plastic tumblers and a jug of milk. "Anybody?"

Alexander and Rachel declined the offer, so he gave glasses of milk only to Jessica and Rick. He returned the unused glasses and the jug to the kitchen.

"He's very useful," the succubus said, offering what she considered a compliment. She could think of no higher praise for a human man.

"He's a bit more than that, but, yeah. He's a nice guy."

Rick sat up with some difficulty, leaning a bit on Rachel, and they ate in silence for a while. Alexander finally asked, "What's taking Ariel so long?"

"Ulug is probably hiding from him, even though I told him not to," his mother said. "Honestly, I don't know what possessed me to bring an Utukku to the surface in the first place. They're so erratic."

Curiosity was so hard to resist. Jessica asked, "Utukku? What's that?"

"A type of demon," she answered. "A drone. They're basically worker bees at the bottom rung of life in the hive."

"So what are you, the queen bee?"

Lily spoke then. None of them had realized she had been awake and listening. "She wishes. The First Fallen has consorts, but there is no queen in Hell."

It seemed to Jessica that she heard a silent "yet" at the end of Lily's words, and she and Rachel shared a knowing look. Clearly, the older succubus had heard it, too. Rick and Alexander seemed oblivious. Somehow, she wasn't surprised by that.

"I have to say," Lily sighed, "being locked up in here is very, very boring. I don't suppose anyone would like to have sex to pass the time?"

"I don't think now is the time for that," Yu Kun said, coming into the room.

"I would have expected that from *you*," she pouted. "You Buddhists think you're so above that sort of nasty physical stuff, don't you? You keep trying to meditate away your libidos."

The monk took no offense. If anything, he looked amused. "I don't believe you are as familiar with my faith as you think you are."

"Then prove me wrong."

His smile broadened. "And how might do I that?"

"By having sex with me."

Li appeared behind his master, looking uncomfortable. The Englishman laughed. "That's ridiculous, Lily. That's simply not going to happen."

"Why not?"

"Lily," Rachel said firmly, "drop it and shut up. Nobody wants to hear your sniveling."

"But I'm *hungry*."

"So am I. Live with it." She gave up on the unappetizing sandwich and put it aside.

The younger demon tossed her head and rose from her chair. "Alexander, what about you?"

"He is not interested," his mother replied.

"Well, then, Rachel, dear... how about it?"

She leaped to her feet and charged the other demon, striking her ferociously with clawed fingers, driving her to the ground. Lily gasped and covered her head with her arms, but Rachel simply moved her attack down her body, kicking her in the ribs. The others, including a very unsteady hockey player, rushed to stop the attack.

Jessica managed to get an arm around Rachel's neck while the others grappled with her in any way they could, and it took all of them together to overpower the succubus and pull her away from her victim.

Alexander went to Lily as Rachel spouted curses and invectives in the language of the Pit. He was joined by Yu Kun, who gave her a quick once-over like a battlefield medic. "She has broken ribs and some nasty cuts on her face, but she'll be fine," he told the room.

"You could have killed the child," Alexander hissed at his mother. "What were you thinking?"

"You don't want to know what I'm thinking," she spat. "How dare you question me! I order you to end any relationship you have with that creature, and with her child. *Do you understand?*"

If he had been a full-blooded incubus, receiving a direct order from his mother, he would have had no choice but to obey. Unfortunately for Rachel, he was his father's son, as well. He glared at her. "No."

Her eyes pinched and for an instant, a red flame seemed to burn in them. *"What did you say?"*

Rick put a hand on his lover's shoulder. "He's part human," he said softly. "He has free will."

She was shaking with rage. "I hope you know what you're doing." She looked from her son to Lily, who was sobbing in pain on the floor. "Keep her away from me."

"*You* stay away," he countered. He accepted a towel from Li and started attending to his lover's wounds. Rachel stormed away into the nearest bedroom and slammed the door.

Jessica looked at Rick. "What was that all about?"

He shrugged, mystified. "I have no idea."

He followed her into the bedroom, closing the door behind himself. She was pacing like a caged tiger, her wings fully extended and her face contorted with rage. He had rarely seen her look more demonic than he saw her now. For a heartbeat, he was afraid, but he overcame his human reaction and went to her, grabbing her by the biceps and stopping her in her manic walking.

"Rach," he said, "what's the matter? What was that all about?"

"She nearly killed our son," she bit, "the very day we got him back. How many times will we have to lose him?"

"I – we – I'm sure it was an accident."

She shook off his hands. "No succubus ever feeds by accident." She jabbed a finger through the air, pointing toward the closed door. "She is hiding something, I know it. It's just a matter of time before she tries to hurt Alexander again, or you."

Pieces fell into place for him. "You think she attacked me, don't you?"

"Of course I do."

"If she came after me, I think I would remember."

"I love you, Richard, I do, but if you think that a half-demon could stand up to a full succubus' attack, then you're more foolish than I ever thought you were."

He could see that she was gaining control over her anger, pulling it back in just like she pulled in her wings and folded them away out of sight. He took her hands and kissed them.

"I love you, too, baby. And we'll keep her away from Alexander. I don't want to lose him, either, and if she's a threat, then we'll just do something about it."

"Like what?" She looked into his eyes. "If it came down to it, could you kill her?"

He hesitated, just like she knew he would. He looked away. "I..." He took a deep breath and raised his head, meeting her eyes again. "If that's what it takes to protect our son, or you, then yes. I could pull her apart with my bare hands."

Rachel searched his face for a moment then embraced him. He held her close, his cheek against her silken hair. She was trembling, and he did what he could to soothe her. For her part, she stroked his hair, staring over his shoulder in fear and upset.

I cannot have seen what I thought I saw, she thought. *It's not possible...a demon can't be possessed by another demon...*

Rick was talking, bringing her out of her confusion. "I'm sorry Alexander talked back to you. It's because of his human blood, that's all. I guess he had to get something bad from me."

She pulled back and kissed him tenderly. "There is nothing bad about you. Nothing at all. And the human part of him gives him free will, as you said. That's something I can't enjoy. I'm glad he has it." She chuckled. "I just wish he could have found a different way to display it."

He laughed and took her hand. "Think you're ready to go back out there?"

"I'm ready."

"No killing anybody else, right?"

She smirked. "I'll consider it."

"Close enough."

Together, they rejoined the rest of the refugees in their living room bivouac.

⚜

Ulug walked as quickly as he could through the streets. The stench that surrounded him cleared the way, and he found his progress more or less unimpeded by the humans who the sidewalks. With no real obstacles, he made his way in record time to the warehouse apartment that had been Alexander's lair.

The place was still soaked in blood and filled with shattered objects. He personally preferred the new look, because it reminded him more of his home. Between was all well and good, but it was a little too clean for his taste. Sometimes he longed for an old-fashioned blood bath. He'd been able to indulge once or twice since he'd come to the surface, but not nearly enough for his satisfaction. Still, it was lucky for him that New York was hardly short on homicides, and luckier for him that his own killings had just worked right into the mix.

He went into the bedroom area of the apartment and sat on the bed, the only furniture that was still intact enough to support the weight of his oversized meat suit. There was a strange stillness in the air, a sense of waiting that was beginning to make him nervous. Something was not right.

Then he felt it: approaching power, rolling like storm clouds on the horizon, coming his way. The Utukku shrank into the corner, upending the mattress and standing it on end between himself and whatever was about to appear. Rachel had told him not to hide from the angel, but he was too afraid to obey. His kind had never been known for their bravery.

The lair filled with presence, and a palpable sense of evil crept over and through everything. As bad as the approach of the archangel had been, this was immeasurably worse. With an archangel, he could have at least begged for mercy. With this being, he knew that mercy would never be an option.

Lucifer appeared in the center of the lair, calmly examining the debris left by his assassins' work. He saw the miserable mattress fort and detected the cringing Utukku hiding behind it. He was uninterested in peons. With a wave of his hand, he reduced the bed, the mattress and the human body behind it to ashes. The pathetic demon, shrieking, was returned to the Abyss, where Lucifer's loyal servant Nergal waited to deal with him. There would be no more betrayals by this lowly creature.

He felt the angel before he appeared, and he turned to face him with a smile upon his face. This little God-servant was no match for Lucifer's power, but he was a worthier playmate than the drone had been. He looked forward to becoming reacquainted with his little brother.

The angel surged into being near the door, his wings spread wide, his sword in his hand. Lucifer chuckled. "Ariel, my brother," he greeted.

"How nice to see you again. It's been, what? An eternity? You look well."

The angel scowled. "You should not be here. You should still be chained in the Pit!" He raised his sword and pointed it at the devil. "You will be sent back."

"Really, now. Sent back? By you?" He sighed. The reunion was not as enjoyable as he had hoped. "I think not."

With a thought, one focused moment of ill-will, he engulfed the holy being with infernal flame. Ariel howled and thrashed in pain, his anguished cries shattering windows in every building on the street. He rushed at Lucifer, intending to grapple him into a burning embrace, to share the pain with his tormentor, but the Adversary simply vanished, teleporting away and leaving him to burn.

The fires were too hot to last for long. Ariel took one last tortured breath and commended his soul back to his Father, then dissolved, leaving only ashes and a pile of singed feathers.

CHAPTER SIXTEEN

*A*bove, Below and Between

Michael burst into the refugees' house, his flaming sword in his hand. His expression was grim, and he wasted no time with the affectation of mortal speech.

The Beast is loosed upon the land, he said in every mind, his tension making him revert to older speech patterns. *There is no protection for you here. I must take you to a safer place.*

He did not wait for anyone to agree. With a surge of power, he took them all into the immaterial plane that was the angels' highway. The next breath they drew was in a cavernous room, cool and walled with stone. Marble statues of saints stood like sentries along the perimeter of the room, watchful and waiting, the instruments of their martyrdom in their stony hands. Medieval-looking torch sconces dotted the walls at regular intervals, their light dim in the darkness of the room. It was a grim place.

Jessica doubled over in pain, clutching her abdomen. She fell to her knees beside a startled Rick and started vomiting. The hockey player crouched beside her, trying ineffectually to help somehow. He looked at the angel.

"Help her!"

Michael looked sorrowful. "I cannot."

Rachel made a disgusted sound and came to the stricken woman's side, supporting her physically so she wouldn't collapse into the mess. "Look around for a blanket or something," she told Rick. "She's going to be feverish very soon."

"How do you know?"

"Because I know. Now do it."

He scrambled to obey, and the others fanned out, too, searching their new surroundings. There were four heavy wooden doors along one wall, and all but one were locked. Within the open room, Li found tables, chairs, and a pile of tablecloths all stacked together as if a catering company was waiting to set up for a party. He grabbed the stack of linens and returned to the open room.

"There are tables in here," he called to Rick. "Maybe she can lie on one of those? I don't see anything else."

The hockey player went into the room Li had just exited and came out with a round folding table, rolling it on its edge. Yu Kun helped him set it up.

Michael had vanished during the commotion. Alexander, whose feet were tingling uncomfortably, looked around him in dismay. "Where's Lily?"

"I don't know, and I don't care," his mother replied, gathering an unconscious Jessica up in her arms. "Put some of those linens on that table, and use more as sheets. We're going to be going through a few."

The men obeyed her directions, and she came to the table with her motionless burden. Li asked in a tight voice, "What's wrong with her?"

Rachel's feet were blistering. Gritting her teeth through the pain, she said, "She's having a miscarriage. The power of this place was too much for the baby."

"Where are we?"

Rick and Yu Kun spread the tablecloths three-deep on the table, and the succubus put Jessica down as gently as she could. Li tucked a rolled-up cloth under her head as a pillow. Rachel stripped her from the waist down and covered her with three more tablecloths. She was already beginning to bleed.

"Watch her," she said. "I'll find a doctor."

Li stopped her and repeated his question. "Where are we?"

"Jerusalem. The Monastery of St. Francis." She shook her head. "I have to go. I can't stay here anymore."

She vanished from sight, leaving behind footprint-shaped scorch marks.

Below and Between

Lucifer entered the little house on Long Island, stepping through the wards set by Ariel as if they were merely curtains. He found the succubus, Lily, waiting for him on her knees, her head bowed in respect. He stroked her hair.

"Have you been a good girl, my dear?"

"Yes, master. I did everything you asked."

"Excellent. And when you were in the whelps' minds, what did you learn?"

She thought back to everything she had pulled out of Alexander's and Rick's heads. "The woman Jessica is pregnant with Yeter'el's child," she reported. "And Rachel knows where to find Pinem'e. She also says that she opposes you, my lord."

This much was already known to him. "Go on."

"They believe Alexander to be the one to challenge you for your throne."

"Amusing, but unlikely." He smiled and stroked her hair again as if he was petting a cat. "Go on. Who else is helping them?"

She replied, "The monks from the Buddhist monastery next door."

"Truly?" He was interested in this news. "It is unlike Buddhists to be involved in our little squabbles. They're usually so disinterested. Why are these involved?"

"The younger one is in love with Jessica," she said, "and the leader of the monks, he calls himself Yu Kun, is actually an Englishman. He has the wings on his wrist."

He chuckled. "Oh, I see. So their pathetic little team of crusaders is branching out, is it?" He stroked her hair. "Well, no matter. We have a team of our own. What else?"

"Three of the archangels have appeared to Rick Buchanan and the succubus Rachel."

"Which three?"

"Michael, Gabriel and Raphael."

He nodded. "Uriel still remains uninvolved, then."

"Yes, Master."

"What else?"

"There is nothing else."

"No?"

"No."

He gripped her hair and pulled her head back so that she was facing him. "And what about the child you carry? Do you still believe it to be the true Pretender?"

"No, my lord." She whimpered. "Please don't hurt me."

Lucifer considered her plea. "I won't hurt you," he told her, "if you can do one more thing for me."

Her eyes were tearing, both from the pain of her wrenched neck and from pure fear. "Anything, my lord!"

"Go back to the Abyss and find Naamah and the other succubus queens. Tell them everything you've done for me, and you will be rewarded."

"Thank you, Master!"

He bent and kissed her on the mouth, passionate and obscene. He released his grip on her skull and pulled away. "Now go."

Lily wasted no time jumping back into the incorporeal between-space, both to obey and to escape. Lucifer chuckled to himself.

"Still lying to everyone you meet, are you, brother?"

The voice came from behind him. He had expected this. His chuckle died, but he kept the smile on his face. Turning slowly, casually, he faced the new arrival.

"Hello, Michael." He gestured toward the sword that blazed in his brother's hand. "Still playing with toys, I see."

"I could say the same to you."

"She has served her purpose. Now my consorts need a little fun. There's nothing wrong with sending my mates a plaything now and then, is there?"

Michael took a step forward. "You need to stop what you are doing and return to your realm. It is not yet time for the final confrontation."

Lucifer sat down on the couch, crossing his legs and stretching out his arms. "I wasn't aware that it was you who kept the timetables."

"You know who keeps the time. I still serve Him."

"And in my own way, so do I."

"You serve nobody but yourself."

"Poor Michael. All these years and you haven't been able to come up with any new lines, hmm?" His smile died. "Put that sword away. We both know that if we start fighting now, this precious world Between will be destroyed. None of us wants that, least of all Him."

The archangel hated to admit when his older brother was right, but this was one of those times. He extinguished and sheathed his blade. "Go back," he ordered again. "This is not the time."

"I agree. I don't want the confrontation to happen yet. You see, I have more to lose than you if the world is destroyed. I gain more worshippers all the time, while you and your master are becoming quaint curiosities."

He was insulted. "There are millions of faithful in this world."

"Yes, millions. But the human population is over six billion. You do the math. All those other souls have to belong to someone." He gestured to himself. "It's really very easy. I don't have to attack heaven. I just have to wait for the throne to fade away because nobody's feeding Him with worship anymore. You will all be so much dust, and I will still be here."

Michael turned his back. "You never change."

"No, and neither do you. That's why this war will never end. You and I were both created on the same potter's wheel, and that wheel just keeps spinning and spinning..."

"And you just keep talking and talking. You love your own voice. You always have." He walked away a few feet then turned again. "I know what you did in Ephesus. You will not succeed."

Lucifer gave an oily chuckle. "I already have. My child is growing inside your child. Rich, isn't it?" He saw the surprise on Michael's face. "Oh, yes. I know. Even archangels sin, don't they? Only now you have the option of being forgiven. I guess our Father has mellowed in his old age." He tilted his head, studying his brother. "Tell me... was her mother a good lay? I might have to go and find out for myself."

Another sword, glowing with crackling blue energy, came crashing down at him, and he dodged with barely a hair's breadth to save him. Another archangel stood behind the couch, his fiery eyes blazing. Lucifer was much less pleased to see this brother.

"Uriel," he greeted. "Long time no see."

Michael stepped forward, a dagger materializing in his hand. He sank it up to the hilt in Lucifer's back. His brother shouted in surprise and pain then vanished back to the Pit. He met Uriel's gaze and said, "Thank you, brother. It's time to seal the doors."

"You let him talk too long," he chided.

"I know." He began to fade into incorporeal mist. "I always did."

Jessica awoke in horrible pain. She curled on her side, her hands over her cramping middle, trying not to let anyone see her reaction. She prided herself on her pain tolerance; after all, she couldn't have gotten as far as she had in karate without being pretty tough. She had never felt pain like this, though, a shredding sort of agony that seemed to cut her to the bone. It was all she could do to stay silent and not cry. Li had wanted to hold her hand, but she'd sent him away. His kindness was appreciated, but she wanted to be alone with this.

The two monks sat silently across the room, their backs against the cool stone wall between two statues. Alexander sat alone not too far away, fretting over his mother and his missing girlfriend. Only Rick was in motion, pacing from one end of the vault to the other, his steps echoing. The sound of his own movements was maddening, and he wanted to bolt the way Rachel had. Something within him was burning, and he would not have been surprised to see a hole being eaten away in his middle from the inside out. He looked at Yu Kun, then at Li, and anger flashed like a heat wave up his back and to his scalp, setting all his hair on end. He hated them both.

Yu Kun was watching him, his cool eyes judgmental and appraising. Rick seethed under the weight of the elder monk's stare. *What kind of Buddhist joined up with a Christian angel, anyway? He's a fraud, a charlatan, a liar. And he's standing in judgment of me?* The spiteful thought rattled in his brain. *Who the hell does he think he is?*

Another thought came to him, this time in a voice he'd never heard before. *Get rid of him.*

He looked at the monk and saw the wings emblazoned on his wrist. They seemed to glow in his vision, icy blue and electric. He wanted to cut them off. He wanted to stand over Yu Kun and watch him bleed then do the same to Li.

The voice returned. *And Jessica? What will you do to her?*

His response to himself surprised him. *Nothing. She's useless.*

And Alexander?

He looked at his son. *He's weak. I can destroy him.*

Yes, the voice whispered. *So why don't you?*

He was startled out of his distracted introspection by the arrival of a pair of nuns in the traditional habit of the Poor Clares, wearing their white wimples and raven-black robes with heavy crucifixes around their necks. They stepped out of thin air, carrying basins and medical supplies, and they went to Jessica's side. The other voice inside Rick's head receded, and he had to take a moment to steady himself, feeling disoriented and dizzy as if he had just awoken from a long and dreamless sleep. He went to the sisters.

"Can I help with anything?"

The older of the two peered at him through John Lennon eyeglasses. "No, thank you, child," she said, her voice heavily accented with some Eastern European dialect.

A wave of power washed over him, and he nearly staggered. An angel stood in the center of the room, his wings folded, his brown skin gleaming in the light from the sconces on the walls. Rick remembered him from Alexander's resurrection. It was Raphael.

"Step aside," he requested, his voice soft. "Let me work."

Rick stepped aside, knowing that if he did not, he would have been swept out of the way by the angel's power. He felt strange and distant as a part of his mind retreated as far away from the newcomer as it could go, hiding deep within him. He slowly walked to where Alexander was seated and dropped down beside him, sitting with his back against the wall and his legs bent before him, echoing the others' positions. His son glanced at him.

"Do you think she's all right?"

It took him a moment to process the words and understand the question. When it sank in, he asked, "Who, Jessica, your mother or Lily?"

"All of them."

"Lily and Rachel are survivors," he said, shrugging. "I'm sure they'll be okay. And as for Jessica – she's in good hands."

The archangel was standing beside Jessica now, his hands on her abdomen. The young woman was bravely trying to hide the tears in her eyes, but when the angel pressed down, she whimpered. Rick felt sorry for her. The nuns stood back and prayed while Raphael worked, and at a signal, one of them reached up under the sheet and took something away. She put it in the basin and vanished through one of the three mystery doors, opening it with a key that hung from her waist. The other nun set about finding Jessica's clothing while the angel performed some sort of magic to clean away the mess.

Alexander spoke quietly. "He's the one, isn't he?"

Rick shook his head to clear it. "Who?"

"The angel. He's the one who brought me back to life, isn't he?"

He heard a scratching sound, small and irregular, like a rodent in the walls, except that the scratching was on the inside of his skull. His head ached with it. He forced himself to pay attention to the outside world and nodded. "Yes."

His son rose to his feet in a surprisingly fluid motion and walked bravely to where the archangel stood. Raphael looked at him with a mixture of patience and curiosity, spreading his wings to form a screen behind which a miraculously recovered Jessica could dress away from masculine eyes.

Alexander hesitated when he was ten feet away, almost overwhelmed by the power that was emanating from the angel. He knelt.

Raphael folded his wings again while the nun took Jessica and the soiled tablecloths through the now-unlocked door. "Do not kneel to me, child," the archangel said gently. "I am not to be worshipped."

"I'm not worshipping," he said. "I'm... I'm trying to express my gratitude. You restored me after the tizalem attack. Thank you."

The angel considered him for a moment then extended his hand. "Rise, Alexander. That grace was from God and God alone. I was only the channel."

The young incubus took the angel's hand and stood. Their eyes met, and they stood that way for a long moment, hand in hand, gazes locked. Finally Raphael nodded and smiled, and Alexander stepped away. He looked as if there was a great deal he wanted to say, but instead he only repeated, "Thank you."

The scratching sound was back. This time, it was in the wall right behind Rick's head, almost as if a rat was trying to eat its way through the stone and into the back of his neck. He considered pounding on the wall to get it to leave, and it occurred to him that rats shouldn't have been able to claw and scramble through stone walls.

He shuddered in a sudden chill and moved to another section of the room.

Raphael turned to them. "Jessica will be brought back to you in time. My brother will be here shortly to explain what must happen next."

He vanished in a flash of rosy light, leaving behind the faint scent of incense. Rick gagged on the smell. The scratching was in the floor now, circling him. He looked at the others, expecting some reaction, but none of them acted as if they even heard it. He didn't understand how they could overlook something so loud.

As suddenly as it had started, the scratching stopped. He felt the need to move, an urge for physical activity overtaking him. Without a word to any of his fellows, he darted to the door the nuns and Jessica had gone through.

Alexander cried out after him, "Wait! Where are you going?"

There was a short staircase on the other side of the door, and he took it two steps at a time, heading up toward the light and freedom.

At the top of the stairs was an open door, made of heavy oak with cast iron hinges. He burst through and into the vestibule on the other side. The heady scent of incense clogged his throat, and he could feel something crawling up the insides of his legs, as if insects had burrowed through his skin and muscle and into the bones beneath. He ran faster.

A trio of monks appeared before him, but he bowled them over and kept running, his foot falls loud in the prayerful hush. He didn't know where he was going, but the buzzing in his head seemed to have a map, and he followed where it led. He found two more long hallways and a gate, and then he was free, out in the sunlight and amid the bustle of another tourist throng.

He dodged around a middle-aged woman who was trying to take a photograph of the monastery gate, then shoved his way through the crowd and kept running. Angry shouts followed him, but he paid no attention, barreling through the Christmas season crowd. He heard wing beats, leathery and wild, falling into place on either side of him, and he ran faster, exhilarated. He had never run so fast, been so strong, or felt so free. He careened through street after street, skidding around corners and avoiding catastrophe by a hair when he darted out in front of a taxi. The driver laid on the horn, but the sound faded as he crossed the road and ran into another alleyway.

Invisible hands grasped him by the arms and lifted him, and he felt himself dissolving into the traveling space between realities, carried away and down by his unseen companions.

Is this him? An unfamiliar voice was speaking in his mind, but not to him.

Yes, another voice, this time from inside him, replied. It was the same voice he had been talking to before, the one that seemed to be riding him like a rented donkey. He felt distantly annoyed and insulted, but found that he had no strength to complain. Rick was no longer in control. *We need to take him back to the Pit and bring him to Yeter'el. Then he can end this and we can begin our return.*

He had no idea what they were talking about, and he struggled for a moment, trying to own himself once more. *Silence him,* a third voice ordered, and then he heard nothing.

Chapter Seventeen

*B*etween

Herman and Brooker left their car at the curb and walked up the sidewalk leading to the rectory door. The rectory was a little unassuming house attached to the church by a breezeway lined with dormant rose bushes. A simple pine bough Christmas wreath hung on the door, and lights were hung along the roof line. In the front window, Herman could see a ceramic nativity set that looked like it had been painted by a six-year-old, all splotches and colors running outside the lines. He stepped on the welcome mat with its printed angels and knocked on the door.

He expected a housekeeper, but the door was opened by a burly, open-faced man who looked more like a farmer than a priest. He flashed his badge. "Detective Lloyd Herman, NYPD Homicide Division. This is my partner, Detective Alan Brooker. We're here to see Father Fitzpatrick."

The man extended a beefy hand. "Then you're here to see me," he greeted. Herman had expected an Irish accent and was honestly a little disappointed at how unremarkable the man sounded. "I'm Tim Fitzpatrick. Please, come in." The two detectives entered the front hall, wiping their shoes on the mat and letting the priest take their coats. He was all smiles and energy. "Could I offer you gentlemen some coffee, or maybe hot chocolate?"

"I'll take a coffee," Herman accepted. He'd never turn down a chance to drink the nectar of the gods on someone else's coin.

"Great." Fitzpatrick smiled and gestured to the living room, where a cheery fire burned on the hearth. More pine boughs draped the mantel, with more shoddy decorations hanging from the green needles. "Please, have a seat, and I'll be right back. Would you like cream and sugar?"

"No, black is great." Herman looked around the hallway. There were dozens of photographs of Fitzpatrick with various parishioners, including several groups of smiling kids in sports uniforms. A framed, yellowing photograph of a white-haired old woman took pride of place in the center of the accumulation of memories, hanging right beside a Celtic cross that was draped with a black-beaded rosary. "Your mother?"

"Grandma," he said, smiling. "God rest her soul. Detective Brooker, how would you like your coffee?"

"Like I like my women, sweet and blonde." He flushed in the wake of his own inappropriate words. "Sorry, Father."

"No, no apologies. I may be a priest, but I certainly understand appreciating the charms of the ladies. I was a teenager once, too, y'see." He winked at Brooker. "Please, make yourselves at home. I'll be right back."

The detectives went into the living room and sat on the narrow couch. The cushions sagged on broken springs, and the nubby upholstery was worn and threadbare in spots. There was a wing-backed armchair near the fire, and a writing desk was set up under the front window, bathed in natural light. The rest of the room was lined with book cases and one fairly new-looking CD player. The whole room gave Herman the feeling that he was paying a visit to a maiden aunt.

Fitzpatrick came into the room with two steaming mugs of aromatic coffee, and the detectives accepted them with murmurs of thanks. As the priest extended his left hand to the older detective, his sleeve rose up, revealing a strange tattoo of a winged cross. Fitzpatrick sat in the wingback chair and crossed his legs, still smiling.

Herman said, "I noticed your tat. Don't often see priests with tattoos, do you?"

"It happens, especially when those priests started their adult lives with the merchant marine." He smiled more broadly. "There's one priest I met in seminary whose whole back was covered with a really elaborate portrait of Our Lady of Sorrows. It was really beautiful."

Brooker sipped his coffee. "Good. I mean, the coffee is good. Thanks."

"No problem. It's my biggest vice: I love expensive coffee blends. That one comes from Cameroon. It was brought to me as a gift by one of our missionary brothers."

"A nice gift," Herman said.

"Yes, it was." Fitzpatrick watched them for a moment then decided to get to the point. "I assume that you're here because you got my letter."

"You assume correctly."

"Then I think that I can offer you a gift, as well, Detective. I have information about the killing at Saint Martha's Medical Center."

He nodded and put his mug aside, then reached into his pocket for a notebook and pen. "So you said. What information do you have?"

"I know the girl who was killed. She had suffered an injury and had lost her memory when your patrolman – Officer Shea, I think it was – found her. It was kind of him to take her to the hospital for care."

"What was her name?"

"Junie Rabelais. She was originally from France."

"How did she get to be wandering naked down the street?" Brooker asked. "And if she had family, why didn't anybody come forward."

198

"I can't answer your first question right now," the priest answered calmly, "and as for the second, sadly, I didn't know her whereabouts until after she had already been killed."

Herman made notes. "Who do you think killed her?"

"A demon."

Both detectives froze and gave him identical looks of skeptical derision. Only the older man put his doubt to words. "A demon?" he echoed. "Really?"

"Yes, really." He smiled. "Gentlemen, you have wandered into a situation you probably were never meant to encounter. But encounter it you have, and I have been asked by the powers that be to give you information and honest answers to your questions."

Brooker glanced at Herman, who shook his head. "The powers that be?" the younger detective asked. "You mean the bishop, or the Vatican?"

"I mean God."

The two visitors exchanged looks, and Brooker added a slow head shake to his expression.

"God."

"Of course. He's my boss, you know."

"You mean God speaks to you directly?"

Fitzpatrick smiled. "Well, not directly, no. He communicates to me through the Archangel Gabriel."

Herman closed his notebook. "Okay, padre. Thank you for contacting us. If we have any other questions..."

"I'm not mad," Fitzpatrick said, "and I will be able to prove everything I tell you. All I ask is that you hear me out."

The younger detective's cell phone bleeped in his pocket, interrupting the priest's addled ramblings and saving the day. Brooker jumped up to take the call in the foyer, speaking quietly. Herman tucked his notebook back into his coat's inside pocket.

"Thank you, Father Fitzpatrick," he said, standing. "I think I've heard all I need to hear."

"No, you haven't. Not even close."

Brooker returned to the room. "They've got a new one on the Upper East Side. We need to get over there pronto."

He'd never been so relieved to hear of a homicide. He nodded to the priest, who was still sitting calmly in the chair, his hands folded neatly in his lap. "Good bye, Father."

The two men left the house and made their way down to the car. As soon as they were buckled in and Herman was steering back out into what would now be rush hour traffic, his partner whistled and twirled a finger at the side of his head.

"Wow, what a freakshow that guy was, huh?"

"No doubt." He shook his head. "What's this new call?"

"Someone stuffed a body into the sewer lines under an apartment building."

"What, the drain was that big?"

"I don't know. I guess we'll see when we get there."

Herman chuckled. "Hopefully nobody there is talking to angels."

Below and Between

Rachel appeared in Pinem'e's cloister, startling the aged being with her sudden arrival. He wrinkled his nose at the smell of her burning feet and uttered words in the language of the angels. The sound grated on her ears, but the effect was healing, and she sagged with relief.

"Thank you," she said. "I knew you would help."

"Only to stop the smell," he said. "I never could abide the smell of burning flesh." He sprinkled powder over the manuscript he had been copying. "What happened to you?"

"I was in a monastery and convent on Mount Zion." Pinem'e laughed. It was a creaky sound, rusty from disuse. She scowled. "I'm glad it's all so funny to you."

He wiped tears from his eyes. "The thought of you in a convent ... it really is priceless, you must admit." He chuckled. "Why did you go to a convent on Mount Zion, of all places?"

"It wasn't by choice, I promise you." She sighed. "I was taken there by Michael, along with my mate and my son and a couple of Buddhists and a woman who was pregnant with what I thought was the Anti-Christ."

The Watcher shook his head. "Buddhists and the Anti-Christ on Mount Zion? What was Michael thinking?"

"Well, the Buddhists are on Michael's squad, which makes no sense to me. As for the child, it was demonic, but it was no Anti-Christ."

"How do you know?"

"I know because being on ground that holy killed it."

He nodded. "I see." He blotted his page then picked up his quill again. "Well, you've got your feet back, and I'm busy, so if you don't mind..."

She didn't take the hint. "I still need your help."

The look he gave her was scathing. "I'm not feeling very cooperative right now." He gestured toward his book. "I have work to do."

Rachel persisted. "It's just one question. The sooner you answer, the sooner I leave you alone."

"You do know how to drive a bargain," he said, his mouth twisting into a wry smirk. "What is your question?"

"Can a demon possess another demon?"

"No."

"But a demon has possessed my mate."

She sounded desolate, and the tone surprised him. He put his quill back into the ink pot and turned to face her. "Your mate was the half-blood that you had with you the last time, yes?"

"Yes."

"Well, that explains it." He went back to his illuminating. "It's his human half that is possessed. His incubus half cannot be taken by

201

another demon, except for Lucifer, of course, who can take anything he wants ...

and frequently does."

"So if he's only half possessed, then it's possible that he can cast the other demon out?"

"In theory." He sighed. "I thought you were leaving. How many more questions do you have?"

She ignored his irascibility. "How do I get the demon to leave him? Rick is important."

"To you."

"To all of us."

"He's just an ape, Rachel," he said, his tone that of a parent scolding a child. "He can never be as important as all that."

"Oh, but he is. He's got a greater destiny than you could ever understand."

He dipped the quill in the ink and let the excess drain back into the glass bottle. "Don't try to pretend that you know all that I understand. I can think and have thought circles around you and your kind for centuries."

"Yes, and that's why you sit here all by yourself now with no power and no influence in the infernal realms," she snapped back. "All that thinking doesn't do you any good when you have nobody to impress."

His face darkened. "There is still someone I am trying to reach."

"God doesn't care about you and your penance," she scoffed. "That's not the way to get salvation, and you know it."

"Do you have any more questions, or will you leave now? Your voice is as annoying as a gnat in my ear."

She walked over to him and stood behind his bench, leaning against his back with her arms around his waist. Her cheek pressed to his and she said, "Tell me how to get that other demon out of my lover."

"Do you know who that demon is?"

"No."

"That's the first step. Learn its name. Once you have that, you will have power over it. Once you have that power, you can cast it out. Simple as that."

She ran a hand over his chest. "I don't think it will tell me its name."

"That's where you're wrong." He gently pushed her hand away. "It only possesses half of him. That means that it has not been able to hide its identity fully within his. Lay with him, feed from him, and when his ape half is sated and snoring like a pig, you will be left with just the demon. If you pleasure him well enough, you will have access to the demon's mind, too." He drew a slow, steady letter on the parchment before him. "You *do* know how to be that pleasurable, don't you?"

She bit his earlobe. "You know perfectly well that I do."

"So you think."

"So I know."

"Any more questions?"

She released him, a bit stung that she had been so easily rebuffed. He hadn't had this will power before. "Not right now. I'll be back, though."

"What luck."

Rachel kissed him on the cheek. "Don't pretend that you don't like me, sweetie, because I know you do."

She teleported out again. It was only when he was certain that she was gone that Pinem'e allowed himself the luxury of a genuine smile.

Above, Below and Between

The two sisters brought Jessica into a little side chapel and left her there alone, seated on one of the heavy wooden pews, facing a sorrowful-faced crucifix high above the stone altar. Brass oil lamps were suspended from the vaulted ceiling on delicate chains, burning softly against the approaching night. There were no windows.

Behind the altar was a beautiful golden object that looked like a cross between a doll house cathedral and a very elaborate trunk. It had two doors in the front that were tied closed by a red silk cord, and a large cross dominated the top. It was beautiful and mysterious, and if she really looked, it was also ever-so-slightly glowing.

She leaned forward and put her face into her hands. She had no idea what had happened to her life. In the past month, she had gone from being in control of her circumstances, even if they were fairly difficult, to being completely at the mercy of forces she didn't even understand. Where was she supposed to go from here? Her schooling could possibly be picked up again, because she didn't think she'd lost that much time, but law school was not something that could be danced through without some dedication. She worried that this little enforced break had taken her so far off the rails that she'd never be able to return. She couldn't even really remember what class she was taking. The bizarre turn her life had taken seemed to have erased it all from her memory.

She had lost her job, she was certain. Given the nature of her boss, that was hardly something to cry over, but still... it had not been her plan. None of this had been her plan. This new reality was very, very difficult to wrap her head around, and it seemed completely unfair.

She wasn't the sort of person to wallow in self-pity or to sit and have a cry when things got hard. Right now, though, she really didn't know what else to do. She was at her wit's end, and sitting here in a strange church by herself was the last straw.

What in the hell is going to happen to me now? She ran her hands up onto her scalp, gripping the hair briefly before she sat up, forcing herself to look ahead. Whatever was going to happen, she had to face it, and withering when the world was going crazy around her was really not an option.

She wished Li was with her.

In the aisle just in front of the altar, a white orb of light appeared, hovering there as if it was waiting for her to notice it. She focused her gaze on it warily and watched as it expanded and brightened, turning from a dot into an oval of blazing light. In the oval, she could see a darker spot emerging, taking shape into something bipedal and human-like, if you overlooked the wings.

Great. Another angel.

The glow receded and left him standing there, his wings gently folded behind him and a look of serenity on his face. She had never seen any human being with skin so perfectly black; he looked as if he had been carved from jet, and he gleamed like a jewel. He was beautiful and surrounded by silent power. She suddenly felt both safe and very, very small.

"Blessed art thou, Jessica. The Lord is with thee."

A chill passed over her, and she hugged herself. "What?"

He smiled gently and walked to her, going down onto one knee before her. For a ridiculous moment, she felt like he was about to propose marriage, and it frightened her to death. He took her hands, and his skin was dry and warm. She looked into his face and all of her fear melted away.

"Rejoice, for Allah giveth thee glad tidings of a Word from him."

She suddenly recognized this moment from an old art history class she'd taken three years ago. She pulled her hands back as if he had burned her. "You're Gabriel," she identified.

He nodded.

"Oh my God. This can't be happening."

"But it is," he said simply.

"No, it's not. I have to agree, right? I mean, even Mary had to agree to get pregnant with Jesus the first time you did this. Right?"

His answer was simple and without any discernible emotion. "Yes."

She shook her head. "This really can't be happening. You have the wrong girl. I'm not a virgin, and I was... I was just pregnant with some *thing*, and... No. Just, no."

He looked momentarily surprised and released her hands. "The words I have just spoken to you are ancient, Jessica, but they are still true. You are blessed, and the Lord God, the Merciful and Compassionate, is much with you."

"Not like that. Please... not like that."

Gabriel explained, "The first annunciation brought news of the first coming of the Savior. It was a dark time when evil reigned nearly unopposed, and there was much need for help from our Heavenly Father. That help came in the form of Jesus Christ."

"I know the story," she said, hushed.

"You are descended from the fruit of that first birth," he told her. "Your mother was the daughter of many daughters in the line of Morwenna of Cornwall and the Lord Jesus Christ. You are truly the Lord's child, not just in the spirit, but in flesh and blood. You hold within yourself the Blood of the Lamb."

Jessica inched away from him down the bench. He let her go, but he continued to speak.

"I have not come to you to tell you that you will be overshadowed by the Holy Spirit and caused to be with child, but the news I bring is just as great. Be not afraid, Jessica. Be of good cheer, for within you can be the seed of the wellspring of a new world."

Half-remembered sermons from church visits with her grandparents ran through her mind, and she shook her head. "No. You can't do this to me."

"Will you listen, at least?"

Another person appeared in the church, seated on the pew across the aisle from the one Jessica was occupying. She was a small woman, dark-skinned with raven hair, and she wore tattered robes. She had a sweetness to her face, but Jessica recoiled from her. *Now what?*

Gabriel introduced the newcomer. "Hazrat Rabia will offer you her wisdom now."

"Child, you think too much of yourself and not enough of the God who loves you," the woman gently chided. "Open your ears and put your love of yourself aside. It is only by loving God completely that you can know love at all."

Jessica managed to scoot away from Gabriel and hopped up to her feet. She shook her head, looking at the woman, then at the angel. Without another word, she turned and ran out the door and into the hallway beyond.

Gabriel and Rabia faded from view, matching looks of disappointment on their faces.

Below

Rick felt like he'd been run over by a Zamboni.

He rolled onto his side and coughed, his body spasming painfully. He was not surprised to find blood in his mouth. He just wished he could remember why it was there. It must have been one hell of a game.

He opened his eyes slowly, not entirely certain where he was and a little afraid to find out. When his vision cleared, he knew that his trepidation was entirely justified. He was in a place that made black seem bright, somewhere that was more cave than room. It smelled like burned meat and dried piss, with a little sulfur thrown in for flavor. He coughed again, choking this time on the stench instead of the blood in his throat.

His muscles contracted again, pulling him involuntarily into a fetal position then twisting him. His body was behaving like a stranger, as if it hated him and was trying to throw him out of itself. He clenched his teeth and his fists and closed his eyes again.

A feminine voice spoke in his ear. "The pain will pass in time. Your body is trying to adjust to moving between planes. Sometimes the first trip as an adult will hurt."

Cool hands stroked his forehead, and for a moment he thought that it was Rachel. It wasn't her voice he had heard, though, and the hands he felt were smaller, the touch different than the one he'd come to know. He coughed and cramped again, then managed to open his eyes and really look.

A succubus was kneeling beside him, naked in the dim red light, her bat wings motionless behind her. She was beautiful, of course, which went without saying; she was also sad, and there was a shimmer of power around her. Whoever she was, she was very, very old.

He managed to ask between clenched teeth, "Planes?"

"Yes," she said softly. She leaned over him and kissed his temple. "You've been brought physically into the Abyss."

He went cold, his heart pounding in his ears. He had been here before, and when his father had released him, he'd sworn to do everything he could to ensure that he never came back. He tried to sit up but failed to master even that much motion. The succubus put her hands on his shoulders and easily pushed him back to the ground.

"Stay still," she scolded. "It'll be hours before you're able to walk."

Rick tried to speak, but another spasm hit him, and he managed only to grunt. His fear and his pain were equal adversaries, and they were trampling him to death. He was trapped in an unresponsive body and in grave danger, and all he could do was lie down and twitch. Panic was only a half-step away.

The succubus wrapped herself around him, spooning up behind him and holding him tight. She tugged at his energy, leeching just enough off that he fell unconscious again. She still held him in her arms, pinning his limbs in place.

Asb'el strolled into view, sipping at a glass filled with something that glowed an angry orange. "Well?"

"He'll be all right," she answered. "He just has to adjust. He's only half-blood... you should have realized what would happen to him if you brought him here."

He shrugged. "If he's as special as everybody thinks, then he'll come through. If not? Then I brought you a fabulous dinner. Either way, you should be happy."

"I'll only be happy if he lives," she said. "You know how much depends on this."

Asb'el sat on a nearby throne-like chair that had been carved out of the rock. "He has a son, and if not his son, then there will be another."

"Yeter'el's line ends with him. Your betrayal saw to that."

He examined his fingernails. "Wah."

"You're such a bastard," she grumbled. Rick's body contracted again, pushing his breath out of him in a painful-sounding rush. She ran a solicitous hand over his arm. "Poor thing. He has no idea, does he?"

"Not a one. I looked into his mind while I was riding him, and he is completely clueless. He knows what he is, of course, and he's fed before, but the rest? He's an idiot."

"Not an idiot," she corrected. "A blank slate."

"And who will do the writing, Naamah? You?"

"Who else?" She hugged the half-human incubus through another convulsion. "If what we think is true, then he'll be my mate, won't he? The least I can do is mold him to my needs."

Asb'el looked into the corner at the two heaps of flesh and broken bone, still alive but hardly living. There was so little left of Yeter'el and Lily. He finished his drink and said, "Why don't you let me call an Utukku to take the trash out?"

"No!" She raised her head, her dark eyes flashing dangerously. "If they're taken, they could be healed by sympathizers. They have to remain here."

He sighed. "Well, can I at least bury them? They're unsightly."

"Go ahead. I don't care. I just don't want any of their friends to find them."

"Not a problem." He smiled and held out his hand, creating a shovel out of thin air. He directed the floating tool to the corner, where it dug a deep pit. He gave another flick of his wrist, and the shovel heaped the two demons into the hole scoopful by scoopful, mixing their pieces together into an infernal soup. Another gesture made the summoned shovel fill in the pit with rock and soil. He strolled over and took pleasure in tamping down the soil, banishing his tool back into the nothingness from which it had come. He gave the pile one last stomp and walked away.

Good riddance to bad baggage.

CHAPTER EIGHTEEN

*B*etween Herman and Brooker arrived at the scene and were whisked down into the basement by a uniformed cop. He spoke as he led them. "The custodian found the mess when he came down here to get hinges to fix a door upstairs. He's waiting over here to talk to you."

"Great. Did he touch anything?"

"No, he says he called us right away and just sat down and waited."

The detectives found the man sitting on a folding chair at the bottom of the stairwell, fidgeting and trying very hard not to look at the body that the crime scene techs were busy photographing.

Herman introduced himself and his partner, shook the man's hand, and said, "So, you're the one who found him, huh?"

The man nodded. "Yes. I come down to get tools and find him there. I notice the stink first."

The open sewer had a stench all its own, and the detective could certainly understand why that would be the first thing a person would notice. He nodded. "What's your name, sir?"

"Juan Enrico Gonzáles," he answered. "I'm legal. I have papers."

"Not concerned," Herman said, writing in his little notepad. "How long have you worked here?"

"Twelve years."

Herman nodded toward the corpse. "Do you recognize the victim?"

"Yes. It's Rick Buchanan's friend, Andrew Kozlarek. Rick Buchanan live here, in this building. They play together on same hockey team." He shook his head. "Such nice guys. They gave me tickets to a game to take my son."

"Is this a pro team?"

"Yeah. New Jersey Devil Rays."

Herman looked at Brooker, who shrugged his ignorance. "You a big hockey fan, Mr. Gonzáles?"

"Not before, but once I meet Rick and Koz, yeah, I start watching. My kid, he's a big fan. He follows the Devil Rays real close."

Brooker asked, "Do you know of any arguments between Rick and Koz? Any sort of problems they were having?"

"No. They were best friends." He shook his head sadly. "Rick gonna be so sad."

"Is Mr. Buchanan home?"

"No."

The older detective made a note. "Did anybody see Mr. Kozlarek arrive at the building?"

"I dunno. Maybe Billy, the doorman," the custodian guessed.

The uniformed officer who had escorted them down the stairs volunteered, "This is a controlled-entry building. Anybody who comes in has to go through the doorman first."

"Is the doorman available?"

"Yeah, he's in the security office."

"Great. I want to talk to him."

In the alcove, the crime scene techs and the guys from the medical examiner's office were working together to get the body out of the pipe. It took a lot of maneuvering, but they managed to pull Kozlarek's corpse out with a wet slopping sound, putting him directly into the body bag so they could contain at least a little of the smell of the sewage. Even from where Herman was standing, he could tell that the hockey player's neck had been snapped. From the looks of things, he had been a big, powerfully built guy; it must have taken someone equally hearty to overpower him. *Maybe another hockey player*, he thought. *Maybe someone he didn't expect to attack him.* He decided that all he wanted for Christmas was a one-on-one conversation with this Rick Buchanan person.

They asked a few more generic questions of the rattled custodian then went upstairs to the security office. The doorman, Billy, was sitting with another detective, Sal Weintraub, and the building management company's rent-a-cop. They were looking at closed circuit security videos of the people who had come and gone through the front door.

Herman asked, "Is this the only camera view?"

"No," the building security officer said. "There's a camera in the custodian closet and in each elevator, one over each of the service entrances, and one on every level in the stairwells."

"That's a lot of cameras."

"Yes, sir," the security guard replied, nodding. "We've got a lot of wealthy residents with a lot of valuables. The company takes our residents' security very seriously."

"Why's there a camera in the closet?"

"To watch for theft. Tools are expensive."

"Are all of those cameras being recorded?"

"Yeah. I can get you all the tapes."

"Please do." He looked at the grey-and-white images on the bubble-shaped screens. "The camera in the custodian's closet, does that face in or out?"

"It's on the inside, facing into the room."

"Any angles on the hallway outside?"

"No, not unless the camera over the service door might have caught something."

Brooker commented, "Sounds like a lot of video time in the next few days."

"There he is," Billy said suddenly, pointing to the screen. "There's Mr. Kozlarek."

The screen showed the hockey player talking to Billy briefly then coming into the vestibule with a cell phone in hand. He looked concerned in the recorded image.

"Did he say why he was visiting?" Herman asked the doorman.

"He was concerned about Mr. Buchanan. He'd left the team when they were on a road trip in Winnipeg, and he was checking up on him."

"This Buchanan, was he sick or something?"

"I don't know. I never saw him."

"Doesn't he normally come in through the front?"

"Yes, sir. But I didn't see him come in. It might have been when someone else was on shift."

That made sense. They'd have to check the videos. "Okay, thanks. See if you can get those recordings to us right away."

"Sure thing."

Weintraub asked, "So, Billy... Kozlarek and Buchanan... were they close?"

"They were real good friends, yeah. Mr. Kozlarek came over a lot. I think they were roommates on the road, too, if I remember what Mr. Buchanan said once."

"Same team, then," Herman said, verifying the information.

"Yes."

"Were they just friends?" Weintraub asked. "Was there anything deeper going on between them?"

Billy looked at the detective blankly then laughed. "You mean, like, were they gay? No, sir, they most certainly were not. I saw a lot of ladies come in and spend the night with Mr. Buchanan. I don't know about Mr. Kozlarek, but Mr. Buchanan is quite a ladies' man. They were friends, but not, you know, *friends*."

"Just asking. This day and age, you can't be too sure."

Herman put his notebook away. "Can we go up and check on Mr. Buchanan, see if he's here?"

"Sure," Billy said. "He's in the penthouse suite, east side."

"Great. Thanks."

The two detectives took the elevator to the top of the building. On that floor, there were only two apartments, one on each side of the corridor. The door on the west was closed and looked perfectly fine. The door on the east side, though, was slightly ajar. Brooker put on some latex gloves and handed a pair to Herman. This didn't look like it was going to be a standard investigation call.

Herman tugged on the gloves and knocked on the door. "Mr. Buchanan? Hello?"

There was no answer, and they really had not expected one. He knocked again, and the door swung completely open, giving them a full view of the apartment within.

At one time, it had probably been pretty nice. Now it looked like a hurricane had been let loose inside it. The furniture was literally smashed into kindling, and the sizeable collection of high-end electronics looked like it had been hit by lightning. Scorch marks and carbon streaks marked the floor and the ceiling, and a gash had been cut in the wall between the living room and the bedroom. It looked like the work of a long blade, like a sword.

A sword?

Brooker led the way inside, stepping around to the left toward the kitchen area, while Herman went farther into the front room. There was dried blood on the carpeting, all of it in one spot. He bent to examine it when his partner called out.

"Hermie," he yelled. "You've got to see this."

He went into the kitchen and stopped short at the sight of the marks on the kitchen floor. A sharpie lay discarded in front of the refrigerator. It had apparently been used to draw a vast tracery of

214

occult scribblings on the linoleum. There was salt scattered everywhere.

"What the hell?" Herman said, perplexed.

"I have no clue. Looks like we might need to call in the special cult unit."

"Christ. What was this guy into?"

"I don't know." Brooker walked away. "I'm gonna check the bathroom and the bedroom."

The older detective crouched down with his notebook and did his best to sketch the arcane drawing. It was all weird symbols, circles and lines, and it made no sense to him. He'd never seen anything like this before. He decided that his rendition was as good as it was going to get, and he put his notebook back into his pocket. The evidence guys would be getting photographs, anyway.

Brooker came back into the kitchen. "Nothing," he said. "Looks clean."

The unspoken "no more bodies" was both a relief and a disappointment. It was a relief, because that meant they only had one victim to deal with. It was a disappointment, because that meant that the owner of this apartment was now their number one suspect, and if he was running, it would be hard to catch up. Rich athletes could run faster than middle-aged detectives as a general rule.

"I wonder if the neighbors heard anything," Brooker muttered. "One way to find out..."

Herman waited while his younger partner went across the hallway and knocked. There was no response, so he knocked again, and again. Finally he came back in.

"Nobody home," he announced. "Now what?"

"Call the cult boys," Herman said. "I've got a hunch."

"Oh, God," Brooker groaned. "You thinking you're Sam Spade again?"

"If the fedora fits, buddy."

"Fuck you."

"You should be so lucky."

He left his partner to call in the Odd Squad and headed down to street level. He needed to head back to Long Island. Something told him that Father Fitzpatrick might have a word or two to share about this mess.

Above, Below and Between

Jessica headed as quickly as she could back to the basement where her friends were waiting. When she burst into the room, Li leaped to his feet and met her halfway across the floor, anxiety clearly written on his face. "What happened?" he asked, alarmed.

She shook her head. "We have to get out of here. Now."

Yu Kun and Alexander both rose, as well, and the older monk said, "No, we have to wait. There is more information coming and we must all hear it."

"Screw their information," she snapped. "I'm not staying here one minute longer. I'm not playing their game."

"What game?" Li asked.

"They're scaring me. They want something from me that I'm not willing to give them, and I'm afraid they'll take it if I say no."

The English monk objected, "No, they aren't that way."

"You don't know that," she countered. "You don't know them any better than I do."

Li frowned. "You've been through a lot. Shouldn't you rest?"

"I'm fine. I do *not* trust them, and I'm leaving. Period."

Alexander came to her side, ready to run. "Let's go then," he said. "Did you see the way out?"

"No, but I'm sure we can find it. If we can't find a door, there's always a window."

The young incubus licked his lips nervously, then said, "I can probably get us out of here, but it'll take a lot out of me, and I'll need to feed right away to keep running." Jessica and Li looked at him, uncomprehending, and he explained, "I'm almost all demon. I can teleport like my mother can, but I can only do it twice per month if

216

I'm alone, once a month if I'm taking someone else. I think I can take both of you, but it'll be difficult. It's not something I usually do."

She grabbed his hand. "Just don't put us in the middle of any walls."

Li asked, "You can definitely take her, but you're not sure about taking both of us, right?"

"Right." Alexander nodded.

The monk stepped back. "Then go. We'll catch up with you."

Jessica shook her head. "Li, no. Come with me."

"I'll find you." He took her face in his hands and kissed her. "Now go."

Alexander squeezed her hand, and she looked at him, nodding. The incubus took a deep breath and closed his eyes, and then they were gone.

"Why did you do that?" Yu Kun demanded. "Why did you encourage her to go? She needed to stay here and listen to what Gabriel had to tell her."

The younger monk gave his master a look somewhere between apology and defiance and left the room.

⚜

Alexander took them as far as he could go, which was only a few hundred yards away. They found themselves standing in a shuttered souvenir store in Jerusalem's Old City, the doors locked for the night. Cheaply made clay oil lamps and "replica" antiques filled the rough wooden shelves, calculated to look like something out of a sand-and-sandal movie. The incubus bent over with his hands on his knees, panting for air, sweat beading his brow from the effort of their travel.

"Good job," she congratulated, patting him on the back. "You all right?"

"Will be," he answered between huffs. "You?"

"Better now." She went to the front window and peered out into the street. "Looks like everybody's gone home for the night." She could hear music and some actor's sonorous narration over

217

loudspeakers, blasting through the night air. It was like being in earshot of some sort of Biblical Disneyland.

Alexander managed to stand up, but he still hadn't caught his breath. He put his hands on his hips and tried to will his heart to slow. "They'll find you," he warned.

"Yes, they probably will," she admitted. "But I don't have to make it easy on them."

She fiddled with the antiquated door until she managed to open it. Operating the latch had been much harder than it should have been, and it made her wonder if maybe the angels had found them already and were putting barriers in the way. She pushed the door open and gestured to Alexander.

"Come on."

The two of them headed out into the street. There was a crowd gathered near a tall wall where pictures were being projected, using the ancient masonry as some sort of movie screen. The narration continued, and the noise of the voice and the background music helped make them feel like they were hidden. They ducked into the throng and made their way through to the other side with some difficulty.

Alexander stopped her before they emerged on the other side of the audience. She started to speak to him, but he held up a hand, shushing her. The fear in his eyes did more to silence her than anything. She looked around, trying to see what had frightened him, but there was nothing that she could detect.

Then she saw the shadows move.

"Oh, shit," she said, grabbing his hand. "Run!"

He didn't need to be told twice. His strides were longer, but she was well-trained from her martial arts practice, and they kept pace through the alleys, running toward light and away from any innocent bystanders. They turned one corner, then another, dodging around Christmas season pilgrims and racing from one alley to another. They raced around one building and started toward another when they came face to face with a blank wall blocking their way. The alley filled with moving shadows, arms raised, misty claws ready to rip. Behind them, they heard a whispered, whistling laugh, and they knew that they were trapped.

Alexander turned to Jessica, his eyes wide, and they just looked at one another, preparing for this to be their last moment on earth. The shadows crept closer, and they braced for the attack, but then a wave of evil passed over them all, and even the tizalem shrank away. There was a flash of black light in the dead-end alley ahead of them, and then that flash resolved into the strikingly handsome form of what looked like a human man.

The incubus beside her gave a little cry and dropped to his knees, pressing his forehead to the ground in utter supplication. Jessica stepped back, alarmed by her companion's behavior and afraid of the dark grandeur that surrounded this new arrival like cologne. The man stepped forward, offering her his perfectly manicured hand.

"Jessica Norgren, I presume."

She did not accept the handshake. "Who are you?"

He smiled. "I have many names. You can call me Nick."

She took another backward step. "How do you know who I am?"

"I know everything about you, my dear," Nick said. There was something incredibly appealing about the way his eyes twinkled, about the curve of his lip and the strength so evident in his muscular body. Enticing images of herself having sex with him ran through her mind, and she chased them away in anger. Nick chuckled. "I knew everything about you even before you were born." He looked at Alexander in curiosity. "And you, boy. You were dragged into all of this by your meddlesome mother. No doubt she never told you the things she was volunteering you for."

Alexander's voice was muffled by the ground as he replied, "No, my lord."

"Hmm." He crouched beside the young incubus and put down a hand, cupping Alexander's chin and encouraging him to look up. He obeyed. Nick looked into his eyes and smiled gently. "Poor boy. Pulled this way, pushed that way... it's no wonder you're confused. And you are confused, aren't you?" The incubus nodded, tears standing in his eyes. "I thought so. You've always done what your mother told you because you have no free will to resist her, isn't that right? But no – you have a little bit of free will, inherited from your father. And you used it to defy her about the succubus Lily, didn't you?"

The younger man wilted. "I'm sorry, Master. I meant no disrespect to you..."

Nick kissed him on the lips. There was a promise of obscenity in that kiss, a carnality that made Jessica look away. She started to retreat farther, but the dominant demon – for she was certain that was what he was – held up a hand.

"Not so fast, my dear."

She froze where she stood, rooted in place and unable to move. She could only watch as Nick caressed Alexander's face.

"Master," Alexander said in a quiet, desperate voice, "I do not want to oppose you. I worship you, as I was raised to do."

Nick kissed him again, running his hand through the other man's dark hair. "You are a good boy," he said at last, "and I am not angry with you. In fact, I think I like you. You need to go home and wait for me there. We need to become more acquainted, you and I. Would you like that?"

Alexander nodded. "Yes, Master. Very much. Thank you."

The older demon released his hold on the other man's face and stood. "Go home, Alexander." He waved one finger, and the incubus blinked out of existence, vanishing back into the Abyss. Nick turned his attention back to Jessica. "Now, then...where were we?" There was a feeling of air displacement, not really wind, not really a vacuum, and then Gabriel was standing behind Nick, a wicked-looking curved dagger in his hand. Nick did not turn around.

"Release her," the archangel commanded.

"Or what? You'll stab me in the back like Michael did?" He clicked his tongue. "Not very sporting."

"I will do what I must."

Nick laughed. "You and I both know that you are no match for me, Messenger. Go back to your Father and give him my regards, won't you? Jessica and I have things to discuss, and as they say, two's company, three's a crowd."

He raised his hand as if to work more infernal magic, but Gabriel caught him by the wrist. "Release her," he repeated. "I cannot fight you, no, but one is coming who will."

"Not," he said, freeing his wrist, "if she continues to say no. You and I are both bound by the rules of this ridiculous charade."

The moment Gabriel's hand closed on Nick's flesh, Jessica felt the hold on her dissolve. While her would-be captor was distracted with the archangel, she turned and fled for all she was worth, running back into the crowd watching the show at the Tower of David.

Nick smirked as he heard her running away. "There," he told his little brother. "Happy now? She's on the loose, and so are the tizalem. I hope they don't find her before you do."

Gabriel scowled and said, "You wouldn't dare. She is Jesus' descendant!"

"True. And how many of His descendants do you think I turned to ash in Germany? *Arbeit macht frei*, my brother."

The archangel disappeared, and the Devil laughed to himself, mentally calling the tizalem off the trail. This was one quarry he wanted to hunt a different way.

CHAPTER NINETEEN

A bove and Between

Gabriel caught up with Jessica at the Jaffa Gate. He appeared directly in front of her, stopping her cold. She shouted in surprise and dropped back into a fighting crouch, her hands raised defensively.

"Get away from me!"

He held up his hands. "I mean you no harm."

"Sure you don't. You just want me to get pregnant with the next I-don't-know-what." She raised her hands a little higher, this time more aggressive than protective. "That's not going to happen."

The archangel spread his arms out to the side. "You do not understand the importance of what is being asked of you or of your very special nature. We can turn to no one else. You are the last of your line."

She nodded, jaw setting. "That's right. Last of the line. That means no babies, no new Messiah, no nothing. Do you understand?"

He bowed his head and stepped aside. "Do you realize the consequences of your refusal?"

Jessica straightened and walked closer to him. "Is this where the guilt trip comes in?"

"Call it what you like. The truth is that if you do not obey this call from God Almighty, your Creator, then all of the world will perish in flames."

"That's going to happen anyway. Just ask Al Gore."

"This is no time to be flip!" His shout rattled the rooftops and shook the very ground beneath her feet. She cringed but managed not to fall. "Do you really believe that your petty concerns are worth more than everything God has made?"

A taxi stopped for her, and she gave it the barest of glances before opening the door. "I think that if God's big plan will fall apart based on what a law clerk says and does, then He's got some bigger issues to deal with." She sat in the cab and started to close the door.

Gabriel yanked the door out of her hand. "Where do you think you're going to go?" he asked. "You are unfamiliar with this city, and you have no money."

She scowled, but had to concede. She climbed back out of the taxi and waved it away. "You just picked a hell of a time to get practical."

"Let me take you back to Li and Yu Kun," he said. "At least let me reunite you with your friends. If I do that for you, will you listen to me for ten minutes?"

She crossed her arms. "Seven."

"Fine." He shook his head. Modern people were so much more difficult to work with than they were at the first annunciation. He offered her his hand, palm up. "Shall we?"

Reluctantly, with a truculent glare, Jessica took his hand and went where he led.

Jerusalem's Old City was packed with people, not all of them holy, righteous, or even sane. It was those who were bad, or addicted, or in some other way vulnerable who wandered away from the rest of the crowds and who were taken by the devil's favorite soldiers.

Thirteen human bodies under new management assembled in the souvenir shop where Lucifer was waiting for them. He had no doubt that Jessica had by now been located by Michael and his ilk, but he knew that she was still defying them. That defiance was what made her soul still ripe for the picking.

Telepathically, he showed each of the assembled archdemons the images of the young woman's face. "This is the one," he told them. "Do not kill her. Find her and bring her to me in Rome."

His followers bowed and scattered like bad omens. He sat back and smiled, his mind already racing through the city with Jessica, watching the show.

Above and Between

Father Fitzpatrick opened the door before Herman even reached it, his smile just as friendly as before. The detective greeted him.

"Hello, there, Father. I have some questions for you about another case. Do you have a minute?"

"Of course." He closed the door and waved his guest back to the front sitting room. "I'm actually very glad you came back. I'm afraid we left off the last time on sort of a bad foot. More coffee?"

"No, thanks." Herman sat down in the same place on the couch he had occupied earlier that day.

Fitzpatrick asked, "Where is your partner?"

"He's handling something back at the station. I wanted to come down and ask you some more questions."

"The drive from Manhattan to Long Island isn't for the faint of heart this time of day," the priest smiled. "Must be pressing."

"It is." He handed Fitzpatrick the sketch he had made of the scribbling on Rick Buchanan's kitchen floor. "What do you make of this?"

He studied the sketch, and the warmth on his face chilled drastically. "Where did you see this?"

"At a murder scene." He studied the priest's reaction. "What is it?"

"It's a protection sigil called the Seal of Solomon. The story is that King Solomon used the magic in a book called the Key of Solomon and imbued a ring with a Seal, and that ring gave him power to control demons. This sigil is part of the Seal. The person wanting to be protected draws this and either traps the demon in the center of the sigil, thereby keeping the demon trapped there, or the person sits in the center of the sigil himself, keeping the demons at bay. This version is slightly different than the usual types, though. This one has infernal script around the outside instead of the usual Enochian."

Herman shook his head. "What is Enochian?"

"The language of the angels, named for Enoch in the Old Testament."

"And infernal script, I assume that's for the other team?"

"The language of demons, correct." Fitzpatrick's face was grim as he handed the drawing back. "This confirms my worst suspicions. You have stumbled upon something very, very dark, indeed."

He looked at the sketch, then turned the page and scribbled some notes. "So do all priests have this kind of knowledge of the occult, Father?"

"No," he admitted. "Only some. I have been an exorcist and demonologist for nearly two hundred years, and so I have some special knowledge."

Herman's head snapped up and he looked at the priest in shock. "Two hundred years? What the hell? That's impossible."

"I was 50 when I died," he said quietly. "But I have been in God's service for two centuries."

"What?"

The priest sighed. "There is much you need to know. It's good that you're sitting down."

Herman couldn't decide if he wanted to stay and listen to the man's ravings or run while he had the chance. Curiosity won out over self-preservation, as it usually did for him, and he stayed. "I'm listening."

"I was born in Ireland in 1759. I came to the New World in 1791, specifically to the colony of Maryland, to teach at St. Mary's Seminary and bring the Word of God to the natives. It was in the New World, during the War of 1812, that I came to grief. I was sailing with the American Navy as a volunteer ship's chaplain aboard the USS Chesapeake. I was killed by the English in a battle in 1813."

"But you're not 50, and you're certainly not dead," he objected. "What kind of bullshit are you trying to feed me?"

"It's not bullshit," the priest replied. "Not at all. I'm telling you the truth. I died in 1813, and now I'm serving God as an angel."

Herman's mouth dropped open. "An angel."

"Yes."

"So you're telling me that you were once a human being, but now you're dead, and you've turned into an angel who works on Long Island as a priest?"

Fitzpatrick smiled. "Exactly."

"And that's not bullshit?"

"Not at all."

"I always thought angels were angels and humans were humans and the two were never the same. I mean, that's what I was taught."

"Some people have that misconception," the other man said mildly. "Some human souls are offered the chance to continue on with their service to God in the guise of minor angels."

Herman laughed outright. "I do *not* fucking believe you."

"I suspected that you wouldn't. You're a detective, not someone who accepts things on first blush. You require proof."

The room was suddenly flooded with white light, as if someone had turned on a spotlight and aimed it at his eyes. The detective raised his hand and squinted into the light, trying to see what was causing this new development. The light subsided, leaving only sparkling dots in his field of vision and a blond man in a white trench coat standing in front of the fireplace.

"Detective Lloyd Herman," the priest said quietly, "I'd like to introduce you to Saint Michael."

Below

Rick opened his eyes slowly, hoping that his memories of being in the Abyss had been some sort of concussion-fueled hallucination. What he saw disabused him of that hope, and he took a deep breath to steady himself. This was nothing he was at all prepared to handle.

He was lying on a pile of silk pillows and covered with the softest blanket he'd ever encountered. In the dim red light, he could see a full-sized mirror and an ornate chest of drawers on the far side of the room. There was nothing else of note in the place.

He sat up and swung his legs out of the bed, taking a moment to let the spinning in his head slow down enough for him to walk. He was naked, which really didn't surprise him, and around his left wrist was a plain brass cuff bracelet, close-fitting and soldered shut. It wasn't going to be coming off without tools and possibly some bloodshed. He didn't really want to know what it signified, but he knew he'd find out sooner rather than later.

So, this is hell, he thought to himself. *Again.* The atmosphere of the place was oppressive, full of unspoken anguish, desperation, and abject terror. He remembered it all far too well.

He heard a soft whimper behind him, on the other side of the cushions. He spun at the sound, startled, and saw the imp lackey that always served Yeter'el. Instead of being its usual annoying self, it was looking at him with huge black eyes filled with sorrow and tears.

"What's the matter with you?" he asked it.

"Master," it cried. "Master."

"What about your master?"

The imp flew to a bare corner of the room and sat down to weep. Rick shook his head in confusion. The little creature lay down as if to hug the ground and repeated, "Master. Master."

"Get out of here!" a female voice shouted, shooing the imp out of its despondent little vigil and all the way out of the chamber. It was the same powerful succubus who had been caring for him before. Now that he was thinking clearly, he recognized her: the Queen of Hell, one of Lucifer's two consorts. He was in the presence of infernal royalty.

"Naamah," he said, lowering his head in respect. "I'm honored."

She smiled. "You're darling. How did you ever come to know me on sight?"

"My father," he said softly. "He taught me a lot when I was a kid, back before we parted ways."

She sashayed up to him and took his face in her hands, looking down at him. "Such pretty eyes. How are you feeling?"

"Dizzy, and confused," he admitted. "How did I get here?"

She sat beside him, her hand on his knee in that overly familiar way that succubi tended to have. "Asb'el and his minions brought you to me. They found you in Jerusalem, running mad. They knew that I have certain healing abilities and thought that I could help you." She kissed his cheek. "Do you remember anything at all?"

He remembered plenty, but nothing he felt like sharing. He lied, "No."

She smiled again, but there was a dangerous flash in her expression. "Well," she said, knowing that he was being less than truthful but letting him run with it anyway, "your memories might return in time."

He looked down at her hand, which had moved up to rest on his thigh. "Will I... uh... will I be returned to the surface?"

"Well, that all depends, doesn't it?"

"On what?"

"On you."

She slid over to straddle his lap, her arms on his shoulders. "Are you going to be a nice and grateful boy, or am I going to have to tell my mate about how mean you were to me?"

Rick definitely didn't want that kind of trouble. He broke into his brightest smile. "Hey, gratitude is my middle name."

Naamah chuckled throatily and started kissing him. Rick had never felt so trapped.

Not far away, in another chamber on the lowest level of the Pit, Alexander paced. The room was luxurious nearly to the point of parody, with kingly furnishings and the affectations of imperial splendor. The famed perfumed pleasure dens of the Persian court could not have held a candle to the apartment where he found himself.

Despite the beautiful appearance, the place smelled of death and decay. There was an undertone of rot beneath the incense that hung in the air, and it turned his stomach. There was old blood here, and desiccated souls, and things he thought it better not to try to identify. No matter where he looked in the four-room suite, he could not find a door or any means of escape. He did, however, find ingenious bondage rigs and torture devices, and his insides trembled at the thought that the Prince of Darkness was on his way to "share" those experiences with him.

He tried calling his mother, but she didn't answer; most likely, she could not hear him. Her power was only a lightning bug next to a forest fire when compared to the magic that Lucifer could wield. There was nobody stronger than him, and nobody who could or would come to his aid.

He stopped searching and stood helplessly before a life-sized oil painting of the Evil One himself, faithful in every detail to the horror that lurked beneath the beautiful face. Alexander shuddered at the avarice and depravity that shone in the portrait's eyes.

"Good God," he said, turning away.

Good God.

There was only one being stronger than Lucifer, and that was the one who had consigned the Devil to the Pit in the first place. Alexander knew that he was about to commit the worst kind of treason, but he was out of options. No matter what he had told his erstwhile king, he had no loyalty to Satan any longer, not after he had sent the tizalem. He could still remember the claws and the teeth and the pain. He had nowhere else to turn.

He knelt in the middle of the room and folded his hands the way he'd seen people do in films on the surface. Bowing his head, he prayed to a distant God for deliverance.

Above and Between

In the wake of Jessica and Alexander's strange exit, Li walked. He wandered the ancient corridors of the unfamiliar building, passing statues of strange people and religious items that he didn't understand. Every door he found was barred or locked, except for one, which he finally found after an exasperating series of left turns down dead-end hallways.

It was a tiny doorway, barely taller than him and only slightly wider, and the door itself was the same wood and iron construction as all the other doors in this medieval place. There was a flickering, golden light in the room beyond the door, and the scent of roses wafted out to where he stood. Hoping for some kind of garden exit, he stepped over the threshold.

It was just a little room, barely ten feet square, furnished with flat wooden pews and a brass and wood crucifix on the wall to his left. There was a young man sitting on one of the pews, a thorny twig sprinkled with mint-green leaves dangling from his fingers. His clothing was simple and almost non-descript, and Li overlooked it completely. Nothing about the man was noteworthy, at least until he lifted his face and looked at Li.

He had seen eyes that wise and compassionate only once before, when he had been privileged to attend a lecture given by the Dalai Lama at the Manhattan Center. It might have been that association, or that old-beyond-years look, or maybe something else about the young man himself, but Li trusted him immediately. For the first time in days, he felt like everything was beginning to make sense.

"You look troubled," the man said, his voice as gentle as his demeanor. "Please, sit down. Perhaps I can help you."

The young monk hesitated then sat down. "Thanks. I don't mean to disturb your meditation."

"You're very welcome. I'm always ready to talk to people, especially when they need help."

Li ran a hand over his head and sighed. "I don't know what's going on anymore," he said. "I'm so confused, and scared, and I don't know what to do anymore. Everything used to be so calm and certain, and now everything is up in the air. I hate this."

It was unlike him to volunteer his emotions, and unlike him to unburden himself to a stranger, but in this moment, with this man, it felt right. The man nodded. "Sometimes life can be confusing, especially when we are confronted by things we don't expect. You've been given a very difficult task, and you've seen things you never thought that you would see. It's natural to feel overwhelmed and upset." He looked at Li kindly. "It's no sin to feel vulnerable."

"I know that. I just… I always try to reason my way through fear, but there's nothing reasonable about this situation." It occurred to him that he should have been asking how this man knew anything about what he'd been confronted with, but at the same time, it felt like a given. He didn't think too hard about it. "Everything I knew and thought I was has just…gone sideways."

The man nodded again, but this time he stayed silent, letting Li work through his emotions on his own for a moment without interference. After a few moments, the man said, "You've never believed in God before, have you?"

"I wasn't raised in that sort of world," he answered. "Some Buddhists believe in God, but I never really have. I wasn't told about God. I was always taught that self-mastery and the elimination of desire would end suffering, not that there was some huge being in the sky that would do everything for us if we prayed the right way."

"Have you eliminated desire, Li?"

He hesitated. "How do you know my name?"

The man looked down at the thorny sprig in his hands, twisting it lightly, the spines on the stem doing him no harm. "I know everyone who comes into this place," he said softly.-

He decided he would just accept that explanation. "I thought I had eliminated it," he said, answering the man's question finally. "I was wrong."

"What desire did you find that you still have?"

Li looked down at his own hands. They were loosely clasped before him, still and listless. He whispered, "I found that I desire to be with a woman, and I never desired this before."

"And this desire leads you to suffering?"

"Yes."

"Because you can't have her? Or because you can't help her?"

"Both." He shook his head. "No, that's not true. I think she wants me, too. At least, she's doing things that make me feel like she does. But I don't know…" He gestured helplessly. "Anyway, it's mostly because she's in a terrible fix that I don't understand, and I can't help her out of it."

"How do you know?"

He frowned in confusion and looked at the man. "What do you mean?"

"I mean, what if you could help her out of her fix? What then?"

"Then I'd help her."

"What if helping her meant hurting yourself?"

It was a very loaded question, but Li was not afraid of it. "Then I will help her. True love extends outside of one's own concerns. Love of humanity has to be greater than love of self."

"And love of one's beloved? Where does that fall?"

His voice sounded like someone else's as he answered, "Above everything else."

The man nodded again. "Sometimes the greatest sacrifices are the ones nobody ever knows about. Do you believe that?"

"Of course."

When the man spoke again, his voice was heavy with regret. "Would you give of yourself to help another person, someone who isn't Jessica?"

"Yes."

He answered without hesitation. The man smiled, and there was a glimmer of pride on his face. "The sacrifice that will be asked of you will benefit not just Jessica, but the entire world and all of humanity."

Li took a deep breath and raised his chin. "Then let it be done."

The man turned to him and offered him the stick he had been holding. When Li looked, the thorns seemed harder than plant material, and glistened with something that looked deadly.

"There was a time when there was a sacrifice required of me, and in a moment of weakness, I begged my father not to make me drink from that cup. This is not a cup, Li, but the end result will be the same. Will you take this, of your own free will, knowing that you will die, but that with your death humanity will live?"

The monk stared at the twig, a million images and thoughts racing through his mind: things he had never done, things he would have liked to do again, people he wished he could bid farewell. He took a deep and steadying breath then looked into the man's eyes.

He did not answer with a word. Instead, he closed his hand on the thorns and let them pierce him, injecting the gleaming poison on their tips. There was pain at first, and the feeling of burning up from the inside out, but then everything was light and air and he was free.

When the light receded, the room was empty, but the scent of roses still remained.

CHAPTER TWENTY

*A*bove and Between

Gabriel returned Jessica to the basement room where Yu Kun was waiting. She looked around and asked, "Where is Li?"

"He followed you out," the English monk replied.

She turned to the archangel. "We have to go and get him. We have to find him."

Gabriel's face was sorrowful as he shook his head. "No. We will not be seeing him again."

Her voice was tiny. "What?"

Yu Kun's composure broke, and he sank to his knees, his head bowed. He made no sound, but his shoulders shook. He already knew.

The angel told them, "Tsung Li no longer lives."

Jessica ground her teeth and cried, "No!" Without thinking, she lashed out, kicking and striking the angel, who simply let her do it. She battered him then stopped, sobbing. "You sons of bitches, what did you do to him?"

"He has sacrificed himself in the name of the greater good." He made no move to hold her as she cried. Any attempt would have been shrugged off, anyway. He watched as she turned away. "He is not the first to fall in this fight against the Evil One."

They simply wept for a long time, and Gabriel let them grieve. He stood in silent sorrow until Yu Kun finally gained enough control to ask, "His body?"

The angel softly said, "Consumed."

Jessica turned on him, her face red from tears and anger. "Consumed? What the hell do you mean, consumed? Somebody ate him?"

"The energy that ended his life also ended his physical form," he patiently explained. "His body is gone."

The monk nodded, his face looking gray and old. "It is well," he said quietly. "He would have wanted to be cremated. It is as he would have wished."

She wiped her face. "I can't believe he died willingly. He never had a death wish, not ever."

"There is a difference," the angel said, "between a death wish and a willing sacrifice."

"Why?" she asked, her voice keening. "Why did he sacrifice himself?"

He looked her in the eye. "He sacrificed himself for you."

Her head spun as if he'd struck her. She sank down to her knees, her eyes brimming. "I don't... I never... Why?"

The room began to fill with angels. Michael appeared, and Raphael, and a stern male angel with fiery eyes and Asian features. Michael said, "He understood that we stand on the brink of destruction, and he acted to tilt the balance in our favor."

Raphael said, "Will you listen to us now, Jessica? Will you honor Li that much?"

"Don't you dare make him part of whatever game you're playing," she hissed. "Don't you dare steal him like that!"

Yu Kun reached out and put a hand on her shoulder. "Rise above your anger," he advised. "This is a time for hearing and a clear mind. The grief can be worked through later."

She shoved his hand away. "Who asked you?"

Michael nodded to his brother. "Gabriel, please. Your message."

"The Dark Child has been conceived. Satan has impregnated a virgin with his infernal seed. Even now, the Dark Child makes his presence known in the mind of his unfortunate mother, and he will eventually drive her mad, as all incarnations of the Anti-Christ have done in the past. If a Child of Light is not conceived to counter him, then all will be lost. The only blood line that is strong enough to bear the new Child of Light is the blood line of the first, Jesus of Nazareth. You, Jessica, are the last woman of that blood line who can still bear children, and so this task has fallen to you.

"The Prince of Darkness has opposed us and will continue to oppose us until the Child of Light is born. Once the child is born, he must step back and allow him to grow. As with Jesus of Nazareth, Satan is only allowed to contact the Child of Light once that child is an adult. If we can keep you secure until the birth of the child, then we may still have a chance.

"Satan means to bring his child to maturity and then loose him like a plague upon the world, wreaking havoc and destroying everything that God has created and loves. The Child of Light will counter his evil and will help to build and heal, and ultimately the two will battle as it was foretold. The Child of Light, if he is strong, will overcome the forces of darkness and the Lord's grace will spread over the land, and Earth will be at peace for the first time since Eden's gates were sealed."

Jessica wrapped her arms around her legs. "And Li? How is he involved?"

"His soul will be used to weaken Satan so that he will be unable to assail you until the Child is born."

"So you've taken a peaceful man and turned him into a weapon," she hissed. "That is obscene."

"He will be the power that helps to protect you and your child."

Her voice was harsh as she spat, "I have no child."

"No," Michael said, "not yet. You have not yet agreed."

"And who's going to be the father?" she asked. "Do I have a choice in that?"

The stern-faced angel spoke. "I am Uriel, the Fire of the Lord. You must think beyond yourself now. This is no longer the time to be selfish and small. You must think of the human race as a whole, as Tsung Li did, and look beyond your own petty needs and concerns."

His words stung, but she wasn't going to show him that. "I'll take that as a 'no'." She clenched her fists. "I don't trust you. You could all be hallucinations, or the devil himself making his demons look like angels. How can I believe a word you say? How can I believe you're the good guys when you kill my best friend and then force this kind of thing on me?"

The angels looked at one another, sharing some sort of inaudible conversation. Finally, Raphael spoke. "Do you believe in God, child?"

She set her jaw and looked away. "I don't know."

"If you do not believe that God exists, then what will convince you? What proof do you require?"

"I want to see Him. If He's God, then I want Him to prove it to me. Do something only God can do. Let me have a glimpse of that infinite intellect."

Yu Kun sighed. "Jessica..."

"No," Gabriel said, silencing the monk. "Saints, too, have required proof when their faith was shaken. Jessica, you will be shown that which you have requested."

She started to make a sarcastic comment, but then fell silent with a gasp. Her mind seemed to blast open, unfolding from the inside out, spreading out to encompass the room. She saw the angels as blurs of light in human shape. Without turning her head, she saw Yu Kun at every age he had ever been or ever would be. She saw the floor plan of the convent where they sat and saw the cellular structure of every brick in every wall. In a flash, the vision widened, and she could feel the rush of life, of rivers and insects and the tiny dust motes on the air that were part of the living world. She could feel the heartbeat of the earth and hear the stars singing. She could see all the way back and all the way forward to the brilliant explosions on both ends of creation, the birth and the death of everything. She suddenly knew everything that human minds had ever known, could do everything that human beings had ever done. She was a newborn, she was a mother, she was an old lady, and the whole time, she was a carbon atom spinning from rock to amoeba to reptile to soil and then to rock again. She knew everything. She understood everything.

The power of the flash of ultimate knowledge shook her, and she began to convulse, words in every language falling from her lips as she contorted on the stone floor. She was larger than the universe, and she was smaller than a grain of sand. She was the grain of sand, but then she was a supernova, and all the time the beat-beat-beat of the pulse of all existence rang in her ears. Her mind kept expanding, running wild, tearing at the seams. There was too much for her mortal brain to contain, too many sensations for her nerves to process. She screamed.

As quickly as the incredible vision began, it was gone, and she was left gasping for air, sprawled on her stomach with her fingers curling into the ground like claws. She *knew*. She knew it all. Before she came completely back to herself, she thought she heard Li's voice, telling her he loved her, and she began to weep again.

Gabriel spoke again, his voice the only sound in the room other than her ragged breathing. "You have had your glimpse," he said softly. "Now do you believe?"

Stunned, she could only nod.

Jessica slowly sat up, pulling herself up into a sitting position once again. She pressed her palm to her sweat-sheened brow, checking to see if her skull was still intact.

Gabriel spoke his age-old words. "Fear not, for thou hast found favor with God. The Holy Ghost shall come upon thee, and the power of the Highest shall overshadow thee. Therefore also that holy thing which shall be born of thee shall be called the Son of God."

From a hidden place deep inside of herself, Jessica replied. "Then let it be done to me according to His word..."

Between

Brooker sat and cued up the tape from the custodial closet's security camera, fast forwarding until he got to approximately the time that they guessed Kozlarek had been killed. For a long while, he found himself watching mops and buckets doing absolutely nothing, and he was beginning to think this tape would be a wash. Finally, though, the recording showed the door opening and someone coming into the closet. The person was huge, easily 6'6", and with dark hair so close-cropped that he looked almost bald. Brooker watched the recorded image rummage in the tools, waiting to see the man's face. When the suspect turned and faced the camera, he almost fell out of his chair.

He paused the player and scrambled out of the video room and over to Herman's desk. He banged through the drawers and files until he found the witness sketch of the man they thought had been dumping bodies in the subway. He grabbed the artist's rendering and returned to the video room. His hand shaking with excitement, he held the picture up to the screen.

It was the same face.

He fumbled through the other tapes until he found the one for the camera that filmed the place where the hockey player's corpse had been stuffed into the hole. He watched the same massive man pounding his way through the concrete with a wrench, impossible strength on display, before he shoved Kozlarek into the opening he had created.

"Holy shit," he muttered, fumbling for his cell phone with the other hand. "Hermie's gonna love this one!"

Herman drove toward the station, his mind full of everything but work. The new wing tattoo on his inner left wrist itched a little, but that was probably because it was still buzzing with the energy it had taken to create it. He rubbed at it absently with his other hand.

He believed what he had been told. He was a skeptic, and he was hard-nosed, but he was also reasonable, and when an archangel comes and recruits you to fight in the Apocalypse, it's a little difficult to say no. It had been hard for him, at any rate.

The letter from Father Fitzpatrick was on the passenger seat beside him, the squiggly line and the X face-up. They had told him that the squiggle was really the map of a coast line, and that the X really did mark the spot where the final battle would take place. It was hard to believe that the showdown between God and the Devil would be taking place fifty-five miles into the Atlantic Ocean, but he supposed that God and the Devil could probably fight just about anywhere they pleased.

His cell's ring tone startled him, and he swerved in traffic, nearly losing control of the car in his abrupt return to the mundane world. He grabbed the phone and answered the call. "Herman."

"Dude, you're not gonna believe this." His partner sounded excited, almost giddy.

Try me. "What?"

"I've got the tape from the Kozlarek dump site. The guy who shoved him down the toilet is the same guy who's been dumping bodies on the subway. He matches the witness picture almost exactly."

He sounded so thrilled Herman couldn't bear to tell him that he already knew. He knew about Ulug, and he knew about demons and succubi and incubi and their victims, and God, but he needed a drink right about now. He was no actor, but he managed to sound interested instead of off-kilter when he responded, "Really? Are you sure?"

"Totally sure. You've got to get back here and see this."

Brooker hung up on him, which was what he did when he was excited. Herman just put his phone away.

He was never going to look at his job the same way again.

Naamah left him lying on his back, breathless and nearly overcome with physical pleasure. Rick stared at the ceiling, glad that she was gone and waiting to get some sensation back in parts of his body that weren't located in his groin. His head vibrated with the energy he had taken from the Queen, and if he hadn't been high on afterglow, he certainly would have been high on the buzz.

He heard a soft rustle, and then he heard his father's imp weeping. He managed to prop himself up on his elbows, looking into the corner where the little creature was stroking the dirt and muttering mournfully.

"What's with that corner, huh?"

The imp wailed and pointed to the dirt. "Master!"

"Buddy, you used to speak in complete sentences. Why don't you give that a try, huh?"

Rick rolled onto his side, still tingling. He felt so good, he almost forgot to be upset that he had been dragged into hell against his will.

The imp took a deep breath and said, "Master ... is hurt ... and buried here!"

It was the mother of all buzz-kills. His head cleared a lot faster under the influence of the surprise. He had never thought anything could hurt his father. Yeter'el had always seemed invincible.

"How?" he asked.

It gave a shudder and shook its head. "Punished. The King of Hell, he punished him. And he is buried, along with *her*."

"Her?" he asked, panicking. *Rachel...?*

"Lily."

He hesitated, uncertain how to proceed. "What do you want me to do about it?"

The imp flew across the room and attached itself to his neck and shoulders, hanging there with claws sunk into his skin. "*Dig. Him. Up!*"

He knocked the imp aside with a snarl. "Ow! Little bastard," he cursed. "What was that for?"

It landed on the dirt mound again, cowering. "Don't be angry, son of Master," it begged. "Please, save him. Poor Master!"

Rick managed to stand. "I don't know. I've never been that fond of dear old Dad," he said, "and I'm fresh out of shovels. And as for Lily? She can stay planted, as far as I'm concerned."

The little devil spat. "Don't care about *her*. She is why Master was hurt. Leave her, let her suffer." It turned its pleading eyes back to Rick. "But Master. Master is good to me."

For the first time, he considered the little being. It must have been hard to be a tiny little pipsqueak of a fiend in a place like hell. Probably everybody had always used him for a hockey puck, knocking him around and hurting him just for kicks. If Yeter'el had been good to him – and honestly, Rick had never seen his father treat the imp like anything other than a family pet – then that would have been cause for a great deal of devotion. He wondered if the imp loved his father, and if a demon like that could feel love at all. The way the little thing was wibbling, he was willing to bet that it actually loved his father very, very much.

He sighed. He'd always been a soft touch. "Find me a shovel," he said, "and I'll dig him out."

The imp flew to him, kissed him on the lips, and then it was gone.

Alexander had never prayed before. He wasn't even sure that he was doing it correctly. He had said every prayer he could think of, including some that he'd learned from television and in books. Still there was no response. Finally, in desperation, he prayed in his own words.

"God, I don't know if you can hear me, or if you even care about people like me. I suppose I've been a very bad person, done some horrible things. I promise you, I will be a better person if you get me out of here. I will never eat another soul again for as long as I live, I swear, if you just get me out of here. Please, God. Jesus. Allah. Anybody?"

Still nothing. With a sigh, he got up from his knees and began to pace again. The base of his neck was tickling, and he reached back to scratch at it. To his surprise, a bright blue spark attached to his skin, shimmering like an opalescent droplet on the tip of his finger.

It danced there, warm and innocent. It reminded him of the baby souls that made up the Wall, the main watering hole here in the Abyss. He turned his hand, watching the blue dot run over it, and when it reached the center of his palm, he closed his fist. He did not intend to consume it, but it seemed to have a mind of its own, and it sank into his flesh.

Now that he had absorbed it, he knew that it was a soul, and a very spiritual one, as well. The energy ball raced toward his solar plexus, sparkling all through him as it went. He had never tasted a soul that agreed to be a meal this way. It felt and tasted different than any other spirit he had ever consumed before. Its nourishment reached down into all of the dark spaces in his own heart, healing them, sealing up the cracks, making him whole. Just before the last of the little volunteer was fused with him, he recognized its last earthly incarnation.

"Li?"

CHAPTER TWENTY-ONE

*B*elow

Rachel was not a stupid demon.

She had been around long enough, and had been savvy enough, to cultivate certain friendships and exchange favors until there were a few powerful demons who owed her. She needed to find out the name of the demon that had possessed her lover, and she needed to do it without walking up to him and asking. Subterfuge was the name of the game, as it always was where her kind were concerned.

She returned to the Pit and went to the Wall. Everyone who was everyone came here, and she knew that sooner or later, she would encounter someone she could manipulate.

Imps and lemures crowded the outer edges, the spots where exposure to the elements of the Abyss had begun to corrupt the soul energy that surged in the glowing gelatinous mass that stretched the width of the largest cavern in the Pit. She ignored them. They were just minor players, barely more than lackeys, and they generally knew nothing. The lemures particularly were prone to just staring and complaining about how their mortal families had abandoned them. She didn't really care to hear their whining.

The center of the wall, where the soul energy was the purest, was where the strongest of the strong came to have their refreshment. An archdemon was already there, drinking deeply while his cadre of shedim kept watch. He was exactly who she'd hoped to see.

Putting on her prettiest smile, she spread her wings out and shed her clothing. Nobody wore clothes in hell, anyway. She shimmied a bit then strolled over to where her old acquaintance was relaxing.

"Adramelech," she greeted cheerily. The archdemon looked up, surprised, Wall liquor dripping from his lips. His mule-like body shivered when he saw her.

"Rachel," he cooed. "How good to see you again." He extended a hand to her, his claws clicking together as she took his fingers in hers. He tapped his hooves and spread out his tail, ebony peacock feathers spreading in a gaudy display. His tail wasn't the only part of him that was responding to her. She was glad to see that she had made an impression.

The succubus leaned forward and kissed him on the lips, pressing her body against his. His snake's tongue danced into her mouth, and she accepted it, even gave it a teasing nibble before he pulled it back. She smiled.

"It just so happens that I've been missing you," she said. She ran a finger down the matted fur on his chest. "I wonder... can we have some time *alone*?"

He looked back at his shedim and barked an order to them. They closed ranks around them, walking as a phalanx of body guards as Adramelech swung Rachel up onto his back and carried her away from the Wall.

She wrapped her arms around his neck and blew hot breath into his ear, making his flanks quiver. He grasped her hands in his own and said, "So after playing with the mortals, you've come to find a real man, eh?"

"Definitely." She squirmed a bit against him, letting him feel her, and said, "It's pathetic, really. The last one went and got himself all possessed. Useless to me then, really."

"Only a splash of demon in him, then, I'll wager."

"Oh, no. He's half. Yeter'el's boy."

Adramelech let out a braying laugh. "That's funny! I'll bet Asb'el is the one that did it. He's the only one powerful enough, and anyway, he's wanted to replace Yeter'el for years." He pitched his voice lower, sharing secrets to impress her. "I heard that he's going to get his wish."

She hugged him more tightly. "Really? Why is that?"

"Because the boss has punished Yeter'el with the Broken Pit. He's not going to be worth anything. I'll bet that Asb'el stops playing with your toy as soon as he hears."

Rachel laughed. "I don't really care. He can keep him now. Incubi and the Watchers are so dull, anyway." She rubbed a hand over his hairy shoulder. "Give me a *real* demon any day...."

"Oh, I will," he promised. "I will."

Above and Below

Lucifer loved Rome. It had been his favorite city for centuries. He had enjoyed himself here on many occasions, and he knew the place well. He had traipsed up and down all of the hills of Rome, waded in the Tiber, and had come to think of the city as his home away from home.

He casually toured his old haunts, stopping by a dairy store and curdling all of the milk just for laughs. There was a time when he could really get the humans riled up with little tricks like that. He'd just curdle milk, blight a crop or two, and then drop a word in the right power-mad magistrate's ear, and it was witch barbeque for dinner. He missed those days.

He strolled along until he reached St. Peter's Square, taking a moment to lay his hand against the red Egyptian obelisk that stood at the hub of the wheel that decorated the square's pavement. He could feel his hidden agent stirring inside, and he moved on, satisfied that his influence in this place still remained. Ahead, on the steps of the basilica, a tour group was assembling to tour the public areas of the Papal palace, and he joined them. He had developed a real affection for tourists in the past few days. He enjoyed their company.

The tour wound its way past endless masterpieces of art that the Church had graciously accepted, sometimes at knifepoint, from the best artists of their day. He recognized a few pieces – he had, after all, given their makers the ability and inspiration to create them. It was like touring his own museum honoring himself.

At one point, he separated from the tour group and walked toward the Papal apartments via an old and disused escape tunnel. He was well acquainted with the ins and outs of this building. He had been here so many times.

He reached the Pope's private living space and sniffed. There had been someone very holy here within the last decade, making the whole place stink. He was considering ways to correct that when he felt it a sudden pain lance through his soul like lightning.

There was someone praying in his domain.

The pain turned into rage, and he went back to the Abyss, abandoning whatever mischief he had been planning. There would be time to ruin the Vatican later.

Below

The imp brought a shovel, and Rick started to dig, hoping against hope as he did that Naamah would spend a little more time away. He was pretty certain that the Queen of Hell would be very annoyed with him for digging up her bedroom floor.

It didn't take long before he encountered something squishy and wet. His lip curled in disgust as he exhumed the bodies that were buried there, taking their pieces out handful by soggy handful. The imp stood guard at the doorway and chittered nervously while he dragged out a seemingly endless supply of gnarled chunks.

He felt around in the hole he'd dug then straightened. "I think that's all of it. Do you know which pieces are him and which pieces are her?"

"No." The imp's lower lip trembled.

"Aw, geez. Don't cry. We'll figure this out. How are we going to get them reassembled? I don't have that trick up my sleeve."

"Lillith?"

Rick scoffed, "Right. Why would Lillith help us?"

"You don't hear any gossip, do you?"

The hockey player rolled his eyes. "Spill it."

"The King of Hell put her aside. They quarreled, and he cast her out of his inner circle. He keeps only Naamah as his consort now. Sometimes he forgets and thinks Lillith is still here, but that tells you how little he cares for her. He doesn't even remember that he's thrown her out."

"Okay," he said, wondering when hell had turned into an episode of *The Young and the Restless.* "So...where is she, and how do we get these pieces to her?"

"By the wellspring," it said. "She keeps a cavern there."

"The wellspring?" he echoed. "Where is that?"

The imp laughed at him. "You don't know anything, do you? You've been away from home for too long."

Rick glowered. "This is *not* my home." He looked down at the mess at his feet. "I just lived here for a year or so...."

With a flutter of its stumpy wings, the imp flew up and toward the door, telling him as it went, "I will call an Utukku with a bucket. Then we can go."

"You're assuming Naamah will let me leave."

It gave him a derisive look. "No chains that I can see," it said. "Besides, she got what she wanted from you."

He didn't know if he should feel relieved or used, so he settled for feeling awkward. "Okay, well, hurry up. I don't want her to come back before we get these pieces out of here."

Lucifer burst into his apartments with a roar of fury, tackling Alexander and bringing him crashing to the ground. With claws and fists and the horns on his wings, Satan pummeled and ripped the hapless incubus, raging all the while. Alexander tried to protect himself, but he was too weak to defend against the onslaught. He earned only a broken arm and an even angrier devil for his efforts.

Inside of himself, he felt the purity he had absorbed beginning to move. The power rushed up through him, and he found himself grabbing Lucifer's face in his hands. He darted in and pressed his lips to the mouth of the First Fallen.

At first, he thought that Lucifer would just break him, but his newfound power, pushed by something even greater, held the devil fast like unbreakable chains. He felt a coiling in his gut, like his own soul was making room, and then he let instinct take over. He opened his incubus' energy maw and began to feed.

Red-hot power fueled by rage and generations' worth of pride splashed against his throat, and he fought to swallow. More and more poured into him, and he took as much as he could take, draining all of the excess power he could reach. The part of him that had been bolstered by Li's soul expanded, opening bottomless wells that he could fill with this stolen power, and he stuffed himself full to bursting, leaving the devil depleted.

Depleted was not the same as defeated, however, and with a cry of fury, Lucifer grabbed Alexander's head and twisted. His neck broke cleanly, and the power drain ended. Satan tried to pull his power back from the body in his arms, but a shockingly bright light rose out of it, a pure soul propelled by all of that stolen energy straight up through the ceiling of the chamber and beyond.

He had been duped, and worse, he had been crippled. He found himself unable to rise and unwilling to call for help. He shook with impotent, frustrated rage.

He had been angry before, but he had never been angry like this.

Rachel and Pinem'e made their way into the chapel at his monastery. The succubus was twitchy and uncomfortable, feeling unwelcome in the house of Christian worship. She hung back by the door to the vestibule, ready to run in an instant if the burning in her bones became too much to bear. Her Watcher companion, though, was well accustomed to this place, and he knew every groove in the stone steps that had been worn by countless feet. He went to the center of the church and knelt, making the Sign of the Cross and bowing his head.

"Saint Michael the Archangel, defend us in battle. Be our protection against the wickedness and snares of the devil. May God rebuke him, we humbly pray, and do Thou, oh Prince of the Heavenly Host, by the Divine Power of God, cast into hell Satan and all the evil spirits who roam throughout the world seeking the ruin of souls."

The archangel appeared at the altar before his words had even been fully pronounced. Rachel took a step backward as Michael approached the kneeling demon priest.

"Brother," he greeted Pinem'e, extending a hand. "It has been a long, long time."

The Watcher pressed Michael's hand with both of his own, bending to press a kiss to the archangel's wrist. "Brother," he responded tearfully. "Can you intercede on my behalf with our Father? For five hundred years, I have served him faithfully, never asking anything, keeping away from the bad influences that led me to my fall. Please... can you ask our Father if I may at last return to the glory of His presence?"

Rachel had never seen her old friend weep before, and it made her uncomfortable. She looked away. His older brother, though, offered him a kind smile and a gentle hand on his head, almost like a blessing.

"Pinem'e, when you and your fellows disobeyed Him, you broke His heart. But He can forgive you, if you prove yourself to Him."

"Tell me what I must do! I will do anything."

"Peace, brother." Michael looked up at the succubus who was hovering ever closer to the door. "Rachel, come closer."

She went pale, but she obeyed, walking as demurely as she could manage. When she got within arm's length of heaven's general, she knelt.

The archangel considered her for a moment. "Tell me truthfully – when was the last time you consumed a human soul?"

Her palms started to sweat. "It's been years. I don't remember the last –"

"Now is not the time to lie to me, child."

She winced. "1847."

"Ah." He nodded. "And this soul, to whom did it belong?"

"I don't remember. Some man."

Michael smiled tightly. "Brother, would you like to remind her?"

Pinem'e shifted nervously. "It was a farmer named Rudolph Ericson. He raised barley and goats in Sweden." He glanced at Rachel, whose face was growing more ashen by the second. "He was your descendant, brother."

"Yes. My descendant. My son's great-grandson's great-grandson. Do you remember him now, demon?"

"I do." Sweat trickled down between her shoulder blades. *No wonder he tasted so delicious.*

"And why did you stop after him, demon? Why no more souls after that?"

She thought back, wondering why he was asking her about her past when that was the last thing it seemed that they'd want to talk about. She remembered St. Petersburg in the winter, the way the ice crystals shimmered like diamonds on the trees, and the way Vladimir had sparkled brighter still in her eyes. She remembered troika rides and imperial balls and laughter. She hung her head. "I fell in love with a mortal," she answered honestly. "And after that, I could never see them just as food again."

Michael nodded. "I see. And what did you learn after you stopped consuming souls?"

"I learned..." She licked her lips, even though her tongue felt dry. "I learned that I could survive on energy alone. I learned that I didn't need to take souls to feel satisfied."

"And yet you raised your child on the innocent souls of children and taught him to feed like any other demon," the archangel accused. "Why?"

Pinem'e was looking at her, and she wanted to hide. "Because he has a great destiny, and to reach his potential, he needed to be strong. He needed to have his demonic powers at their fullest strength."

"Destiny. I see. And what is his destiny, Rachel?"

She looked down, cringing from the disapproval in the powerful being's voice. "I thought... I thought he would be the one to challenge Lucifer for his throne."

"And why did you want this? Was it so that you would gain power as the mother of the new Satan? Was it so that you could be the hand holding the reins, controlling your boy?"

"No!" Her head snapped up, and she looked into Michael's eyes defiantly. "I would never do that to my boy. No, I wanted him to take down Lucifer so that... so that there might be an end to this constant warfare."

The archangel narrowed his eyes, but turned away from her. He looked at his brother. "Why did you call me here, Pinem'e? It wasn't just to ask for my intercession. You know as well as I do that there are others more suited to granting clemency than me."

The Watcher took a deep breath and finally released his grip on Michael's hand. "We need your help. Lucifer and his minions have taken both Rick and Alexander bodily into the Pit, and neither of us can reach to the level he has taken them. We need to bring them out, but we can't do it without assistance. We are only two against all of the devil's forces. We wouldn't stand a chance."

He looked from the Watcher to the succubus and back again. "So you called me out of concern for her mate and her son."

"We called you out of love," Rachel interjected. "I love them both. I want them both to be safe." She considered trying to seduce the archangel into compliance, but rejected that thought immediately. Not only was she convinced that he would be gravely offended by her advances, she was also sure that if he accepted her offer, she would probably be burned to ashes by his touch. Angels of his rank were not to be tampered with lightly. "Please," she finally said, speaking simply and without games. "Please help us save them."

Michael looked at her, then at Pinem'e. "Will you both sacrifice to have this happen?"

The Watcher spoke for both of them. "Anything."

"Will you give up your immortality and live as mortals, as humans?"

Rachel was appalled, and she chided herself for that selfish reaction. Her son and her lover needed her, and without them, life would be unfit for living. She nodded. "Yes."

Pinem'e asked, "You mean as full humans? With the chance to be forgiven and to return to God after we die?"

"Christ died for all men so that sins would be forgiven. If you become a man that would include you."

The Watcher lunged at Michael and embraced him, weeping in pure joy. "Yes, yes, yes! God bless you, Michael! God bless you!"

His brother hugged him and looked at Rachel. "And you?"

She swallowed the lump in her throat and nodded. "Yes. For my child, for the man I love, yes."

He nodded. "Very well, then."

Between

Gabriel took Jessica and Yu Kun to Queens, materializing with them on the steps of the rectory at St. Benedict's Church. The door opened immediately, revealing a startled Father Timothy Fitzpatrick.

"What a surprise!" he said, holding the door open wide. "Come in."

They filed in and went into the sitting room when the priest silently bade them to sit. The archangel wasted no time.

"Timothy, these people need to stay here under your protection. They will be pursued."

Fitzpatrick nodded gravely. "I understand." The archangel blinked out of existence, and he told his guests, "I'll find you both rooms, and then I'll see about getting us all some dinner."

Yu Kun said quietly, "I need to return to my monastery. The brothers need to know about Tsung Li."

"Gabriel said you'd be pursued," Fitzpatrick objected. "You won't be safe."

"I can take care of myself, Father." He put a hand on Jessica's shoulder, then turned and left the house.

She turned to the priest. "How are you messed up in all of this?"

He showed her the tattoo on his wrist. "I've been messed up in this for a very long time, my dear." He saw the shadows in her eyes and asked, "Are you very tired? I can just bring a tray up to you if you'd rather take your dinner in your room."

She nodded and wiped at her eyes, which were insisting on leaking. "I'd like that very much."

Fitzpatrick escorted her up the stairs and into a modest guest room. She sat on the bed and stared at her hands as the priest listened to a voice in his head. After a moment, he told her, "There is a bathroom attached to this room, right through this door, and linens are in the Welsh dresser in the hallway. There's a phone here, so help yourself if you need to make any phone calls." He looked at her, compassion in his eyes. "I'm so sorry about your friend."

She almost lost it. "So am I."

He gave her a gentle squeeze on the shoulder, then left the room, closing the door almost silently as he went. She waited until she heard his footsteps reach the bottom of the stairs. Once she was certain he wouldn't hear, she hugged the pillow to her chest and began to sob.

CHAPTER TWENTY-TWO

*B*elow

The imp returned with a pig-faced monster and a large box that looked like it was made out of braided long bones. Rick loaded the bits and pieces of his father and Lily into the box, and the imp covered it with a silky cloth very reminiscent of coffin lining. The Utukku carried its burden and led the way out of the room, grunting at them to follow. The imp happily flew along beside his master's remains, and Rick trailed along behind, looking over his shoulder all the way.

When he finally looked forward, his gaze fell onto the box in the worker demon's hands, and he struggled to understand the things that he was feeling. Yeter'el was his father, and he had a strange sort of instinctive loyalty to him because of that fact. He was also the author of the most frightening and painful experiences in Rick's young life, and he hated him as much as it was possible for one person to hate another. Why, then, was he taking this trek, chancing the wrath of the Queen of Hell and traipsing through level after level of the devil's domain, just to get his father's pieces glued back together? He didn't know. He only knew that in that box, imprisoned in those shreds of flesh and bone, his father's mind was still coherent, and that was a torture that he couldn't countenance.

They walked for what seemed like hours, taking the sloping ramps that snaked between the disparate levels of Hell, descending as far down as they could go. With every step, the atmosphere became more oppressive, the sense of dread and dripping evil more pervasive. Rick was no coward, and he had been to his fair share of bad places, but these levels of the Abyss were worse than anything he had ever imagined. This was where nightmares came to die.

It was cold, now, and clingy-damp like rotting vegetation. Something that should have been a bat but most certainly was not flew over his head, trailing tendrils of something unspeakable. He crouched, too tall to stand comfortably in the narrowing corridor. He had no idea what was on the ceiling, but he was absolutely sure that whatever it was, he didn't want it in his hair.

The path they were on took a sharp bend to the left and dead-ended on a cliff overlooking the original Lake of Fire into which Lucifer had been thrown at the time of the first fall, and into which the prophets said he would be flung again. It was a vast, bubbling cauldron of red-hot molten rock, a caldera wreathed in sulfurous fumes and heat distortion. From where he stood, Rick could feel the heat on his face. The imp flew to him and hovered over his shoulder.

"The wellspring," it said, looking down into the chasm. "She is close."

The Utukku snorted and grunted, then shoved the box and its noisome contents into Rick's hands. He staggered beneath the weight. "What the hell, man?" It waved a pudgy hand at him, then trudged back up the ramp, back into more familiar levels of the Pit. Rick turned to the imp. "What, he's just leaving?"

"Too afraid. The wellspring is powerful. And Lillith … she is powerful, too."

"Do you know how to get there?"

"Of course."

"Is it far?"

"No. Just down there, on the shore of the lake. Beautiful."

Rick raised an eyebrow. "Beautiful? Are you fucking kidding me?"

The imp looked surprised. "No kidding."

He looked down. The lake was easily five hundred feet below him, and if there was a beach, it was very, very narrow. There were no ladders and no climbing ropes to help them reach the bottom, and even if there were, he didn't know how he was going to climb down and carry three hundred pounds of intelligent hamburger with him. The imp was watching him expectantly, and he knew that he had to do something.

He did the only thing he could think of to do. "Hey! Lillith!"

The rocks around him hissed, as if they were surprised by his audacity. Even his tiny companion covered its mouth with its hands. Apparently, one didn't just summon the former consort of the Prince of Darkness by bellowing her name. Too bad nobody had told Rick that before he came down here.

A smell like carrion reached him, faint at first but growing stronger. Black mist rose out of the ground where he stood, weaving around his ankles and climbing up his legs with an almost physical icy touch. He took a step back out of the tangible cloud and collided with the cavern wall. Space was at a premium in this neighborhood of hell.

A cloud of yellowish gas began to seep out of the lake and rise like mist. It gained speed as it gained size, and he regretted his shout. He hadn't considered that there might be more things lurking down here than just Lillith. Now he had called their attention, whatever they were.

The cloud began to take shape. It was roughly reptilian, with pterodactyl wings and a gaping maw. As it came closer, it consolidated into a draconian form with leathery wings and a whipping tail. Mist became flesh, and the roiling yellow became sickly, jaundiced eyes and scales. The dragon flapped its wings and hovered directly in front of him. Rick's heart pounded in fright. The imp was long gone.

A voice in his head demanded, *What do you want?*

He answered out loud, because panic made him stupid. "I need to see Lillith."

Why? The dragon's nostrils flared then closed. Its pupils contracted. *What's in the box? An offering?*

"No."

There was a rumble in the dragon's chest, and then it spat, shooting pin-like shards of glass at him. The projectiles pierced into his skin like the spines of a cactus, and he shouted in pain, using the heavy box to protect most of his body from the attack. The dragon reared up as if to strike again, and a feminine voice spoke quietly at Rick's ear.

"Stop it, Baphomet."

He was standing with his back pressed against the cave wall, and yet a small, cold hand was touching him between the shoulders. The dragon hissed and retreated sullenly as Lillith faded out of the stone. She wrapped her arms and wings around Rick and the box, collecting her visitor and his burden in one move. He shivered, and then they were standing on the lip of the boiling lake.

The heat was intense. He could feel the small hairs on his legs and arms shriveling and burning away. He couldn't bear to open his eyes into the blast, and he turned his face away from the worst of it.

"You're still mortal," she said, sounding both surprised and intrigued. "Very well. We'll go somewhere else."

He was overtaken with the sickly sensation of a different kind of teleportation, and he felt profoundly ill for a moment. In a flash, though, the sickness faded, and he found himself standing in a neatly-decorated and almost prim apartment. He recognized the New York skyline through the picture window and nearly wept with relief at being mostly home.

The box did not make the trip, but the torn bodies of Lily and his father did. The pieces fell to the floor with a horrible slurping sound, sliding down his body and bouncing up against his ankles. He jumped back, disgusted.

Lillith laughed. She was sitting on a black leather chaise lounge, dressed in a long black negligee. She tossed her flame-red hair. "You're so squeamish."

"I – uh, well – yeah, I guess." He looked down at the accumulation and grimaced. "That's just really, really gross."

She leaned back seductively, curling up on the furniture with her long legs stretched out over the upholstery. "So what brings you to the wellspring, little boy? Are we having an adventure?"

"Lady, I'm a lot of things, but I am *not* a little boy."

She raked her gaze over his body, taking in the sights. She smiled. "No, you certainly are not. But that doesn't really answer my question, now does it?"

"I was looking for you."

"I got that far. I want to know *why*."

She was staring at him in open appraisal, measuring him with her eyes, and it affected him. He was embarrassed by his body's response and tried to cover himself with his hands. This sudden modesty amused her capitally, and she laughed again, longer and harder than before. He flushed, his embarrassment redoubled.

"What's your name, little boy?"

He squirmed. "Rick."

"And what does Rick want with me?" she purred, sitting up a bit straighter.

"I need your help."

"Ah! Now we're getting some answers." She rose and sashayed over to him, enjoying his discomfort. "What help did you need?" She ran a finger from his shoulder down to his hand, which was doing an increasingly poor job at concealing his excitement. Sometimes he really hated being male. "Did you need help with this?"

He flinched away from her finger before she could touch anywhere more personal. "No, no, not with that."

She pursed her lips and looked him over one more time. "Too bad. Then with what?" She gestured at the bloody heap at his feet. "With that?"

He nodded vigorously. "Yes. Yes, with that. That's actually two people, and I was sort of hoping that you could… that you could…"

"That I could put Humpty Dumpty and Dumpty Daisy back together again?" she finished for him.

Rick sighed. "Yeah."

Lillith shook her head and walked around him, her hand skimming along his skin, still damp with sweat from the proximity to that burning lake. She licked a salty drop away from between his shoulder blades then continued to examine him like she was buying a used car.

"Honey," she finally said, "you know that you have to make it worth my time."

"I don't have much," he mumbled.

She looked down again. "I wouldn't say that. Do you know how long it's been since I had a strong body between my legs?" He shook his head. "Suffice it to say that I would very much like to make your acquaintance. I won't even eat you. Well … not in the bad way, anyway."

"Is that all you want? 'Cause that's a pretty slim deal," he said, then kicked himself. *Stupid. Don't do her negotiating for her!*

Lillith stood in front of him, her feet buried ankle-deep in the gore, and looked into his eyes. He looked back. Finally, she smiled. "No," she admitted. "That's not all. I want a gift."

"What gift?" he asked, almost afraid to know.

"You'll have to figure out for yourself what I'll find most appealing. Do a little research, Rick. You *can* read, can't you?" He nodded dumbly, and she chuckled. "Then read about me, and bring me a present worthy of the service that you're requesting."

The way she said "service" made him tremble. His will power was breaking, and she knew it. She stepped a little closer, letting her breasts brush against his chest. The scratchiness of the lace she wore was maddening, compelling and enticing all at once.

"That can wait for later, though," she said, leaning up to kiss him. "This comes first…"

Naamah stole into Lucifer's private quarters, buzzing with the energy she had "borrowed" from the half-blood incubus she had left sleeping in her bed. There were things her mate had hidden from her for years, and the time was swiftly approaching when she would need to know where they were. She wanted to find a talisman he had made using the last feather his angel wings had shed before his transformation had been complete. It was the last link between Lucifer and God, and if it could be taken, then his importance to the Creator would be broken. It was the emblem of his rank and position here in Hell, and she meant to have it for herself.

She did not expect to see him lying on the floor in his gallery. She also did not expect to find the physical corpse of a partial-blood incubus cooling beside him. Lucifer looked gaunt and depleted, almost desiccated. She felt her eyes widening.

"What happened to you?"

She knelt beside him, her hand on his burning forehead. He was too weak to speak, but there was rage in his eyes. She opened her mind to his, and he let her see the attack he had suffered from the augmented Alexander, showing her the incident from the young partial demon's prayers all the way through to the departure of the consecrated soul that had given him such strength.

He expected her to be angry, to cry for vengeance, or to offer him solace. Instead, she pulled her hand away from him with an expression that was somewhere between wonderment and joy.

"He really was the One," she said, "wasn't he?" She looked at the fallen body and whispered. "He could pray down here. Nobody can ever pray here. And He helped him." Her eyes fell once again onto her mate's face, and they hardened. "You're no longer the strongest. You've lost."

Lucifer opened his mouth as if he meant to speak, but no sound emerged. She could feel a tickle in her mind where he was trying to contact her to communicate with her there, but she ignored it and refused him entry. She stood up and stepped away from him.

"It's finally happened, just like the prophecy said it would."

She turned her back and started exploring the conjoined rooms, upending and ripping apart everything that interfered with her search. Finally, hidden in a niche in the wall, she found the talisman, the white feather still gleaming with a purity that was completely out of place in the Abyss. She went back to Lucifer's side and held her prize before his face.

"Looks like you don't get to keep your crown," she purred. "Too bad."

The Queen of Hell slipped the talisman's cord over her head, letting the feather hang between her breasts. It burned her, but she enjoyed the pain. Power surged through her, and she felt her mind opening with all of the knowledge that came with being the Adversary of mankind. Lucifer managed a quiet moan as he felt that knowledge leaving him, and she laughed in delight.

For the first time in centuries, things were going to change.

Above and Between

Yu Kun let himself into the monastery house through the back door and went directly to his bedroom, where he shut himself inside and locked the door. He didn't want his followers to witness his distress.

On the table beside his bed, he had a single photograph in a simple wooden frame. It showed himself as a younger man sitting with a happy, smiling child on his lap. That child, a boy he had literally purchased in a rural village in China, was Tsung Li, the closest thing to a son that he had ever known. "Michael," he whispered through his tears, "explain it to me. Why him? Why did you take my boy?"

No answer came. It was no surprise. He picked up the photograph and clutched it to his chest. Mindful of the other monks, trying to be as silent as he could, he allowed himself to weep.

He heard Li's voice quietly speaking from the corner of the room. "Don't weep for me, Master."

Yu Kun whirled toward the sound and sat staring in shock. Li was standing by the window, surrounded by a glimmer of sunlight despite the growing darkness outside. He gave the English monk a gentle smile, wisdom shining in his dark eyes. Yu Kun gaped.

Li said, "I understand, now. I understand all of it." With an almost bashful smile, he held out his arms, and a pair of snow-white wings unfurled behind him. "You see? I'm all right. Don't cry."

He finally found his voice. "Are... are you back? Are you..."

"Alive? No, not exactly." He folded his wings again, and they disappeared into his back as if they had never been there. "But I have come back to continue my work."

"What work?"

Li looked happy when he answered, "I'm Jessica's new guardian angel. I'll take care of her and the baby until he's old enough to meet his destiny."

Yu Kun whispered, "She's with child, then?"

"Yes."

"Will she be able to see you?"

"I hope so."

He hated that he was weak enough to ask the question. "Will I see you again?"

The new angel nodded. "I'm sure of it." With another little smile, he faded out of sight.

CHAPTER TWENTY-THREE

*B*elow and Between

Lilith left him sweat-soaked and half dead, and it was hours before he could manage to drag his pathetic self to the shower. The place was outfitted with products suitable for both genders, which was a very good thing. He hated having to shower with some chick's body wash and smell like flowers the day after a one-night stand.

This had been no normal fling, though, as the gashes in his back and the bite marks on his chest could attest. Muscles in his back and shoulders were aching like he'd been through the mother of all bag skates, but the claw marks made standing in the hot water jets a dodgy proposition at best. He washed, shampooed and rinsed as quickly as he could, displeased by the pinkish tinge the water took on. Apparently, his back was bleeding. *Joy.*

He pulled a towel out of a closet in the bathroom and wrapped it around his waist, then grabbed another to rub his hair dry. He had just finished that mundane task and turned to look into the mirror when it occurred to him that for all the effort he'd just put into entertaining the Queen Bitch of the Abyss, he'd never had the chance to ask her to help his father.

Rick went back out into the apartment and stood in front of the wide picture window, looking out at the sparkling lights of Manhattan. The city was really something to see at night. Unfortunately, dark windows were also reflective, and he could see the pile of body parts on the carpet behind him. His stomach turned, and he decided he'd had enough of this place for one day.

He wanted to go home, but how he was going to accomplish that was an open question. He had no clothes, no keys, no phone, no money, no identification. There was only one thing left to do. Hopefully Lillith had a land line.

He found a phone in the kitchen, mounted on the wall beside the refrigerator. He knew the number by heart and dialed it at speed. The ringing seemed to go on forever, and he was preparing to leave a voice mail message. Then someone picked up.

"Hello?"

He didn't recognize the voice. It was purely American, with no trace of Koz's Czech accent and not at all what he'd wanted to hear. "Koz?"

"Uh, no... he's, uh, he's not here. Can I take a message for him?"

He sensed the person on the other end reaching for paper and a pen, and there was deception in his silence. Rick was suspicious.

"No, that's okay. Thanks."

The other person tried to keep him on the line, but he hung up as quickly as he could.

Above and Between

Brooker was cursing at a cell phone when Herman finally came back to the squad room. His partner looked up in irritation. "What, you had to walk back from the Island? Took you long enough to get here."

"Traffic," the older man defended lamely. "What's the matter?"

He held up the cell phone. "This is Kozlarek's phone. And somebody, I'm betting that Rick Buchanan person, just called."

"What's the number?"

"Blocked."

"Hell."

"Yeah." Brooker scratched his head. "Fuck."

Herman sat down heavily at his own desk and stared at the picture of their suspect, the one who was really a dead body possessed by a demon, the one that Michael had told him was now so much charcoal in the warehouse district. He wondered who the man had been before the demon took him, and whether he had family looking for him.

"That's him," his partner said triumphantly. "We're running his face through the data base right now. Hopefully he's got some priors and we can figure out who he is."

"Good work," he said, but his tone was distant. He was visibly absent-minded, listless and staring into space. His partner frowned in concern.

"You okay, man?"

The older man took a deep breath. "Yeah. Fine." He rubbed his forehead. "I just, uh, I've got something on my mind."

"Wanna get a drink after work?"

It was the guy's version of "do you want to talk," and he appreciated the effort. "Nah, that's okay. I just need to get some sleep, that's all."

Brooker sat in silence for a moment, scrolling through mug shots on his desk computer. Finally he said, "You know, you've been hitting it pretty hard for a while, now. You've got some days coming. Why don't you talk to the chief, take tomorrow off? Wouldn't hurt, y'know."

Herman nodded, using his own computer to call up information about Maine. "Yeah," he mumbled. "Maybe I'll do that."

Naamah met Lillith at the shore when she returned to her exile post. Lillith looked surprised to see her, and when she saw the talisman around the other demon's neck, her eyes widened in shock. "Where did you get that?" she demanded.

"Where do you think?"

"Does he know you found it?"

Naamah laughed and laughed as if Lillith had just told her the funniest joke ever. Her mirth was lost on her fellow demon who just crossed her arms. She took a whiff of her compatriot then smiled, herself. "You smell like Rick Buchanan."

"So do you, sister."

Her smile turned hard. "So it seems that once again we share a male."

"Oh, don't be cross, Lil," she said, wrapping her arms around her neck and kissing her lips gently. "We just have similar tastes in meat."

The talisman brushed against Lillith as Naamah leaned into the embrace, and she hissed in pain. The feather left a black smear of charred skin. She kissed Naamah, her tongue darting into her mouth to taste where else her lover had been. "How did you manage to take it?"

The older demon smiled in pure, delicious pleasure. "He's in no position to stop me."

"What do you mean?"

She touched her, caressing Lillith's body as she sing-songed, "There was a little mixed blood incubus from the Watcher line who sat in his room and *prayed*." When the other demon pulled away in surprise, she caught her and pulled her close again. "He prayed, and his *prayer was answered*." This time when she pulled away, Naamah let her go, meeting her eyes. This was the best game of I've-got-a-secret that she'd ever played.

"Answered?"

"Yes. And the answer gave him the strength to suck the power right out of Lucifer's bones."

The younger demon shook her head, amazed. "That's not possible. That can't be true."

"Oh, but it is. He managed to snap the part-blood's neck, and his soul *went up*. Yes! *Went up*. Do you know what that means?"

"The Watcher's Messiah has come," she breathed.

"And there's a channel open to Above." Naamah's eyes gleamed. "The weak ones will say that this is proof that He has finally forgiven us, and that we're going to be redeemed back into the City of Heaven. You know what I say?"

Lillith smirked. "It's a insertion point."

"Yes," the older demon said, shivering. "At long last, we finally have the in-road to take the Throne once and for all. If He's forgiving demons, then He's getting weak, and the time to strike is *now*."

They embraced again, kissing passionately in their mutual excitement. This time, Lillith didn't mind the burning of the talisman. She ran her hand along the cord that held the feather, feeling the power tingling even from that contact.

"So we can start telling the lesser ones about this, and let them crowd the highway," she purred. "Then, when the angels are all distracted with the influx of the newly redeemed, we can take the greater ones and hit Him where it hurts."

Naamah's answer was an enthusiastic kiss, devouring Lillith's mouth with her own. When they parted, they were both breathless, their faces bright with lust. The older demon touched Lillith's breasts and whispered, "I've missed you. I was so angry when he cast you out."

"You could have come to visit."

They looked into one another's eyes, and then there were no more words.

Above and Between

Father Fitzpatrick brought a tray into Jessica's room, offering her a bowl of delicious-smelling tomato soup and a grilled cheese sandwich. He put the food down on the dresser and said, "It's not much, but then, I'm not much of a cook. My housekeeper will be here tomorrow, and she can cook much better than I can."

She was still hugging the pillow. Embarrassed, she put it aside. "It's okay. Food is food, right?" She stood up and gave him a shaky smile. "I'm not really all that hungry, anyway."

He nodded. "I understand, but you need to keep your strength up." He showed her a little brass bell that stood on the tray beside a glass of milk. "I'll let you have some privacy. If you need me, just ring this, and I'll come running."

A memory of watching *It's a Wonderful Life* with Li rose in her head and threatened to make her cry again. "Every time a bell rings, an angel gets his wings," she said, quoting the famous line.

Fitzpatrick smiled. "That's a sweet thought, but thankfully, it's a much quieter affair. There'd be bells ringing constantly. Can you imagine the noise?" He chuckled. "Well... if you need me... you know. Enjoy."

She walked him to the door. "Thank you."

"Don't mention it."

Jessica locked the door behind him then considered the meal he had brought. It smelled wonderful and looked appetizing, but she knew that it would taste like sand right now. Eating was the last thing she wanted to do. She poked at the food just so her host wouldn't feel that he'd wasted his time. She could only tolerate a few bites before she abandoned the tray all together.

She paced briefly, but lacked even the ambition for that much activity. She could not believe how much she hurt. She had never lost a friend to death this way.

The only thing she wanted to do was to find Li and shake him until he woke up, to make him breathe again, to bring him back. The thought of the rest of her life without him made her feel helpless and empty. She was starting to cry again, and it was making her angry. She hated being a stereotypical female and had fought against it all of her life. Now here she was, reacting to the loss of her best friend like a typical sloppy female.

"Jessica," a voice gently chided, "grief is hard enough without castigating yourself for it, too."

She looked up and saw Fitzpatrick standing there inside the room. She had not unlocked the door, and she certainly had not opened it. She wiped her face with the heel of her hand.

"How did you get in here?" she demanded. It sounded so much more reasonable than "how did you read my mind?"

He didn't answer her questions. Instead, he said, "You've been through a very trying time, and there are more trying times ahead. You need to be kind to yourself, or you'll never make it through."

She looked away and sat on the bed again. "I can't... I can't believe..." The priest sat beside her and took her hand, holding it between his own. He listened. "We were so close. And I thought we were going to get closer, you know? I mean, I really..." She took a ragged breath. "I love him."

Saying the words brought the pain crashing down on her, and she dissolved into wracking sobs. Fitzpatrick put his arm around her and held her while she cried, not speaking, only supporting her. She intended to choke him if he started spouting platitudes. Luckily for them both, he kept silent.

She cried until she couldn't cry any more. The priest brought her tissues, but she retreated into the bathroom to blow her nose and wipe her eyes. She'd heard once that crying could make a person feel better; well, now she knew that was a lie. She felt even worse than she had before.

She pressed a cold cloth to her face, then tossed it back into the sink and took a hard look in the mirror.

"Suck it up," she scolded her reflection. "You don't have time for this."

Fitzpatrick knocked on the closed bathroom door. "Jessica?"

She hadn't been in here that long. Annoyed, she called back, "Yeah?"

"There's someone here to see you."

She had absolutely no interest in seeing any visitors. She cursed under her breath. "All right," she called. "I'll be right out."

With a blotchy face and a bad attitude, she went back into the bedroom. She started to speak, then fell silent, her voice freezing in her throat when she saw the person standing beside the priest.

She finally managed to squeak, "Li?"

He smiled his accustomed cock-eyed smile and said, "Hi."

She ran to him and wrapped her arms around him, sobbing again but not caring this time. He hugged her, and she took his face in her hands, kissing him soundly. He kissed her back then embraced her. She hooked her arms under his, grasping his shoulders and back with hands intent on not letting go again. "Oh, thank God," she said, her face pressed against his. "Thank God. What happened?"

"It's a long story," he said. "You'd better sit down."

Something in his voice scared her. She sat down. "Li, what...?"

He looked at her apologetically. "I never meant to upset you so much. I just did what I had to do. I had to help protect you, you and your baby." He glanced at Fitzpatrick, who nodded to him. "I'm just trying to take care of you. That's why I was sent back."

Jessica's voice was a pale imitation of itself as she echoed, "Sent back?"

He spread his wings out, and she stared in disbelief. He gave them a lazy beat then let his hands fall down to his sides, and his new limbs drooped a bit behind him as well. "I didn't come back the way you probably wanted me to," he said, "but this is better than nothing, right?"

"You're an angel."

"Yes. A guardian angel."

Fitzpatrick spread his own wings, dove-grey and speckled. "We both are."

Her jaw dropped, and Li said, "We're going to be right by your side from now on. We're going to keep you and the baby safe."

Unconsciously, she put her hand over her abdomen in the posture adopted by mothers from the beginning of time. "So you're not alive. Not really."

"Well... it all depends on your point of view."

Li giggled at the priest's words and quoted *Return of the Jedi*. "You'll find that a great many of the truths we cling to depend greatly on our own point of view."

Jessica laughed in spite of herself. "God, they could bring you back to life as an angel, but they couldn't cure you of your movie obsession!"

He smiled. "I am what I am."

"Great. Now you're Popeye."

"Except without the spinach."

They chuckled together, finding more mirth in the moment than the comment actually warranted. It helped to relieve the tension. When the laughter faded, Jessica asked, "So... now what?"

"Now we take you someplace safe."

"Seems I've heard that before, and it didn't work out so well."

"This time will be different." Li held his hand out to her. "I promise."

Below and Between

Rick hunted high and low in the apartment and found quite literally nothing to wear except his bath towel. Frustrated, he gave up and flopped onto the couch in the living room, turning on the television. He automatically tuned in to the sports news channel, hoping for hockey highlights to feed his ongoing addiction to his game. He found a hockey report, but it wasn't what he wanted to see.

The overly-made-up female anchor was looking into the camera with a look of false sorrow on her face. She intoned, "And now sad news from the world of hockey. Andrew Kozlarek, right winger for the New Jersey Devil Rays, was found dead today in the basement of a Manhattan apartment building. His teammate, Rick Buchanan, is still missing, and now the police are looking for Buchanan as a person of interest in the murder of the Czech superstar."

He stared at the screen in disbelief, not hearing the next report that the reporter droned out. He hurried back to the phone and called Koz again.

The same unfamiliar voice answered, "Hello?"

"Who is this?" he demanded, his voice a growl.

"Who is *this*?" the other man countered.

"You killed Koz," Rick accused, fury making him shake. "You killed him, didn't you? Why else would you have his phone?"

There was a scuffing sound, and then a different voice, one that sounded more tired than the first, came on the line. "Rick Buchanan?"

"Good guess," the athlete snapped. "Who is this?"

"My name is Lloyd Herman," the other man said, "NYPD. We need to talk to you."

His temper flared. "You don't need to waste time talking to me. You need to find who killed my friend!"

"We know who killed him," Herman said. In the background, the first voice let out an exclamation of dismay and surprise. "It was Ulug."

He nearly fell over. With a trembling hand, he dragged a kitchen chair closer and sat down before he passed out. "How do you know that name?" he rasped.

"I know a lot. I know about Alexander and Rachel, and we have a mutual friend." He waited a beat, but the hockey player was too stunned to say anything. Herman said again, "We need to talk to you. Will you meet us?"

His voice was a bare whisper as he nearly dropped the handset. "No."

"Mr. Buchanan, I really think –"

He hung up.

Above and Between

Brooker gaped at Herman as he put the cell phone back down on the desk. "What the hell was that all about? Who's Ulug? Who's this Rachel and Alexander?"

The older detective just shrugged back into his coat, put his sidearm on the desk, and walked away. He left the squad room and took the elevator down to the parking garage. His head was swimming, but he thought he heard what amounted to angelic bat noises guiding his steps. He left his badge on the elevator floor and got into his own car, where he locked the doors and fired up the engine. Michael appeared in the passenger seat beside him, his tall, muscular body barely fitting into the tight space. Herman nosed out into traffic and started driving.

After a few blocks, Michael said, "Turn left, then right at the second light."

He did as he was told. More directions followed, and he obeyed, ultimately ending up down in the tangle of warehouses by Christopher Street in lower Manhattan.

He drove down a dark alley until Michael said, "Stop here."

Herman parked the car and followed the archangel into an apartment in the bottom floor of a non-descript building that had one housed a cartage company. The place was a shambles, and the stench of blood was nearly overpowering. He coughed on the smell but followed his guide farther inside, walking past the destruction in the living room and ending up in the area of the open floorplan that had served as a bedroom.

Much to the detective's surprise, a beautiful brunette woman was lying there on the bed, curled loosely on her side and staring into space. She showed no reaction as they entered the room.

"Lloyd," the archangel said, "this is Rachel."

He nodded to her. "It's a pleasure, ma'am."

She did not respond. When she spoke, it was only to Michael. "My baby is dead. How many times do I have to lose my son?"

The angel bowed his blond head. "I am sorry."

"Did you know this would happen?"

To Herman, she sounded gutted. He'd never heard a woman's voice sound so hollow. The angel answered, "No. I knew it was possible, but I didn't know it was unavoidable."

A tear trickled out of one eye, and she wiped it away. The detective felt like a voyeur. "Why? Why did it have to happen? I just got him back."

"The Lord –"

"No," she said, sitting up suddenly. "Don't say that. I don't want to hear any excuses about mysterious ways." She pinned the archangel with a hateful look. "I want you to tell me why He felt the need to murder my boy twice."

"It was necessary to bring salvation to the Pit," he explained.

Rachel spat, "There is no salvation in the Pit! That's why it exists – to house the souls that God doesn't want."

"He wants them now."

She looked at Herman for the first time, dismissed him out of hand, then turned back to Michael. "He calls Himself the Creator, and that may well be, but He's destroyed more than my kind ever has. He let us sit and fester like boils for centuries, and now He decides He wants to be a Father to us? He can take His mercy and shove it up His all-knowing ass." She crawled across the bed to Michael, grasping his hands when she reached him. "I don't want any part of His hypocrisy. He killed my baby, my favorite, my best baby. I hate Him. I want nothing to do with Him, ever. Do you understand me? I want Him to rot the way He left us to rot!"

The angel shook free of her hands. "You are raving," he said firmly.

She grasped at his waist and came up with his sword, which she brandished at him even while smoke started to rise from her hands. "I've had enough." She held the point of the sword against Michael's chest. "Tell me, *older brother*, is suicide still an unforgiveable sin?"

"I am not your brother, Rachel, and if you kill yourself, there will be no afterlife for you, forgiven or not. You have no soul."

"Liar." She pushed the sword forward. "You know *nothing*. I have a soul, you ass. You just can't bring yourself to look at me closely enough to see it."

Herman spoke up. "Ma'am, put down the sword."

Rachel snapped, "Shut up."

Michael held up a hand to the detective, motioning for him to be still. "If you turn that sword upon yourself, you will simply cease to exist, and God will mourn for the loss of someone He might have saved."

"Sounds like a win-win to me." The point of the blade was digging into Michael's chest, but no blood was coming to the surface. Instead, a soft blue-white light was starting to seep out around the blessed metal. "And if I turn this against you?"

"Then I will smite you with all my power, and you will still cease to exist."

"Sounds good. Let's do it."

The detective tried again. "Rachel, what about Rick?"

She turned on him, swinging the blade around so quickly that he never saw it move. The point rested against his throat. "Don't you dare speak to me about him."

"Why?" he asked. "Don't you love him? Isn't he your chosen mate?"

The succubus shoved the sword into his flesh, and unlike Michael, Herman did bleed. Ruby drops welled up where the point pierced his skin. "He was," she said, "but Lillith and Naamah *took* him."

The archangel's voice was weary. "Give me the sword."

"Only if you promise to use it." She saw the dubious expression on his face and laughed. It was the saddest laugh Herman had ever heard. "I have *nothing*. Do you understand?"

"You have your Heavenly Father."

"Fuck Him."

"Do not disrespect the Lord your God!"

"Not my God. *Your* God." She looked back at the detective and smiled like a barracuda. "What about this ape? Is he one of your Master's chosen puppets?"

Michael sighed. "Lloyd is on the team, yes. He serves God."

Her eyes were manic when she looked at Herman. "Have you ever seen God?"

"No."

"Would you like to?"

"Enough!" The archangel grabbed his sword out of her hands and pushed her back onto the bed. "Stop your raving!"

She sprawled on her back, looking up at the angel with a lascivious grin. "Now that's more like it. I'll bet you've always wanted to be a bad boy, haven't you, Michael? You've always wanted to have a good, long, nasty, hard fuck. Why don't you do it? Or is that something you can't do? Are you a eunuch, Michael? Did God take away your balls?"

The detective turned to his companion. "Why are we here?"

"We came for her." He looked with disgust at the demon who had spread her legs and was touching herself obscenely.

Herman raised an eyebrow. "Why?"

"Because it was ordered." The angel turned back to her. "Rachel! Stop!"

"Why?"

Michael grabbed her face in his hand and made her look into his eyes. "Your son has been redeemed and waits for you in the Celestial Court. Will you join him, or will you leave him there alone?"

Her eyes filled with tears. "What?"

"Repent your sins, Child of God, and be forgiven."

A long moment passed with angel and demon locked in silent communication. Herman could sense the tension between them and could almost see the energy arcing from one to the other. He shifted from foot to foot, feeling awkward and a little afraid. Finally, the succubus sagged, lowering her eyes and nodding her head. Michael released his hold on her face and stepped back.

"May the Lord in His love and mercy help you with the grace of the Holy Spirit," the angel said, putting his hand on Rachel's head. She began to shake. The expression on her face was one of extreme pain, but she grasped Michael's wrist and held it in place, gritting her teeth and hissing in pain. She was burning to death from the inside out. The archangel continued to pray. "May the Lord who saves you from sin save you and raise you up."

With the last of his words, the succubus let out a piercing scream and burst into flame. Herman stepped back, shocked, but Michael kept his hand on her head, ignoring the blaze, continuing to bless her and pray over her. She thrashed in agony but made no attempt to escape his touch. Rachel shrieked one last time then made a sound that could only have been the demonic equivalent of a death rattle.

What was left of her body slumped down onto the scorched mattress and crumbled into white-gray ashes.

The archangel dropped his hand back to his side. "Amen."

In the sudden silence, the detective realized that he was shaking. He ran a hand over his face. "Jesus... why did you bring me here to see that?"

"Because there had to be a mortal witness." He turned to face him. "You, Lloyd, have to tell the story of what you see. These times will be yours to record for all the world to remember."

His breath caught in his throat. "Am I... Are you saying that I'm a prophet?"

"No," Michael said. "You are the first evangelist of the new Messiah. Remember what you have seen."

Herman blew out a slow breath. "I don't think I could forget it."

CHAPTER TWENTY-FOUR

*B*elow and Between

Rick found a bottle of scotch in the apartment's kitchen and handled the painful news of his friend's death in time-honored hockey fashion by drinking himself blind. He was a sodden mess when Lillith returned at three o'clock in the morning, her favorite time of day. She found him laying half on and half off of the couch, his towel discarded, his face smashed into the couch cushion and one hand still wrapped around the neck of the liquor bottle.

Naamah appeared behind her, her arms around the younger demon's waist. She saw the state he was in and giggled. "Hardly what you'd expect, is he?"

Lillith went into the kitchen and returned with a bottle of water from the refrigerator. She twisted the top off and upended the bottle over his head, soaking him in an icy splash. He jumped at the impact and fell off the couch the rest of the way, landing at her feet with an "oof." She tossed the empty plastic bottle aside.

"You're pathetic."

He pointed his finger at her, gun-style, and slurred, "Back atcha."

Naamah spoke a guttural word, and his head was suddenly clearer, although he was still well lubricated. He let go of the scotch bottle and looked up at them. For a moment, he looked alarmed to see the two of them standing together, but he covered it well. He offered his sexiest smile.

"Hi, ladies."

"Get up," Lillith ordered. "We have something to show you."

He stood up and considered putting his towel back on, but decided against it. His body was hardly a stranger to either of them, and he didn't know where the towel was, anyway. "What's that?"

"If we told you, it would take the fun out of showing you." Naamah took him by the left hand, and Lillith took the other. "Ready?"

He knew that whatever they had cooked up together was probably going to end badly. Nervously, he agreed. "Ready."

The next breath he took was in Lucifer's private quarters. The scent of the deepest levels of Hell was unmistakable. The two succubi released their holds and gently steered him into the gallery.

As soon as he stepped over the threshold, he saw his son lying dead on the ground, his neck obviously broken. He could not suppress his gasp of shock and distress, and he had to lean against the wall for support. Lillith went to him and rubbed a hand in small circles on his back, encouraging him not to hyperventilate.

Naamah wasted no time on compassion. "Look down." He did. To his surprise, Lucifer, too, was laying on the floor, his eyes showing that he was awake and alert, but his body visibly depleted. He had never seen the First Fallen before, but in his soul, he knew who he was. The older demoness stood behind Rick and put her arms around him. "He killed your boy," she said, manufactured sorrow coloring her voice. "But Alexander is the one who wounded him."

Lillith looked down at the fallen angel at her feet. "We could have killed him ourselves," she said, "but we thought you'd like to avenge your son yourself."

"Yes," the other demon agreed. "Wouldn't you like to have the honor of squeezing the last light out of the Father of Lies?"

Something in Rick's head snapped. The demons sensed it and took advantage of the opening, spearing their tendrils of temptation and madness into his very soul. He was filled with a rush of rage and hatred, all of it directed at the dissipated creature laying beside his dead son. His body shook, and Lillith and Naamah both held their hands against his back, fueling the black fury as it took control.

"Kill him," the older demon whispered to him. "Kill him for all of us. Take his place."

He didn't care about places. He didn't care about consequences. He only cared that he was hurting, and his pain had turned to wrath, and that wrath was expressing itself in a deep, burning hunger his human half could never know. With a cry, he fell on Lucifer, physically tearing him to pieces while his incubus power, boosted and sustained by the two ancient succubi who were influencing him, stole away the last drops of supernatural life force.

Lightning struck his soul, and the pain was mingled with exquisite pleasure, filling him with intricate wisdom and power. His mind nearly burst from it. Coated in black gore, shreds of the First Fallen hanging from his lips and fingers, he threw his head back and roared.

"The Adversary is dead," Lillith said.

Naamah smiled and placed the angel-feather talisman around Rick's neck, where it glowed red and angry. "Long live the Adversary."

Still trembling, Rick put his hands on the sides of his head, pressing as if he could force his physical brain to hold the sudden influx of memories and magic. He was himself, but he was Lucifer, too, as if he had simply absorbed everything that the fallen angel had ever been. The sensation was intoxicating, and he vibrated with it. He could feel raw potency coursing through him, shooting like sparks from his fingertips.

The succubi watched him closely, waiting to see what he would do and if he would survive the rush. He staggered to his feet, and they stepped aside, giving him room. He turned his eyes to the body on the ground then held out his hand. Alexander's corpse began to glow a steady red, then levitated from the rock, floating up to hover at the level of Rick's waist. A golden box appeared beneath him, and in a roar of sudden flame, he was incinerated, his ashes falling into the urn below. The urn sealed itself then shot over to rest on a shelf, knocking a Persian sword out of the way so it could take the weapon's place.

He turned to face the two Queens of Hell, studying their faces. They had hoped to control him, to rule the Abyss with Rick as their puppet. He had a different plan.

"Ladies," he said smoothly, opening his arms to them. They came to him, pressing against him, and he held them tightly to his torso. "You've been very, very bad girls."

Naamah giggled and rand a finger through his chest hair. "Does it please you?"

He pulled back so that he could look her in the eye. "No."

The two of them had just enough time to be afraid. Then the flames took them, and they were destroyed. He dropped what was left of them to the ground, more dust to mingle with what remained of the First Fallen.

The talisman that Naamah had worn was still intact. He picked it up and wrapped its leather cord around his hand. It tingled, but not unpleasantly. He smiled. He knew exactly what he was going to do with this.

Above, Below and Between

The first thing Rick did with the power he'd gained was to go to the NYPD morgue where they were keeping Koz. He opened the freezer and pulled out the drawer, looking down into his friend's face. He touched the cold, lax face then put a hand over the unbeating heart. Luckily the coroner hadn't come to play yet, so the damage he'd have to repair was minimal.

He knew that as the Adversary, he had no right to give life. His part was only to take. There was one who might have the power to help, though, and he prayed for him to appear.

The words must have been loud, because Raphael appeared almost instantly. "What do you want?" the archangel asked, wary.

"I want him brought back to life. He was innocent and did not deserve to be murdered this way."

"You would take him from Heaven and return him to the material world?"

Rick gave him a pinched smile. "I know he didn't make it all the way up. He's in purgatory, isn't he? Burning off that puck bunny habit, I suspect." He leaned forward. "I'm the Adversary now. I know where souls are going."

Raphael sighed. "This is something I cannot do without permission."

"Then ask your boss. I'd do it, but for obvious reasons, they won't let me in the door."

The archangel looked uncomfortable with this new shift in the modus operandi of the Heaven-Hell debate. "Anything else you'd like me to ask Him for you?"

"Give me back Rachel, too, and ask Alexander if he's willing to come."

"Alexander has been redeemed. His soul is now one with God."

"Ask him anyway."

Again, the archangel sighed. "Anything else?"

"Yeah." Rick held out the talisman. "This is a signet of office, right? Because 'Satan' is a title, not a name, right?"

"Correct."

"And if I put this on, then I'll be lost. Right?"

"Again, correct. Although you have taken such steps that I think you are lost already."

Rick ignored that comment. "And if I don't put it on, then there's a chance that I could go back to being just myself?"

"No." He shook his head. "As long as you command the power of Lucifer, you will never be yourself again. You will never be anything but the Adversary."

"Thanks," he said. "Good to know." He nodded toward Koz. " Could you...?"

Without a word, Raphael vanished.

Above and Between

Michael waited while Herman gathered his few personal belongings and dropped his last rent check off with the superintendent. He felt strangely at peace with his decision. He had always anticipated that when he left the force, he'd feel empty or deprived; instead, he felt liberated in a way he'd never felt before. It was an odd feeling, but not unwelcome.

"Are you ready?"

He turned to the archangel, his duffel bag slung over his shoulder. "Ready."

Michael nodded, and then they were gone.

Above, Below and Between

Rick paced beside Koz's morgue tray while he waited. He had summoned his clothing, wallet and keys out of his coach's office, where they had been sitting in a box under his desk, waiting for his return. Now dressed and properly funded and identified, he was ready to roll. He just needed Koz to wake up.

Raphael appeared again, standing on the other side of the tray. "Your request has been considered, and the Lord has granted life to Andrew Kozlarek, not because you've asked, but because his death was unjust."

"I don't care how He justifies it. Just bring him back."

The archangel placed a hand on the Czech player's chest, and the body was surrounded with a golden-pink glow. The power emanating from the angel was intense, and it was painful to Rick; he took a step back and shielded his eyes from the light. After what seemed like forever, the room returned to normal, and he felt Raphael departing.

He turned back toward the tray, irritated and angry until he saw Koz's chest rise and fall as he took a breath.

"Koz!" He hurried to his friend and felt his strong, steady pulse. "Oh, thank God. Thank you, God! Come on, buddy, open your eyes."

Slowly, his friend did. He looked up into Rick's face and groaned. "Oh my God… what I drinking last night…?"

Rick laughed. "You don't even want to know. Come on… the guys thought it would be funny to play a joke on you. Let's get you out of here."

He helped his friend sit up and climb down off of the slab. Koz leaned heavily on him, his arm draped around Rick's neck. "I feel like shit," he moaned.

Someone slipped under the struggling man's other arm, taking some of the weight off of Rick and helping the man to stand. Rick looked over and saw Rachel smiling at him as she put an arm around Koz's waist.

"You boys and your booze," she chided gently. "Let's get you home."

"Where my clothes?"

"I have no idea," Rick admitted. "We'll find you a lab coat or something so you don't scare anybody."

He looked into Rachel's eyes, and she mouthed, "I love you." Her gaze flickered down to the talisman wrapped around his hand. She stared at it but said nothing further.

They found a set of scrubs and a lab coat in the coroner's locker room and helped Koz get dressed. Rick took Rachel in his arms and kissed her deeply, overjoyed to have her back. When they parted, she smiled up at him.

"Alexander?" he asked.

Her happiness dimmed, but only slightly. "He has a job to do in Heaven. He sends his love and gratitude, but he won't be back. Well, not yet, anyway." She squeezed his hands, then stepped back, telling him, "Go do the other thing you want to do. I'll get Andrew home."

He kissed her again and waited while she escorted his buddy out of the morgue. Once Koz was safely out of view, he willed his physical self away and teleported back to Lillith's place.

When he got back to the apartment, he turned on the television and watched the sports newscast. The smiling bozo behind the network desk blathered his way through football and basketball reports then finally got to hockey, the red-headed stepchild of the professional sports world. Rick stroked the feather in the talisman as he waited.

The graphic in the upper corner of the screen changed into the Devil Rays' logo, and he pointed his hand at the television, flexing his new infernal muscles. "Change it," he said. "Nobody remembers."

He concentrated his will and felt the newfound power in his command exerting itself over the minds of every mundane person affected by the recent strange events. It was difficult, and it took time, but reality shifted to match his intention. Instead of reporting on his disappearance and Koz's murder, the newscaster launched into a perfectly drab retelling of a perfectly unremarkable game the Devil Rays had played in Winnipeg, complete with highlight reel footage of things that had never happened the first time around. It was the ultimate cheat, but he didn't care. Some things needed to be undone.

His next task was to straighten out the mess on the floor. The pieces of Lily and Yeter'el still bled, and he could feel both consciousnesses still attached to their physical forms, a bit worse for the wear. He held out his hands, felt the infernal magic surge, and put them back together.

They were both dazed, but they both knew what had happened and who they had to thank for their resurrection. Lily knelt before Rick and kissed the tops of his feet, and Yeter'el bowed his head in gratitude.

Rick said, "Both of you, get up." They obeyed. He held up the talisman, and two pairs of eyes shot wide in shock. "You know what this is. It's mine now." They started to grovel, but he stopped them.

"I don't want it. All I want to do is get back to my life and play hockey. Naamah, Lillith and Lucifer are all dead. There's a power vacuum, and the archdemons are all going to be looking for this little thing, because that's how they get to be king."

Yeter'el asked, "What is your will, my son and my king?"

"First of all, my will is that you get out of my life and stay there. Second, my will is that you and Lily here take the spots that Naamah and Lucifer just left."

The succubus gaped, and his father started to smile as if Christmas had come early. In a way, it had. "You're giving dominion over Hell…to me?"

"Yes, I am." He threw the talisman to the incubus, who caught it and yelped with surprise when it burned him. "I'm also going to give you a little bit of what I took from Lucifer."

"You took?" Lily said. "You are the One?"

"In the flesh, baby." He beckoned his father forward. "Come here."

Yeter'el came to him willingly, and Rick put his hand on his father's head. They both closed their eyes, and Rick pushed power into the other's body, letting it seep down into Yeter'el and entwine with his soul. When three-quarters of the Adversary's abilities, memories, and strength had passed from him into the incubus, Rick dropped his hand.

Yeter'el gasped. "Don't stop!"

Rick rubbed his hand, which burned with the energy that had coursed through it. A scorch mark colored his palm like the exit point of a lightning strike. He shook it off. "Yeah, I'm stopping. You don't get all of it. You can't be trusted with all of it."

Lily looked from the incubus to the athlete and back again. "But… what will you do?"

He smiled and backed away. "I'm going to go get some lunch, and then I'm going to get ready for tonight's game. I don't want to see either of you, or any of your buddies or henchmen, ever again. Clear? I'm out."

His father shook his head. "No. As long as you hold that power, you'll never be out."

They both knew that the crowning component of the Adversary's being, the part that made him the strongest demon in the Abyss, was still in Rick's control. Yeter'el would be stronger than anything still in the Pit, but Rick would be stronger than his father, at least for now.

"I'm out far enough for my liking," he told them. "Get out of here. Don't let me see either one of you on the surface again."

They obeyed, returning to the Pit to take their new positions. The hockey player looked around at the apartment and decided he would give it to Rachel. Lillith didn't need it anymore.

Above and Between

Jessica was sleeping in the back seat of the sedan while Fitzpatrick drove. Li sat in the passenger seat, looking out at the Atlantic Ocean as it beat against the coast. There was a deep hush in the car, something more than silence.

Fitzpatrick spoke first. "The One has arisen. Lucifer has fallen."

Li nodded. "What will happen now?"

"Only God knows." The angel-priest looked in the rear view mirror at Jessica. "Now we will keep watch."

"And Michael?"

"He and his recruit will find a way to seal the Gate."

The car sped past a sign emblazoned with an artistic rendering of fall colors and fly fishing. It proclaimed, "Welcome to Maine."

"Should we be so close to the Gate?"

"How better to keep an eye on it?" Fitzpatrick countered. "And after all, what's better than hiding in plain sight?"

Li sighed. "Not having to hide at all."

The priest smiled wryly. "That, my friend, is no longer an option."

The deep silence returned, and in the bright morning sunlight, the car rolled on.

About the Author

J.A. Cummings has amassed a large collection of poetry and short stories, which are available on her website. Her first novel, *Nightchild: A Clans Novel*, was published in 1999. The sequel, *Sacrifice*, was released in 2010.

Ms. Cummings currently resides in Michigan with her cats and extensive music collection.

More information can be found at jacummings.com.

www.ingramcontent.com/pod-product-compliance
Lightning Source LLC
Chambersburg PA
CBHW071308170626
46809CB00001B/377